MARG

&

THE

VICIOUS

CIRCLE

MARGAUX

&
THE

VICIOUS

CIRCLE

Book 1 of the Margaux Chronicles

ANNE MCCLARD

Aristata Press

Library of Congress Control Number: 2024912089

Book Design: Anne McClard
Book Cover Design: Anne McClard
Editor: Erin Cusick

ISBN 979-8-9906293-0-1 (paper)
ISBN 979-8-9906293-1-8 (hardcover)
ISBN 979-8-9906293-2-5 (ebook)

This book is a work of fiction. Some of the places described, and historical
moments, are real. The temporal aspects of the story are deliberately vague
and are not intended to accurately represent historical events. All characters
are wholly fabricated, and any resemblance to real people is purely
coincidental.

See last page for printing information.

Aristata Press, Portland, Oregon
https://aristatapress.com

For my mother

MARGAUX

1985

MARGAUX

SATURDAY, END OF OCTOBER

I PEEK through the tiny glass window on mailbox number eleven and see a white envelope slanting across the rectangular expanse.

When I first visited this building a year ago, the wall of old-style brass-and-glass mailbox doors sold me on the place, that and the fact that I could afford this one-bedroom walk-up in Lower Manhattan. The manager said they had planned to replace these mailboxes with more secure ones, but the tenants objected on account of their old-world charm.

Cautiously, I turn the combination lock—twice around to the right to clear the multi-letter code I have set, then left past home to *L*, right past home to *O*, left to *V*, right to *E*. I know—very guessable, but I'm not worried. Who would want to steal *my* mail?

The door springs open. I pull the envelope out. My heart beats faster, and my chest fills with an all-too-familiar dread. The logo in the upper-left corner is familiar, but I can't quite place it. It's a tree enclosed in a circle; the branches form an upside-down peace sign.

Under the logo, in fine print, is the name M. Des

Jardins, one of one hundred and thirty-five agents I queried about my novel. As I recollect, the description of the agency looked promising, something like

M. Des Jardins Literary Agency believes that all writers deserve a chance to be read, no matter how unbelievable their stories. Please send your query to the attention of M. Des Jardins, #9 Rose Garden Way, Mount Hope, Colorado 81229

I'd never heard of a town called Mount Hope in Colorado, despite being raised there off and on from an early age. I spent most of my early life in Peakview, a suburb of Denver, but also lived in a few other places around the state. Of course, there are probably plenty of towns I've never heard of in Colorado.

Undoubtedly *another* rejection letter.

I keep a notebook of the agents I've sent my manuscript to. Each entry carefully lists other works of fiction I believe are similar to mine that the agent represents. I don't remember any of M. Des Jardins's authors. I'll look it up later.

All the queries I've sent meld together—most have gone unanswered. The few responses I've received have been lukewarm at best, insulting at worst. I cross these off the list and try to forget that I received them. One of the more insulting ones read

Dear Miss Andrews,
Thank you for your recent query. You could have saved time and money on the copying and postage if you had bothered to read the description of our agency's interests in fiction. We only represent deserving authors who publish honest autobiograph-ical fiction. Your story, although fascinating, is too strange to be a true accounting of a lived life, especially by a person as young as you.

Almost everyone who has read my novel levies a criticism about its believability, and yet this *is* my story, a *true* fictionalized accounting of *real* events in my early life that led me to the place I find myself in this moment, standing hopeful in front of a wall of metal mailboxes. I tuck the letter in my canvas shoulder bag to read later. No point in meeting Paloma for lunch in a sour mood.

I push open the heavy door and emerge into hazy autumn sunlight. The air is cool but not cold. I lucked out when I found this apartment on Elizabeth Street, practically across the street from the Elizabeth Street Garden. It is a garden in name alone, nothing more than an unloved overgrown parcel of undeveloped land. It does have some beautiful trees that have now turned.

The fallen leaves lie brightly against the backdrop of the gray sidewalk, which is still damp from an early-morning rain. I look down as I make my way up toward Houston in my trademark red rubber rain boots. They are a cheerful addition to the scattered leaves.

Paloma and I are meeting at Veselka. I was surprised when she called saying she had something important to talk about *in person*; she hardly ever comes into the city. She doesn't like driving in town, so she took the train to Grand Central and said she'd take a taxi from there. We're supposed to meet at eleven thirty, but I don't hurry as I walk north. I know she will be late, as a matter of principle. It's a power play.

I stop in my tracks when I see that she's already waiting. This meeting must be important—it's scarcely eleven twenty. She's lovely standing there, with the posture of a ballerina, always perfectly attired. Today she wears her auburn hair pulled back in a loose bun, a few curls left out to frame her beautiful face. She's the only one of us five kids who has blue eyes, something I wished for as a child.

We're sisters, six years apart, and thus have traveled

different roads. We love each other and get along better than many sisters, but over the years a reserve has crept into our relationship. It started to happen when we were still children —in the spring of 1968, a difficult year for the entire family. Then as time went on, the chasm between us grew.

She viewed me as the spoiled youngest child, or so I assumed. Once, when I was still in high school and she was already married and pregnant, I overheard her tell our mother that she thought I was superficial—she said, *All Margie is interested in is how she looks and having fun.* Who doesn't want to have fun?

Recently, unexpectedly, Paloma told me that she had suffered from depression most of her life, as a younger child and in adolescence, when our family's world went topsy-turvy. She still sees a therapist and takes antidepressants.

"Wow, you're here already!" I give her a hug and a perfunctory kiss on the cheek.

"I guess you have come to expect me to be late all the time," she says. "I thought I'd prove you wrong today." She laughs. Her left eye twitches; she's nervous. "I already put my name on the waiting list."

"Oh good," I say. "Well, I'm eager to find out what brought you out of your comfort zone in Darien, on a Saturday no less."

I don't mean to sound as judgmental as I do. She lives a posh suburban-housewife lifestyle, replete with one of those new minivans and a car phone, and is married to John "Jack" Herbert Lattimore III, whom she met through a mutual friend at Yale. They married immediately after graduating.

"Let's wait to talk about that until we sit down," she says. She strokes her purple cashmere scarf with a gloved hand as if it were a cat or some other furry animal.

I have never known Paloma to be without a dog in her adult life. Even when she was a child, dogs played a prominent role, beginning with our magical dog. For a time she dreamt of being a professional dog trainer.

She needs something to take care of, something to love, something that loves her back unconditionally. I'm quite the opposite. I abhor the idea of being responsible for something else, someone else. I have never fallen in love, at least as an adult.

"How are Evan and Abby doing?" I ask.

Her eyes light up at the mention of her children's names. "They truly bring me more joy than I ever could have imagined," she says. "Evan started second grade, you know, and Abby is in first."

"How did that happen so fast?" The last time I went to Darien was more than a year ago—for Abby's fifth birthday party. Paloma and Jack pulled out all of the stops for the celebration. She's giving her children everything she always wished for. Of all the kids, she felt the most cheated by our parents' divorce.

"Maybe you should pop out to our place for a visit," she says. There's an accusation of neglect in there somewhere. "You could spend the night—are you free next weekend?"

Being stuck in Darien for the weekend makes me nervous—all those perfect lawns and gray-and-white colonial houses. The hostess calls Paloma's name. Maybe I can ignore the invitation.

* * *

WE SIT DRINKING OUR WATER. The menu is expansive, but I always get the same thing.

"I'll have a small mushroom-and-sauerkraut pierogi order and a cup of borscht," I say to the server.

"And I'll have a bowl of the vegetarian borscht," says Paloma. Predictable. Always watching her calories. She is quite trim, especially after having had two children already.

Paloma takes the napkin and places it carefully in her lap. "So . . . no doubt you are curious as to my urgent need to talk to you . . ."

"Well, yes, I am," I say. "Why the mystery?"

"It's about your book. I finished reading it, and afterward, I took the liberty of sending it to Mother too."

"Wow, that's rich," I say. "It would have been nice if you'd asked me first."

"The family doesn't want you to publish it."

I try to remain calm. I don't want to make a scene. "When you say 'the family,' you mean *you*, right?" My face flushes. "Or did you send it to Theo, Wendell and Keith too?" Our oldest brothers, Keith and Wendell, barely make an appearance in my novel. They wouldn't care; Theo might.

"Don't get me wrong, Margie, I *love* the book. I am honored that you let me read the manuscript, *but* it is too personal, too *real*."

I make a sound that is somewhere between a laugh and a cry.

"Look, I'm afraid of how it might be perceived. People will know it's about us. It will implicate *our family*. Don't you get that? Mother agrees that it's a bad idea to publish it."

"That's ridiculous, Paloma. Not a soul who has taken the time to read a chapter of my book believes a single word. I have the letters to prove that! Maybe life truly is stranger than fiction."

"We are especially worried about how Theo will take it. No need for me to tell you how fragile he is. I know we always thought he had something—"

"You are reading *way* too much into this," I say.

Why did I imagine my sister would give my book a fair read? She has always looked down on me and the life I have chosen. She lords her English literature degree from Yale over me.

When I told her I wrote a novel, she brushed it off as *that's nice*, and a year later when I gave her a copy of a semi-polished manuscript, she said she would read it if she could find the time. Apparently she found the time.

"Please reconsider publishing it—at least reread it with a stranger's eyes. Try to imagine how it might come across. Imagine it through Theo's eyes."

What might Theo make of the story? The character based on him doesn't come off especially well, at least in the beginning. The mother doesn't look so good either—she's understandably inattentive, some would say neglectful.

In the novel, the character Trace is *not* Theo, nor is Marta my mother. The story draws on real events, but I wholly fabricated the family and the characters. There's *a lot* of embellishment, not to mention all of the peculiar events that nobody but us witnessed and experienced. Still, part of me thinks she has a point.

"I haven't landed an agent for it yet."

Without thinking, I dig into my bag and whip out the envelope I retrieved from the mailbox upon leaving my apartment. I slap it down on the table in front of Paloma.

"Here, this is rejection one hundred and thirty-something. Why don't you open it?" A tear runs down my cheek.

Paloma's expression changes from consternation to puzzlement when her eyes land on the envelope. "How strange," she says. "This logo is similar to the decorative symbol on the iron gate of our house in Peakview."

I dab my cheek with my napkin. "Yes, it *is* similar but not the same, somehow more modern." I used to peek out the iron gate through the leaves of that symbol. I imagined that the gate led to a secret world, and in reality it did.

I pick up the envelope. "Well, here goes nothing," I say, sliding my thumb under the flap to tear it open, but the paper doesn't tear; it springs open as if it holds its own anticipation.

LETTER FROM M. DES JARDINS
SATURDAY CONTINUED

As I PULL the folded leaf of stationery out of the envelope, it vibrates between my fingers. I unfold the letter. The same logo on the outside of the envelope is positioned center-top of the Crane stationery. In every way but one, this letter resembles all of the other letters; it is handwritten, not typed. The handwriting is neat, but not too neat. It is ornate, but not overly so.

Dear Ms. Andrews,

I have just finished reading your novel, One Elysium Street. It thoroughly impresses me, and I would delight in representing it as your agent should you agree. Would it be possible for us to meet in person to discuss the terms? As luck has it, I will be in New York City next week to meet with several distinguished publishing houses. Perhaps we can meet then?

Please give me a call at 303-555-4681 as

*soon as possible so that we can make
arrangements.*

Sincerely,

*M. Des Jardins
Literary Agent*

A surge of adrenaline rushes through my body, and the paper shakes in my trembling hand.

The date is five days ago. That means "next week" is almost here. No wonder M. has suggested a phone call. What does the *M* stand for? Mildred? Marcus? M. Des Jardins's gender remains a mystery, and the handwriting lends no clue.

"Well?" Paloma raises her eyebrow.

"Looks like I might have an agent after all." I hand the letter over to her.

She purses her lips as she reads it, then looks up. "Well, congratulations, I guess."

Is Paloma jealous? She writes too, although I've never read any of her writing. All five of us kids write, but never share. When she was still at Yale, she imagined she would end up in the publishing business, maybe at Knopf or one of the other big publishing houses in New York. She did not aspire to being a housewife.

The server delivers our food. The smell of sauerkraut rises. Revolting. We both pick at our dishes. Paloma always picks at her food. Usually I do not, but I have lost my appetite with all the stress of the earlier conversation with Paloma and from the excitement of reading the letter. At long last, an acceptance!

We sit in a silent bubble, in the midst of clinking dishes and lively conversations at other tables.

Paloma's mouth is set in a frown—she's resigned to the fact that I will, in all likelihood, move ahead with my plans to publish. I'm sure it bothers her that she no longer holds sway over me, the way she did when we were children. Always the controlling big sister, she's lost her power now.

After we finish, Paloma says, "I'm going to say it again, I hope you will reread your manuscript through our eyes before moving headlong into publishing it. I'd hate to see our family torn apart by your ambition. It *is* a good story, and you may have written it, but it is not *your* story alone."

"I'll reread it with that in mind," I say. I certainly don't want to hurt our family. If I had thought it would, I'd never have written it in the first place.

* * *

When I get back to my apartment, I rush up the five flights to 5A. Winded, I unlock the door.

The afternoon sun is streaming in, and dust particles dance in the beams. I take off my jacket and boots and sit down in the straight-backed Morris-style chair in front of my writing desk and my Smith Corona electric typewriter. I can't imagine my life without that typewriter—it's my only true friend.

I have been working on my next novel, a sequel to the first, and the latest news energizes me to get back to working on it.

I glance over my right shoulder at the wall clock hanging above the sink in what passes for my kitchen. It's two o'clock, noon in Colorado. I rifle through my bag for the letter, pull it out, and dial the number with irrational urgency. It's Saturday, after all, and improbable that anybody will answer on the weekend, but maybe they have an answering service. After a few rings, someone picks up.

"M. Des Jardins Literary Agency," a woman's voice says with the studied clip of an administrative assistant.

"Hello," I say. I'm sweating and my mouth is dry. Why am I so nervous? "My name is Margaux Andrews—"

"Of course it is," says the woman. "Who else would it be? We have been waiting for your call." She sounds slightly put out, like my call is tardy.

"Oh," I say, "I'm sorry, I called almost as soon as I received the let—"

"No excuses please. We are too busy for that. M. must leave for the airport in an hour and wants me to ask you if you are able to meet first thing in the morning?"

"Yes, of course, but—"

"No buts about it. Meet M. at the Algonquin Round Table at nine tomorrow morning."

Before I have a chance to respond, she has hung up.

The *Algonquin Round Table*? What *is* that? How on earth am I going to meet a person I don't know at a place I have never heard of? I cross the room and pull out the Manhattan Yellow Pages. I go to the *A* section and scan . . . Alg . . . Algonquin . . . Algonquin Hotel! That must be it. I go to the *R* section and scan for Round Table, thinking maybe it's the name of a restaurant. No luck. I pick up the handset again and dial the number for the hotel.

A woman with an overly cheerful voice answers. "Algonquin Hotel, home to literary legends, how may I help you?"

Home to literary legends! What an odd way to describe a hotel. "Uh, hello . . . I have what may be a strange question."

The woman laughs. "You'd be surprised at some of the questions people ask."

"Well, I am supposed to meet with a literary agent tomorrow at the Algonquin Round Table . . ."

"And what's the question?" she says.

"What *is* the Round Table?"

I pull the receiver away from my ear as the woman releases a shrill peal of laughter. "Oh dear, you must be new in town."

"Well, I've lived here for more than a year."

"Like I said. And from the sound of your voice, you are *very* young."

"I'm twenty-five, but I don't see the relevance."

"Oh, it explains *everything*."

"Well? Can you help me?"

"Certainly," she says. "You will be meeting your party in the Rose Room at the round table. I presume M. Des Jardins is the agency?"

"Yes, that's right." How does she know who my agent is? "The Rose Room?" I say.

"Yes, that is where you will find the round table."

"Oh, okay, and the *round table*?"

"You can't miss it—there's only one," she says. "I recommend that you hop on over to the library to learn more about the Vicious Circle. It will all make more sense to you, dear, after you've immersed yourself in a bit of New York City history."

"Well, thank you for your help," I say.

"You must be special, indeed. M. Des Jardins has not taken on any new clients in the past fifty years. We'll see you tomorrow, and please, no jeans and T-shirts in the dining room." She hangs up.

Fifty years? How old *is* this person? They must be ancient, like at least eighty or something.

I pick up the phone one more time and dial my neighbor Cassie. She can undoubtedly tell me where the closest library branch is.

MULBERRY BRANCH

SATURDAY, END OF DAY

THE MULBERRY BRANCH library is just a few blocks away, and I get there easily before closing at five. I pull the door open. Instantly, the smell of books transports me to the public libraries of my past. It's a small library, like something intended for children's reading groups, not for adults. There are low bookshelves full of colorful books and a comfy reading area clearly designed for little people— improbable that I will learn anything about the Vicious Circle here.

Libraries, and doing research, have always intimidated me. I never mastered the use of the card catalog or the Dewey Decimal System, so I bypass the wall of card-catalog drawers and head straight for the sign that says "Reference Librarian." My feet tread loudly across the polished tile floors. The echo makes the room feel eerily vacant. I step up to the counter but don't see anyone there. A sign next to a bell says "Ring once if you need assistance. Otherwise, help yourself." I tap the bell twice. The sound is louder than I expected.

"Oh! My, can't you read?" a high-pitched woman's voice

says close by, but nobody is there. "The sign says 'Ring *once* if you need assistance.'"

"Hello?" I look around. "Uh . . . sorry, I meant to ring it once."

"Well, why didn't you say so, then?"

Am I Alice in *Alice in Wonderland*? I half expect to see the Cheshire Cat, or possibly the Mad Hatter. Instead, the red curly hair of a small woman appears in motion above the counter and then disappears again. She must be unusually short—perhaps a dwarf? The woman grunts as she pushes an object across the floor. Her head and shoulders pop above the counter as she steps up on a stool revealing her bespectacled face and rosy cheeks.

"How can I help you?" She smiles.

"Well, I was told to visit the library to do some research on something called the Vicious Circle. You see, tomorrow I am meeting with a literary agent at the Algonquin Round Table."

"Well, that is certainly interesting, since the Round Table only exists metaphorically in these times, and the members of the Vicious Circle, well, let's say they mostly have faded into the annals of time."

"Is there a book or something I can read to learn more about it?"

"There are quite a few," she says, "but of course we don't have them here in this branch—and your interview is tomorrow, so ordering one won't do you much good."

"I suppose I could go to the main library?"

"Well, not today. It is closing soon, but—" She raises one heavily lined over-tweezed eyebrow. "Let *me* tell you what I know about it," she says. "If you're willing to wait about thirty minutes so that I can finish my work for the day, the library will close at five. There's a place a few doors down where we can get a drink and a snack. Perhaps I know enough so that you can seem *knowledgeable* when you meet with the *so-called* agent?"

I think for a moment. "Yes, that would be good." *So-called agent?* "I can peruse the shelves for a bit while I wait." I glance doubtfully over at the rows and rows of children's picture books.

"Give me a moment," the librarian says, disappearing from view to look for something under the counter. She reappears in seconds.

"*Or,* you can have a look at *this* book while you wait."

She offers me a book that looks pretty old. A blue cloth-covered volume with gold embossing that reads *Here Lies Dorothy Parker*, or is it *Here Lies* by Dorothy Parker? It looks well read. I open it to see the date of publication—1939. It's a collection of short stories.

"Thank you!" I cross over to the comfy area of the library and take a seat in the overstuffed chair, which I presume belongs to the storyteller for children's literature hour.

The first story, "Arrangement in Black and White," is about a woman at a party for a celebrated Black musician and her conversation with the host. It feels dated—the language, the venue—and it transports me to the atmosphere of an upper-crust party during the Roaring Twenties. Dorothy Parker must have been at this party; *she* must have overheard this conversation. It is so unbelievable that it must be true. Every racist cliché that I have ever heard makes an appearance in her story—and comes out of the mouth of one woman, no less. Phenomenal. Did the woman at the party ever read this story? Did she recognize herself? Did she see what an awful person she had been?

I've begun the second story when the reference librarian appears in front of me. Her hair looks redder than I remembered—perhaps it's the contrast between her hair and her yellow raincoat and boots.

"Well." She smiles brightly. "Are you ready?"

I close the book and offer it up to her. "That sounds nice! Let's go."

"Keep it. I have taken the liberty of checking that book out for you," she says.

Odd. I don't remember giving her my name or my library card. I don't even *have* a New York Public Library card.

"Oh, and here is your new library card." She hands me a card that doesn't look like any other library card I have ever seen. It has the sentence "Knowledge Is Power" typed on one side of it—not printed, typed on a typewriter. On the other side it says "This card is the exclusive property of the holder, entitling them to a free pass at the New York Public Library." No name.

"Put that someplace safe," she says. "We only give those to the truly curious."

I tuck it into my wallet with my identification. I am *truly curious*.

"I suppose if we are going out for a beverage, we should be on a first-name basis—my name is Rosie. My mother named me that for the color of my hair and cheeks."

"It certainly suits you! And I guess I should have introduced myself," I say. "Margaux Andrews—a pleasure to make your acquaintance, Rosie." I put my hand forward to shake, and Rosie reciprocates. Her hand is soft and warm in mine. Her grip is firm, but not tight.

Rosie pulls out a ring of keys, opens the front door, and ushers me over the threshold into the cool evening air.

* * *

WE STOP two doors down from the library in front of an unmarked red door. "Here we are," she says. She taps a rhythmic pattern on the door and turns to me. "That is today's secret knock, different every day!"

"Oh," I say, "is this a friend's house?"

"No, no, this is the place I was telling you about. It's a private club where people discuss seriously curious and funny things."

The door opens a crack; I can see nothing but dark eyes peering out. "Hiya, Rosie, we've been expecting you. Who'd you bring today?"

"This is Margaux," she says, "a bona fide card-carrying truly curious person."

The eyes land on me. "Your card please?"

I look at Rosie. "Oh, I don't carry calling cards, I'm sorry."

Rosie and the person behind the eyes giggle. Rosie says, "Your library card will do."

I dig out my wallet from my bag and fetch the card. A hand reaches out and snatches it. Will I get it back?

The door swings open to reveal an ornately appointed restaurant with a bar, overflowing with fashionably dressed people of many different ages, also notable for their lack of racial and ethnic homogeneity. Above the chatter, the music of a jazz band rises, and as we pass through the restaurant, I overhear several languages being spoken. What a magnificent place—with timeless decor and eclectic furnishings from various eras.

The host seats us at a small round table with built-in seating and hands us each a small menu. "Your server will be here momentarily."

The menu only has two items on it: "Drink" and "Snack." A note at the bottom says, *Drinks and Snacks served between 4 p.m. and 9 p.m., Dinner is served at 10 p.m.*

I glance up at Rosie, who appears to be studying the menu. "This is a curious restaurant, Rosie."

"Yes, it is," she says. "Isn't it delightful? One never knows what to expect here—like life itself."

A tall thin woman approaches the table. "Good evening, Rosie."

"Hello there, Winnie," Rosie says. "I'd like to introduce you to Margaux, my guest for the evening."

She turns to me. "A pleasure to meet you, Margaux."

"Likewise." How odd to introduce waitstaff as if they are friends.

"Have you decided what you'd like to have?" Winnie asks Rosie.

Rosie says, "Yes, I will have the Drink and the Snack."

Winnie looks at me. I flush. Is this some sort of practical joke? I play it straight. "I guess I will have the same thing she is having? Thank you."

Winnie collects the menus and disappears.

"So, did you have a chance to read any of Dorothy's lies?" Rosie asks.

"Lies?"

"*Here Lies* by Dorothy Parker." Either she is lying or she is dead. I assume the former, since a corpse could not have written all of those stories."

"Of course I saw that, but there is also another way to interpret it, as in *her corpus . . . of work*, which is how I interpreted it."

Rosie laughs. "A title is a beautiful thing when done well; it does so much work for the reader, a gentle guide."

Winnie comes back. She sets an old-fashioned cocktail down in front of Rosie and a large glass of red wine in front of me.

"Thank you, but I thought I ordered the same thing she did."

Winnie says, "You did indeed. She ordered the Drink and the Snack and so did you. We always serve the Drink that is most desired, and she wanted an old-fashioned and you wanted a glass of cabernet. You haven't changed your mind, have you?"

"No, a big red is exactly what I had hoped for."

"I thought so," she says, and vanishes.

"How did she know what I wanted?" I ask. "I don't know what I want half the time."

"Isn't it marvelous?" Rosie says. "I have no idea."

Winnie comes back. She places a large wooden board on the table between Rosie and me; it's filled with a variety of cured meats, cheeses, nuts, and fruit, the likes of which I have only seen when traveling in Europe. And then, a fragrant basket of steaming bread fresh out of the oven— what I always desire.

"So you want to know about the Vicious Circle," Rosie says, "and I thought, what better place to come than here— to the Round About."

"Oh, I see what you mean!" We're seated in a perfectly round room. "I wondered what this place was called."

"The Round Table borrowed its name from King Arthur's round table, and the Vicious Circle refers to a loose collective of writers, mostly journalists, who back in the nineteen twenties ate lunch together daily in the Rose Room around a round table at the Algonquin Hotel. These writers were not the literary scions of the day, but they were bright and socially engaged people who enjoyed verbal jousting and outwitting each other; they were cutting, hence the name. Dorothy Parker was one of the founding members and one of the most sharp-tongued, which is one reason I thought her stories would be of interest to you. There were only a few fiction writers in the group, but their writing was mostly based on reality and the social issues of the day."

"Funny, the first thing I thought when I read 'Arrangement in Black and White' was that the author had been at that party."

"Yes, Parker was well known for taking on controversial

topics like racism and sexism in her short stories, and they were often based on her own experiences in the world. She was known for her use of irony as a way to communicate her most controversial opinions."

"I would have enjoyed eavesdropping on her round table!" I say.

Rosie carefully places a piece of cheese and salami on a chunk of bread. "Yes, that would have been fun."

I dig in too. The bread is delicious.

THE ROUND TABLE
SUNDAY MORNING

In spite of having had more wine than usual at the Round About, I wake up refreshed and ready to go in the morning. I go over yesterday's events. Perhaps I dreamt some of it—Rosie, Winnie, the strange restaurant where they serve you what you most desire.

The phone rings. "Hello?" I say.

"Yes," says a woman, "this is Winnie. We met last night at the Round About."

"Oh, Winnie, of course!" This is downright strange.

"I'm calling because you left your library card on the table. I'm sure you'll be needing it!"

"Gosh, I must not have noticed that it had been returned."

"Returned? Returned from whom? Why would someone take someone else's library card?" she says.

"When I got into the restaurant last night they asked for it—"

"How strange. It's a good thing they returned it! Anyway, would it be okay if I drop it by your place later today on my way into work?"

"Sure," I say, "I should be home by then, 202 Eliz—"

"Elizabeth Street, 5A."

"Yes, but how did you—"

"I called Rosie. She gave me all of the details."

"Well, okay then, what time should I expect to see you?"

"How does three thirty suit you?"

"Sounds good," I say. "I'll see you then."

It is already eight twenty-five when I get off the phone. I need to hoof it to get up to the Algonquin by nine. Rosie and Winnie are real, at least maybe. How could Rosie possibly know my phone number and address when I didn't give them to her?

* * *

SUNDAY MORNING IS OFTEN QUIET, especially in Midtown, and today is no exception. Although it is sunny and bright, as I exit the subway, a faint breeze sends a chill through my sweater. I cross over to the sunny side of the street. I should have worn a jacket. I dressed in my best clothes: a midi-length gray wool skirt, a rust-colored cashmere sweater, and high brown Frye boots. Definitely not jeans or a T-shirt! It's what I would wear to church if I were the churchgoing type.

The Algonquin Hotel is an unassuming turn-of-the-century building with a heavy limestone-and-brick facade sandwiched between newer Midtown buildings. Green awnings pop out above the lower windows, and the flags of the United States and New York wave over the door.

A doorman sees me and opens the door with a flourish. "Welcome to the Algonquin," he says, bowing slightly and waving me through with his left hand.

Inside, the concierge says, "Good morning! May I help you?"

"Yes, it is a good morning, isn't it? I am meeting someone at the round table in the Rose Room. Can you point the way?"

He gestures toward the back of the lobby. "Be careful as you go. Hamlet is in an ankle-biting mood today."

"What did you say?"

"Hamlet, the lobby cat. Keep your eyes peeled for him. He's a big orange tabby. Deceptively cute."

Why would they keep a cat that bites ankles in a hotel, especially when so many people have allergies? That's a real liability.

As I make my way through the lobby, I pass Hamlet curled up in an overstuffed chair. His eyes meet mine, and I see him smile, but that's ridiculous. He's big and fat, definitely *not* the ankle-biting type.

The restaurant is busy but not super crowded. I wait at the hosting podium. At the back, six people sit at the singular round table. Maybe the round table is a community table, one of those shared tables restaurants have begun to provide to keep singles from taking up larger tables. Which of the six is M. Des Jardins?

A woman holding menus approaches the podium. "Breakfast for one?" she asks.

"Actually, I am here to meet my party, M. Des Jardins, at the round table."

"Of course, I should have known. Follow me."

Not sure why she should have known. When we reach the table, a young man close to my own age stands to greet me. He's handsome, oddly familiar. "Oh, Margaux!" he says. "I can't believe you are finally here."

"Am I late?" I ask, vaguely embarrassed. All eyes are on me. I thought M. would be alone, but it is clear from the expressions on the faces at the table that they are *all* expecting me. There are three empty seats. Where should I sit?

"No, it's that it's been such a long time since we last saw each other. We were child—"

Suddenly, I know who he is. "Oh my God, you're Kiyo

—Mr. Sakura's grandson!" Mr. Sakura was the caretaker of the house we lived in on President Street in Peakview, the house that inspired my novel. The last time I saw Kiyo was after my eighth birthday. He was ten. The logo makes *perfect* sense now. But who are the rest of the people at the table? Should I know them too?

"Ever since we received your submission at the agency, I have been giddy," Kiyo says.

A woman sitting across from Kiyo laughs. "That's putting it mildly. Kiyo couldn't stop singing his praises of you, and how you were his long-lost childhood sw—"

"Friend," Kiyo says. "Please sit!" He pulls out the chair next to him. "Margaux, I want you to meet the members of M. Des Jardins Literary Agency. *We* are M. Des Jardins." Kiyo opens his arms to the other occupants of the round table. "Two of us are still missing."

"I'm Kacia," says the woman directly across from Kiyo. "We spoke yesterday. Sorry that I was so brusque with you —we were anxious to hear back."

"No problem," I say. "I'm overwhelmed by everything. I thought M. was an actual person." I look around at all of the delighted faces at the table watching my confusion and surprise; they are devouring this moment. The remaining four members of M. Des Jardins introduce themselves—all special agents of one kind or another. My mind can't retain their names as it races with wonder at the revelation that Kiyo, my childhood crush, is behind all of this.

"M. *was* an actual person—Mihana Sakura, my maternal grandmother," Kiyo says.

"What about the Des Jardins part?"

"My grandmother thought it sounded sophisticated, and also, as you know, my grandfather was an avid gardener— roses were his specialty, and he always referred to my grandmother as his perfect rose." Kiyo continues, "I never knew her, but she is the one who started the literary agency many years ago, back in nineteen twenty-seven. She died shortly after my mother's birth in nineteen thirty-five."

"That's so sad," I say.

"My grandfather, who you knew, of course, took over the agency for a time, and then the war came. He and my mother were forced to leave Los Angeles and were sent to an 'internment camp'—a euphemism—in Colorado. They lost everything they had, including the agency."

"Wow, I had no idea."

"And neither did I!" Kiyo says. "It wasn't until my own mother was dying a few years ago that I learned the whole story, including about the agency. I didn't know she had lived in one of those wretched concentration camps as a child."

"You must have felt brokenhearted for her," I say.

"Not at all," Kiyo says. "I felt proud of her, amazed at her accomplishments. She made the most of her life and, as a result, was able to leave me a small fortune. It was she who suggested that I revive M. Des Jardins Literary Agency, which is what I have done. If you agree to it, you will be our first signed author—the first signed author since my grandmother died fifty years ago, when she last signed Dorothy Parker, and I think you know who she was—"

"That *is* a coincidence," I say. "A funny little librarian at the Mulberry branch gave me a collection of her short stories yesterday. I'm definitely intrigued."

"Good, that is what I hoped," Kiyo says. He looks toward the door and smiles. "Oh, and look who's here!"

Rosie and Winnie head toward us; both are grinning. They make quite a pair—Winnie is lanky and lithe, Rosie squat and solid.

"Margaux, I want to introduce you to our Top Dog, Ms. Rose White, and her assistant, Ms. Winifred Green." Kiyo beams.

"But how . . . I thought—"

"Yes, isn't the world a beautiful and magical place?" Rosie says. "And, regardless of what Kiyo says, he is the Head Honcho, not me."

Winnie hands me my library card. "You'll need this," she says, smiling as she takes a seat next to Rosie in one of the two empty chairs. "I still want to see you later. I wanted to make sure you saved room on your calendar for me, and I didn't want to spoil any surprises. I love surprises."

"I do too," says Kiyo. "My grandfather taught me about everyday magic and about making magic too. While some people feed on fear, focusing on every scary thing in life that is in their past and present, and worry about scary things in the future, others focus on the beauty and mystery of it all. M. Des Jardins is only interested in literature that recognizes the truth of magic and celebrates the human capacity for overcoming adversity, which is why we love your story so much."

The server comes and takes orders. I fidget with my napkin.

"Not everybody shares in your enthusiasm for it," I say. "My sister, Paloma, for example."

"Hmm," Kiyo says, "don't let her dissuade you. She has undoubtedly spent her life trying to deny reality by denying the power of imagination to change it."

That's true. Paloma remembers only the pain, and there was plenty of that. She can't see the magic and beauty of our childhood. For her, there was more pain than pleasure. We lived entirely different realities. I sometimes wonder if something bad happened to her in childhood that I don't know about.

"As you may recall from when you sent your manuscript, we ask authors to send them *blind*, without author-identifying information, because we don't want to make biased decisions on whether or not to publish. We don't want to know one's gender or anything about one's ethnic or racial background. We're interested in unadulterated words. When I started reading your manuscript, however, the story instantly transported me back to the house on President Street where I spent so many magnificent days with my grandfather, you, and your family. I knew that there was only one person who could have written it. Because I knew, I recused myself from the decision-making process, leaving the final decision to Rosie. I'm telling you this because I don't want you to think that I showed any favoritism in accepting you."

"And I gave my unequivocal approval, as did the rest of M. Des Jardins," says Rosie. All of the others nod in agreement.

Kacia says, "We were unanimous in our acceptance of your manuscript. We've received three hundred and one manuscripts since opening our doors. Most have gone to the recycling bin after the first chapter."

"I'm flattered," I say. "I don't know what to say."

"Say *yes*," Kiyo says. He looks me straight in the eye. My heart quickens.

"Well, I promised Paloma that I would revisit the novel before publishing it. I don't want to hurt anyone with my words."

Rosie says, "I can certainly respect that."

"And Theo—"

"Needs to face the truth. Don't you think he figured out what happened to Anna a long time ago too?" Kiyo and I had come to the same conclusion about what happened to her the day they found her body—we both suspected that Theo had been involved in her disappearance, but we never spoke to him about it. Instead, we went to my mother and Mr. Sakura, and we all swore ourselves to secrecy to protect Theo. We haven't spoken of it since then.

"I owe it to them to read and make changes to protect them."

"Fair enough," Kiyo says. "Tomorrow we are meeting with several editors from top houses—we think Gottlieb will be interested in you as a new talent."

Gottlieb? Is he talking about taking my book to Knopf?

"Rosie and Winnie are based here in New York," Kiyo says, "so, if you need *anything*, any assistance at all, reach out to them. I think you know where to find each of them, but in case they are not there when you need them, please call me."

Kiyo hands me his business card, which is beautifully letterpress printed on thick rag card stock. I run my finger across his name, Kiyomaru (清丸) Flores.

"*Really*, you can call me anytime for any reason."

The old crush has returned. "I will," I say.

"Promise?" He looks me straight in the eye.

"Crisscross." I cross my singing heart.

ANOTHER PRANKSTER

SUNDAY AFTERNOON

I'M a ball of confusion on my way home, so distracted that I miss my subway stop. All I can think about is Kiyo, how weird it is having him show up in my life after such a long absence. Suspicion sneaks into my thoughts. Why now? Is it serendipitous? Plotted? At least it explains a few things, like how Rosie and Winnie knew so much about me. There was something vaguely creepy about that until it all came together at the Algonquin. Still, I have so many questions.

At the apartment, I bounce up the stairs to the fifth-floor landing, where I stop short. My front door is ajar. The locks and door are intact. Did I leave it unlocked? Unlikely. No, I definitely remember locking both the upper and lower locks.

Without entering, I say, "Is someone there?" Not a peep. Not sure why anyone would answer if they had broken in and were still inside. My heart pounds. I hope they didn't steal my typewriter. God, please.

"Boo!" Theo jumps out from behind the door.

"Fuck you, Theo!" I say. "You're lucky I didn't have a gun or a knife or that I didn't gouge your eyes out with my keys." My mother taught me to hold my keys between my knuckles for self-defense, and I always do, but clearly I lack the instinct to gouge someone's eyes out. Otherwise, I would have done it.

Theo is cracking up. "Ah, come on, it was a joke." He's like a big puppy dog—the sweetest guy you've ever met, but he has no clue what a jerk he can be, especially to me. I'm lucky to have grown into adulthood, given the number of times he endangered my life when we were children; that's one of the focal points in my novel that he may take exception to.

Theo was the only one of us children who ever received a spanking, mostly when he had endangered me in some significant way, like the time he turned off the cold water when our mother was filling the tub for our shared bath when I was four and he five and a half. After feeling the water with his own hand, he said, *Get in! The water is the perfect temperature.* I ended up screaming in pain from the scalding hot water on my feet and legs. Our mother was furious. Too many stories like this to recount—a minuscule number made it into the novel. He wasn't evil or bad—just liked to prank me, and he himself enjoyed danger.

"You almost gave me a heart attack. It's lucky I didn't fall down the stairs," I say. "What the hell are you doing here, and how did you get into my apartment?"

"It wasn't too hard," he says. "When I got here and you weren't home, I sat down on the stairs. After an hour, I decided to knock on your neighbor's door."

Of course. I gave Cassie a key in case I got locked out for some reason. "And she let you in, having never met you before?"

"Actually, when she opened the door, she immediately recognized me," he said, beaming. "She said, 'Wait, don't tell me, you've gotta be Margaux's brother. She didn't tell me that you were *identical* twins!'"

People always say that about us. Other than the fact that I have large breasts and no penis, they say we look alike. I don't see it. When we were children in Peakview, if we had on our winter parkas, our own mother couldn't tell us apart. She shopped for us as if we were twins to keep us from fighting over who got what. In truth, Theo is almost two years older. He has black hair like our mother, shiny and straight. I have lighter kinky hair. We have the same dark eyes. Our mother says the eyes come from her Cherokee grandfather. I get my curly hair from our father's side—my mother said she thinks he had some African blood somewhere, but his family would deny it if it were true, the most racist people she had ever known.

Inside the apartment, Theo has made himself right at home. He has evidently eaten a bowl of raisin bran. The box is still out, as is the milk carton. Typical. I bet both are empty. Theo has always been a bit of a slob, having been surrounded by girls and women who babied him and never expected much of him in the way of doing household chores.

"So why are you here?" I ask.

"Oh, well, I was missing my sisters . . . Actually, Paloma invited me for a visit."

"I saw her yesterday. Why didn't she mention you were coming?"

"Dunno. I got in last night," he says. "She told me you might have an agent for your book. Big congrats! I'm so proud of you."

His genuine enthusiasm puzzles me. Paloma no doubt told him everything, including her thoughts on my novel, but he's not concerned.

"Wow, thanks, Theo. I haven't said yes yet."

"You should," he says without hesitation.

"But here is the real surprise—you know the agent."

"Really? I don't know any literary agents."

"Remember Kiyo Flores?"

"No shit! How weird is that? How'd that come about?"

"Kind of mysteriously." I set my canvas bag down and dig through it to find the letter and hand it to him. "I had no idea it was from him until I got to the hotel this morning."

Theo takes one look at the letter and says, "That logo looks like our old gate!"

"Yep," I say.

"If this is from Kiyo, then who is M. Des Jardins?"

"Originally, it was his grandmother. Now it's a Vicious Circle."

"Whoa, that doesn't sound good," Theo says. "What does that mean?"

"Oh, nothing—Kiyo has teamed up with a bunch of interesting characters who are clever literary pranksters."

I fill him in on all that happened between seeing Paloma yesterday and meeting Kiyo today at the Algonquin Round Table.

"Wow, this takes me back to President Street," Theo says. "Mr. Sakura sure brightened a dark time."

"Yeah, and you know *that* is what my novel is about—dark times. Have you read it?"

"Nah," he says, shaking his head. "Truthfully, I'm afraid to read it, especially after talking to Paloma. Afraid that I might not like it. And then what would I say to you?"

"I think you *will* like it. I wrote it for *you*—well, for you, me, and Paloma, and all that we went through back then."

Theo has a wistful expression on his face.

"Anyway, I would like you to read it before I turn over a final version to the publishers to edit. I promised Paloma that I would reread and rewrite things to protect our family. She's worried about what it might—"

"That's a crock of Paloma shit," Theo says. "Publish it. She's worried about me, I know. I'll be fine. That's what I came to tell you. I've been doing well. The nightmares have stopped."

After they found Anna's body, Theo went into a shell.

Once a daredevil, he became more cautious. Come to think of it, he became nicer to me.

"Okay, but you must promise to read it."

"Maybe I won't, maybe I will," he says, grinning. "On a different subject, can I sleep on your couch tonight? I have a friend to see in the city."

I don't want to pry. Maybe he has a love interest. That would be terrific. To my knowledge he has never fallen in love. He's dated a few hippie chicks, but never for long. He told me once that he'd always imagined Anna was the one, but they were little kids then. Nobody meets their one and only then, do they?

"Sure, that's fine. I have to leave for work early tomorrow, but you can lock up and slip the extra key under the door. Did you already tell Paloma?"

"Yeah, she's not expecting me back until tomorrow."

"Great, do you have time to go out for a snack and a drink at four?" I ask. I told Kiyo, Rosie, and Winnie I'd meet them at the Round About again. Now I know why Winnie needed to return my library card.

"Of course. Nothing I would like to do more."

"Do you have a library card on you by chance?"

"Now that is a real non sequitur! Why? Do I need one?"

"You might," I say. "We'll see." I plop my weighty manuscript down on the counter in front of him. "In the in-between time, feel free to start reading. I'll be doing the same."

ONE ELYSIUM STREET

CHAPTERS 1 THROUGH 5

For Magical Thinkers

I dreamed I moved among the Elysian fields,
In converse with sweet women long since dead;
And out of blossoms which that meadow yields
I wove a garland for your living head.
Danaï, that was the vessel for a day
Of golden Jove, I saw, and at her side,
Whom Jove the Bull desired and bore away,
Europa stood, and the Swan's featherless bride.
All these were mortal women, yet all these
Above the ground had had a god for guest;
Freely I walked beside them and at ease,
Addressing them, by them again addressed,
And marvelled nothing, for remembering you,
Wherefore I was among them well I knew.

— EDNA ST. VINCENT
MILLAY

PEAKVIEW

1968

PEAKVIEW, CO—An anonymous tip has led to the discovery of the body of a young girl in a shallow grave adjacent to the railroad tracks that run to the south of Vista Boulevard. The victim's identity and cause of death are being withheld until next of kin have been notified. There are no known suspects. If you have any information regarding this crime, please contact Detective Harrison at the Peakview Police Department.

— PEAKVIEW GAZETTE, MAY 28, 1968

1

PIGLET (MARGARET)

MAY 1965

TODAY IS MY FIFTH BIRTHDAY, May 30, 1965. I've never had a birthday party before. My grandma Mimi and my aunt Vivi are coming, plus a few of the kids who live in The Apartments. Our apartment is decorated real pretty with paper streamers and balloons. Mama made a homemade cake from Betty Crockett and let us each invite one friend. Willie invited Rob, Birdie asked Catrina, and Tree invited Maddie, a girl he met in kindergarten. I invited Stella, my best friend in the whole wide world.

I'm bored with waiting for the guests to arrive. I've been waiting on the front balcony for forever.

To entertain myself, I squeeze my head between the third-floor balcony bars; it barely fits, and when I try to pull it back out, it gets stuck on my ears. My heart starts to beat fast. I might throw up.

"Birdie! Tree! Willie!" I wait, hoping that Mama doesn't hear me. She'll be *really* mad. *Piglet, how many times do I have to tell you to stay away from the balcony bars? They are dangerous!*

At least this time I'm stuck on the *inside* of the bars. I'll never forget the look on Mama's face when she found me hanging on for dear life to the *outside* of the balcony. I was still little then. Tree talked me into it. *Come on, Pig,* he said, *you can squeeze between the bars.* Once I got to the other side of the railing, I looked down and froze. Other than my shaking legs, I was unable to move. I started to cry.

Piggie, scooch like this. Tree showed me how easy it was, scrambling like a squirrel over and along the railing and back to safety. He made it look simple, like a reasonable thing to try. *Piggie,* he urged, *don't be afraid.*

But suddenly, he disappeared into the apartment. I thought maybe he ran to get help, but no, he left me hanging on for dear life. He musta known Mama was coming up the stairs with the groceries. He knew he'd get a whippin', and he did.

There's a sound behind me. "You're an idiot!" Tree says. I turn my head as much as possible and see a sneer on his face. He's almost seven, thinks he's the boss of me.

"Am not."

"Are too."

"Am not, *you* are."

"I know you are, but what am I?"

"Come on, Tree, help me get my head out," I whimper.

"Only if you promise not to tell on me to Mom or Birdie one time tomorrow."

"I promise." A hard promise to keep. What if he tortures me? I can't bear the Chinese water torture or being his tickle typewriter without telling on him. I don't know how else to get him to stop. He's bigger and stronger than I am.

"Crisscross?"

"Cross my heart, hope to die, stick a needle in my eye!" I poke my pointer finger into my eye.

"Well, okay then." Tree carefully flattens my ears against my head and pushes on the top to get me unstuck. "If I were you, I wouldn't do that again."

"You're one to talk," I say. "Thanks for coming to my rescue."

* * *

STELLA ARRIVES FIRST—SHE always does. She's wearing the same outfit as always: high-top sneakers, jeans, and a T-shirt. She's a tomboy like me.

"I like your shirt!" I say, knowing it'll make her smile.

"Thanks, I wore yellow for your birthday. I know it's one of your favorite colors."

I like how bright it looks against her dark-brown skin. I wish my skin looked like that. I'm white as snow from head to toe. Grandma Mimi told me I'm lucky, cuz I'm a towhead. When I asked her what that meant she said that my hair is the color of flax, like that would clear things up for me.

I grab Stella by the hand and take her over to the coffee table so she can put her present with the others, and then we disappear into the kids' room to play.

It's not long before the sound of chattering voices alerts Stella and me that the party has started.

As we step into the room, Grandma Mimi sings out, "Happy birthday, Princess Peggy." She refuses to call me Piglet like the rest of the family. I'd rather be called Piglet than Princess Peggy any day. I charge over to hug her. I can smell her Chanel No. 5 perfume. "Is Stella here?" Mimi asks, looking around the room.

"Yeah, don't you see her? She's right—" As I turn to point, I am surprised to see that Stella has vanished. "Well, she *was* right there a second ago. Maybe she had to go potty."

"Yes, you're probably right." Grandma bends over to hug me. "Give me some sugar, hon!" She talks different. Mama said it's because she grew up in Mobile, Alabama, wherever that is.

Everybody but Tree's *girlfriend* is here. I'm disappointed because I wanted to meet her.

49

Tree is sitting on the couch looking sad. He's tracing the outline of the flower-patterned upholstery with his finger. I quietly move toward him. "Where's your *girlfriend?*" I tease.

"She's not my girlfriend."

"She's a girl. She's a friend. That makes her a girl-friend." I love the power of words.

"Go away, brat!" Tree balls his hand into a fist with his knuckle poked up. "Or I'll give you a frog on your arm."

Today I know I am safe. It's my birthday, and the room is full of grown-ups. "Dare you!" I look him square in the eye, squinting.

"Why don't you go play with your little invisible friend? Leave me alone!"

I decide not to pester him.

* * *

I'M mad about the party. I thought we would at least play Pin the Tail on the Donkey, or maybe we would have a piñata like we did at Tree's last birthday. Instead, Birdie and Willie are hanging out on the balcony with Catrina and Rob. They're talking loudly and laughing a lot. Curious about what's so funny, I pop out on the balcony. They keep talking as though I'm not there. Stella joins me, thankfully. We both laugh when the big kids do, but we're not sure what's so funny, so we make eyes at each other.

"Piggy-wig," Birdie says, "can you go get me another pop? Root beer."

"Sure!" I turn to go in, and before I have gone through the door, the whole bunch of them scramble down the metal stairs that lead down to the ground floor, making a huge racket.

They ditched me! I yell after them, "I'm gonna tell Mama on you!"

"So what?" Willie yells back.

They laugh as they disappear.

Stella says, "That was mean!"

"Yeah, I know, but at least I have you." I squeeze her hand in mine, and we go back to the party.

* * *

Tree has disappeared into the kids' room. Mama, Vivi, and Mimi are all gossiping about someone named Donna.

"I heard through the grapevine that they are getting divorced," Vivi says.

I know that word. My parents are *divorced*. That's why I don't have a dad. Well, I have a dad, but I don't know him. I've seen pictures of him in his uniform. He lives in another country, Mama says.

Mama sees me standing there with Stella—she always sees both of us, sometimes when Stella isn't with me. "Where have you guys been off to?" she asks. The gossip stops.

"Oh, we were out on the porch with Birdie and those guys."

"Run and go get them! It's time for us to have birthday cake!" Mama says.

I want to tell her they ditched me. Instead, I say, "Okay."

Stella and I go out the front door. We can see the four of them sprinting across the lawn toward our building. They aren't laughing now.

They clamber up the stairs, barge right past me and Stella like we're not here at all. We follow them in.

"Mom." Willie is out of breath. "Something real bad happened!"

"Are you hurt? What's going on?"

"It's Maddie, Mom," says Birdie. "We know why she didn't come."

"What on earth?"

Rob and Catrina say simultaneously, "Maddie's missing."

"They're saying she was kidnapped," Willie adds authoritatively.

"Where'd you hear that?"

Willie looks down at his feet. "Well, we were trying to get away from Piglet cuz she was acting all weird like she does sometimes, making faces and talking to herself—"

"I *wasn't* talking to *myself*," I say. "I was *talking* to Stella."

"Anyways, we went on over to the playground to sit on the swings and talk. That's when we saw all the police cars over at the Smiths' apartment. There was a crowd gathered outside talking."

"We asked one of the grown-ups what was going on," says Birdie. "The lady said she wasn't certain, but she heard that the Smith girl was missing, and they think it might have been a kidnapping."

Mama says, "That's one of the most terrible things I can imagine! Lord, I hope that is not the case."

Aunt Vivi says, "Well, don't go getting all upset about it until we know more."

"Quite right," Mimi says. "There could be a completely different explanation. Maybe she's hiding at a friend's house, afraid of getting in trouble, or maybe she's gone and got lost."

Everybody is real quiet. Tree's crying—something I've never seen before.

"Aw, come on, Tree, everything's gonna be alright. They'll get her back." Birdie wraps her arm around his shoulder.

Mama looks worried.

Vivi reassures her, "Nothing like that could *ever* happen to *your* kids."

"There are too many of them!" Mimi adds. "They're never alone."

But that's not true. Sometimes when Mama goes to school and I am with the babysitter, Trudy, she sends me outdoors to play by myself, especially if her boyfriend is there. Stella usually shows up to keep me company, but sometimes I crouch in the warmth of a dryer vent outside the laundry room all by myself. Someone *could* take me if they wanted to, and *nobody* would know for hours. Maybe I won't do that anymore. Maybe I won't tell Mama that I do that.

We eat our cake, and I open presents. Stella is there by my side the whole time to comfort me. She whispers in my ear, "You will have many other birthday parties, and they will all be better than this one."

* * *

AFTER MY BIRTHDAY, nothing is the same. Maybe that's what being five is like.

The night after the party, we all sit in front of our new television set. We are tuned to channel 2 watching *Gilligan's Island*, waiting for the news to come on. Finally, the newsman comes on with a special report. It is about Maddie.

"Maddie Smith, six years old, is three and a half feet tall and weighs forty-five pounds. When she was last seen, she was wearing a polka-dotted Minnie Mouse pajama set. She is missing her two front teeth, has dark-brown curly hair and brown eyes, and a small mole on her left cheek. If you think you may have seen her, call our emergency hotline at 757-KTVP."

They put up her school photo from kindergarten. I've seen her before at the playground.

"According to Maddie's parents, they put her to bed at

seven p.m. on Saturday, May twenty-ninth. On Sunday morning her mother went to awaken her and found her bed empty. There was no sign of a struggle, and all doors and windows were closed and locked."

Maddie's tearful parents appear on screen. Mrs. Smith is hard to understand through her sobs. "Please, bring our precious Maddie back."

Mr. Smith looks tired. "If you know anything, please come forward now. We have formed a group of volunteers to help search for Maddie. She's a sleepwalker, and we think it's possible that she left the house asleep, possibly waking up someplace unfamiliar."

Mama switches the TV off. "Well, kids, it's been a big day. Time for you all to get to bed."

"But—" Birdie whines.

"No buts about it," Mama says as she herds us to the bathroom to brush our teeth.

* * *

AFTER GETTING our pj's on, we climb into our own bunk beds. Birdie and Willie both sleep in the top bunks. I sleep under Birdie, and Tree under Willie. At first we are all quiet, then Birdie asks, "Where do you think she is tonight?"

I say, "Stella told me she's in heaven."

"That's stupid," says Tree. "Stella isn't real."

"She's real to me."

"Cool it, guys," Willie says. "It's bad enough that Maddie is missing. Let's not fight."

2

MARTA

MAY 1965

AFTER THE KIDS have gone to bed, Marta throws herself down on the couch. The room darkens as night descends; the only light emanates from the silent flickering black-and-white television. She always turns the volume down when the kids go to bed, but still enjoys the flow, cadence, and comforting company of old movie stars. She stares up at the ceiling. What a terrible day.

She studies the popcorn texture above her as she does almost every night while she lies awake ruminating over all of the choices she's made, the choices she is making now. *You're going to raise a bunch of homos!* Doug had yelled at her as she scrambled into the taxi with all five kids in tow. She'd looked back as they pulled away from the curb. He stood there with his hands in his pockets, a look of disbelief plastered on his reddened face. Marta read his expression as, *How could* you *possibly leave* me? He would have been right to wonder. Only an insane person would leave a husband with a promising naval career, a surgeon no less. She didn't have any money, and she hadn't graduated from high school. She worried about how she would take care of five kids without *his* money. At best, she could get a job waiting tables in a truck stop or some dingy diner. She had been *completely* dependent on him. That is what made her decide to get her GED a few months after leaving him. Then with the encouragement of her sister, she applied to college the next year, beginning as a freshman at the age of thirty-five. Maybe she *had* made a mistake in leaving Doug.

At the time, she felt clear about the choice. *Stay or die.*

No, leaving was the right thing. They never should have married, and wouldn't have if she hadn't gotten pregnant. She met him in her last year at Peakview East, and he was in his first year at UP in pre-med, four years older than she. He was attending college on the GI bill, had been a naval aviator in the Pacific Theater—a war hero. Most handsome man Marta had ever seen, and their attraction to each other had been instantaneous. She got pregnant after only one time, her first time, and it wasn't even pleasant. Sex with him was never good.

Over the years the mistakes of the marriage were compounded by her admission of being more attracted to women than to men. Soon after telling him that, the night before she left, Doug came home from work later than usual; he was drunk. The kids were all in bed. She didn't challenge him, didn't ask him where he had been. She simply reheated the Salisbury steak, mashed potatoes, and green beans and put it on the table for him. He sat down and angrily began jabbing the food with his fork. *I spend all day at the hospital, and this is the shit you feed me?* Marta knew better than to defend herself. *I'm sorry* is all she said before leaving the room.

She went into the bathroom and shut the door, made some sounds as if using the toilet. After about five minutes, she ran some water, pretending to wash her hands. She looked in the mirror. The bruises had healed, but she still saw them. Finally, she quietly opened the door.

Doug lay in wait for her in the hall. He grabbed her by

the neck with his right hand and pinned her against the wall, poked her hard in the right eye with his left thumb to keep her from struggling. *If you gave a damn about me, you would throw a fit when I came home late, but you play the pathetic little mouse,* he said.

Marta's heart pounded. *Shhhh . . .* she managed. She thought of Piglet, nine months old, asleep in their bedroom, and of the other children. What would happen to them? Would he kill them too?

A door at the end of the hallway opened. It was Kit, the oldest. *Let her go, you fucker.* The growl in his voice startled her. When had he become a man?

This is none of your business, Son. If you know what's good for you, you'll go back to bed, Doug threatened.

No, Dad, if you know what's good for you, you'll let her go.

Marta couldn't see Kit, but Doug released her from his grip, and she collapsed on the floor. When she looked up, she saw Kit holding Doug's service pistol, pointed straight at Doug, who stood still and stared at his son in disbelief. Doug turned and ran out the front door.

He returned in the morning, remorseful like always, with a bouquet of flowers for Marta. Then, as if nothing had happened, he showered, dressed in his uniform, and left for work. She stayed out of his way.

After he left, she called her mother to tell her she was moving back home. Her mother's silence hurt. *No woman in her right mind would leave a doctor husband. Every woman puts up with abuse from time to time. Why should you be any different?* Marta is different. She wanted more for herself, more for her children. She didn't want to live in fear. She had known for a long time that one day she would leave, and the previous night's events had convinced her that the time was then. She had managed to pilfer enough money over the last ten years without Doug's notice to buy four one-way airline tickets to Denver. Tree and Piglet could sit on laps.

Has she run from one horror only to jump into a different one? Maddie Smith's disappearance weighs heavily. Oh, how Maddie's parents must feel. Marta sometimes leaves the kids at home, not quite alone but without adult supervision much of the time, to attend classes at the University of Peakview. Willie is twelve now, and Birdie is ten, technically old enough to babysit, but they are not all *that* responsible, nor should they be. Plus Tree is a handful. When she *is* home, the kids run wild at The Apartments. Piglet and Tree often sneak off to the playground without her or the older kids, despite the rules. A place that once felt so safe now feels sinister, dangerous.

Marta wishes she had not had all of the trouble with Kit the first year after the divorce, that he hadn't forced her to send him to live with Doug. She could have used his help right now. He was angry—acting out, stealing—he'd become a hooligan. It breaks her heart every time she remembers putting him on the flight to Washington DC, where Doug had been transferred shortly after she left him. Now Kit lives even farther away on a Naval base in Spain. He doesn't write. She's lost him.

Marta gets up and goes into the kitchen, where the wall phone hangs, and calls her sister.

"Hi, Viv, sorry to call you so late."

"It's okay, I'm not doing anything—playing a game of solitaire. What a day, huh?"

"Yeah, that's why I'm calling. I was wondering if you could help with the kids?" She pauses. "And what do you think about asking Mom too?" Her mother had been adamant when Marta moved back to Peakview that she did *not* want to become the de facto babysitter. At seventy-five, she didn't feel capable of keeping up with four kids.

"I'd already thought of that," Vivi says. "Actually, I already broached the topic with Mother."

"What did she say?"

"She said she was willing to help out until things settle down—until we know more about what happened with Maddie."

"Thank you! That makes me feel much better. I'll let you get back to your game."

"Well, okay, hope you can find some sleep tonight, sweetie."

"Me too. Thanks again. I'll talk to you tomorrow."

* * *

WHO KNOWS what is going to happen? Maybe Maddie will show up, and all the worry and speculation will recede in a giant sigh of relief. But until then, it is good to know that Vivi and Mimi will cover while she goes to her classes.

It isn't only the thing with Maddie, though. It's also Tree and Piglet. They fight constantly. Piglet is only five, but somehow she knows *exactly* how to push Tree's buttons, and Tree is mean as a snake to Piglet without provocation, frequently putting her into physical danger. Last year, when Birdie was supposed to be watching the kids, Marta came home from the grocery store to find Piglet clinging to the outside of the balcony railing. She could have fallen and been seriously injured or killed.

And then there is the problem of Birdie and Willie. Birdie has developed breast buds, and Willie has started growing hair under his arms. They can't share a room for much longer. The time has come to find a bigger place, preferably on the ground floor.

The Apartments, the UP married student housing, has been such a godsend. She struggled to find a place to live as a single mother with four children. Understandably, nobody wanted to rent to her. Had she owned a home, *she* wouldn't want to rent to herself. Although she doesn't much relish yet another move, she sets a goal of moving someplace else by the end of the summer. If she's lucky, she will find a place nearby so the kids don't have to change schools yet again. Poor Birdie hasn't gone to the same elementary school for two years in a row. Since their arrival in Peakview, they have moved four times, and to think she thought military life was rough. She washes up the last of the dishes and wipes down the counters.

It's past midnight already. The television crackles with snow. Marta turns it off and finds her way to her bedroom in the dark.

3

BIRDIE (ROBIN)

MAY TO AUGUST 1965

BIRDIE IS the first to wake the next morning. She always wakes with the sun, which is part of the reason Daddy started calling her Birdie, that and the fact that her given name is Robin. He's an early riser like she is. Every morning, with a twinkle in his eye, he would say, *The early bird always gets the worm!* Then he would scoop her up in his arms and give her a piece of candy. It was their little secret. Mama doesn't believe kids should eat candy. *If you eat candy, your teeth'll rot and fall out.* Birdie misses Daddy so much. She misses the way he used to throw her up in the air and play airplane with her. She misses the smell of his aftershave. Why did her mother go and ruin everything by bringing them to Peakview? Life in Norfolk had been nearly perfect.

Birdie steals out of the kids' room without waking the others. Mama is up, she knows, because light spills into the hallway from under her bedroom door. She's probably studying for her finals. Everything is dark and still in the living room, except for the whir of the baseboard heaters. For the first of June, it is cold. She turns on the TV. Nothing is on yet but the test pattern. No matter, she'll wait.

In Norfolk, she had pretty clothes and many lovely toys.

Here in Peakview she has nothing but hand-me-downs from her older cousins. She had to leave almost everything behind when they left. Now, because she is ten, soon to be eleven, Mama thinks she is too old for toys, but Tree and Piglet still have quite a few, so she often plays with their toys when she babysits, and some other times too, when nobody's looking. She's teaching Piglet how to make cootie catchers out of folded paper and how to play jacks.

In the olden days, they lived in a big house with a perfectly manicured lawn. She and Willie played croquet with friends. They had a tree house that Daddy built for them. Here they live in a crowded apartment, not a house. She, Willie, and Kit used to have their own separate bedrooms. Tree slept in the nursery, and Piglet slept in a crib in their parents' bedroom. Now they sleep stacked on top of each other like sardines. It's a good thing Kit got sent away —otherwise he'd be sleeping on the couch. It must be wonderful for him now, living with Daddy in Spain.

There are some good things here in Peakview; it isn't *all* bad. It snows *real* snow, and there aren't any snakes. She doesn't miss the cottonmouths or the big scary black snakes that sometimes curled up on the back porch and surprised her. She doesn't miss the creepy neighbor whose face had been blown up by a grenade or something in some war. Mama said, *He's a hero, honey, don't be afraid of him*, but she *was* afraid of him, deeply afraid.

Now she is afraid of whatever, *whoever*, got Maddie. Her imagination races. Maybe the *hero* lives here too.

The TV flickers to life at around six thirty. It's the morning wake-up show. Not Birdie's favorite, but better than nothing. She hops off the couch and follows along with the lady doing morning exercises on the silent screen. She stands on her tippy-toes, stretching her arms toward the ceiling, bends down and touches her toes. At six forty-five, when the morning news break comes on, she squats in front of the television and adjusts the volume so that only she can hear it.

Maddie's smiling kindergarten picture fills the screen. It's a repeat of the report from the night before. *It could have been Piglet or Tree or me.* Birdie can't stand the thought. She thinks of how often she has been left in charge and ditched the kids to go visit Catrina. *What if someone took one of them? It would have been my fault.* Now she understands why Mama was so disappointed in her.

Birdie goes into the kitchen and pours herself a bowl of cornflakes, adds sugar and milk, and goes back to the TV to sit cross-legged in front of it. Stormy Weather is giving the forecast. Is that his real name? Mama said it was made up, but Birdie likes to imagine his parents naming him that. She is named for a bird, after all.

Finally, it is seven, time for *Captain Kangaroo*.

* * *

"BIRDIE, be a sweetheart and go buy Mimi a Coke out of the machine." Her grandmother holds out her dime-filled hand. "And buy one for each of you too. Willie, you help her."

The heat on this July day is oppressive, so an ice-cold Coca-Cola sounds terrific to Birdie. She's sick and tired of being cooped up at home with either her grandmother or Aunt Vivi all the time. Piglet and Tree are constantly at each other's throats.

Since Maddie's disappearance, nobody at The Apartments lets their kids go out to play. Neighbors have become afraid of each other, suspicious. They gossip about the Smiths—say they think they killed their own daughter. Some say it was an accident; others say it was on purpose. Birdie doesn't think they did it. Why would anybody kill their own child?

Both Willie and Birdie jump up. Birdie gets to Mimi's outstretched hand first.

"The early bird gets the worm!" Birdie taunts Willie.

"At least gimme *my* dime, Bird."

"Well, okay." She gives him two. "You can buy Tree's too."

"I wanna go too," Piglet whines.

"Me too! I wanna buy my own," Tree says.

"I can see I opened a can of worms." Mimi shoos them with her hand. "Go on, the lot of you, but stick together. I don't want any shenanigans, and I expect you back here in less than five minutes."

They all run out the door. Birdie leads the pack as they clamber down the stairs and run over to the laundry room, where the Coke machine is. The familiar scent of Tide laundry detergent wafts out as she opens the door. *Someone* is in there. She peeks her head around the corner.

"It's *her*," she whispers to the others. "Mrs. Smith."

Each in turn peek in to get a look at her. She looks younger than their mom. She looks sad, real sad. She doesn't act like she notices them.

Single file, real quiet, they creep in. All four of them crowd around the pop machine.

"Me first," Piglet says loudly. "I'm the youngest."

Not wanting to make a scene, Birdie wraps both arms around Piglet's waist and picks her up. "Well, okay then, put your dime in the slot and open the door."

Piglet does as instructed. The machine makes a sound when the door unlocks. She opens the door and takes the cold bottle out. After the door closes, the machine locks and a new bottle falls into the spot left behind. Piglet squeals with delight.

"Shhhh," Birdie whispers, "we don't want to bother Mrs. Smith."

But Mrs. Smith still hasn't moved.

Tree, who is taller than Piglet by an inch, has no trouble inserting his coin, and so it goes until they have purchased five Coca-Colas. There is one dime left. Birdie looks at it. Will Mimi notice if she doesn't return it? Without consulting Willie, she pops it into the slot and pulls out a sixth Coke and opens it on the bottle opener.

She moves silently down the row of washers to where Mrs. Smith is sitting and staring vacantly. She sets the Coke down on the side table. Still no response. She pushes it toward her and places her hand on top of Mrs. Smith's hand. Their eyes meet for a moment, telling Birdie that Mrs. Smith has accepted the gift.

The others wait patiently for Birdie by the door.

When they get outside, Willie says, "Birdie, you did a real nice thing."

"She looks so sad. I hope she'll drink it."

* * *

WHEN THEY GET BACK UP to the apartment, Mimi says, "You were gone for more than five minutes. I thought I was going to have to come find you."

They file into the kitchen to open their Cokes. Mimi turns to Birdie. "I gave you *six* dimes. I hope you brought back the change."

Birdie's heart beats faster. "Well, yeah, about that. Mrs. Smith was there, and I bought her a Coke. She seemed so sad—I thought it might make her feel better."

Tears well up in her grandma's eyes. Mimi reaches out and hugs her in a rare demonstration of affection. "You're a sweet child, Birdie Anderson." She kisses her on top of her head. "I am sure you made her feel a bit of happy."

* * *

THE BEGINNING of August rolls around, and life is getting back to normal. Birdie is now allowed to go visit Catrina, and they have permission to go to the playground in groups of four. Vivi and Mimi still come to the apartment to keep a watchful eye on the kids, sitting on the balcony with a view to the playground. They don't watch all that closely, though, since they usually have their eyes on the paper or a magazine, so Birdie's been paying extra attention to Tree and Piglet, making sure they don't dodge out of sight.

Birdie looks forward to getting back to school and seeing her friends who don't live in The Apartments. She'll be starting sixth grade in September and gets to be a crossing guard, an honor only bestowed upon sixth graders. She learned that Mrs. Hugg is going to be her teacher, and everyone knows she's the best. Thank God she didn't get Mr. Christiansen. He's supposed to be real strict.

Today, Vivi is babysitting, and Birdie is curled up on the couch reading *A Wrinkle in Time*. Her mother comes home from school a bit earlier than usual.

"Hey, Viv and Bird!" she chimes as she comes through the door. "I think I've found a place for us to live!"

"That's terrific news!" says Vivi, getting up from the dining room table, abandoning her game of solitaire.

"Where?" Birdie asks. This question is everything. "I hope I don't have to change schools again." Birdie has gone to a different school every year of elementary school. Under the best of circumstances, making new friends is hard for her.

"Nope, you won't change schools. It's a house, and it's a stone's throw from here." Her mother looks pleased with herself.

"Yippee!" Birdie rushes over to her mom and hugs her.

"You want to go see it?"

Birdie jumps up and down. "Yes! Yes! Right now?"

"Yep!" Her mother dangles a key in the air. "It's all ours

—well, on loan, but ours. Run and get the other kids. We'll all go. Viv, you want to come too?"

"I wouldn't miss it."

* * *

THE HOUSE IS within walking distance of The Apartments on an elm-tree-lined dead-end street, but they drive there anyway. When her mother stops the car in front of a tall wrought-iron gate, everybody piles out. In the middle of the gate is a round symbol that looks a like an upside-down peace sign with leaves, and in the center of the symbol is the number one, but there's no house in sight.

Birdie's mother unlatches the gate, and the kids rush through. A beautiful flagstone walkway curves gracefully around a bend ahead and out of sight, but still Birdie doesn't see a house. To the right of the path is an immaculate lawn, with the greenest, most perfect grass Birdie has ever seen. Not a dandelion in sight. *We could definitely play croquet here.* On the far side of the lawn, there is a tall thicket covered in bright-purple flowers. The yard forms a world unto itself. To the left of the path, an amazing flower garden spans the entire length of the walkway, overflowing with flowers and bushes and a wide array of roses. Behind the flower garden stands a tall hedge of some sort. Maybe that is the property line.

"Wow!" Birdie exclaims.

"This is only the beginning," her mother says. "Wait until you see the rest!"

"Marta." Vivi clears her throat. "This is a lovely yard, but how are you going to take care of it?"

"Oh, it comes with a gardener, Mr. Obata."

As if on cue, a man appears from around the bend. He's wearing a white cotton sun hat, sparkling clean white shirt, blue pants, and carrying a spade.

"And here he is!"

"Hello, hello, and welcome to your new home!" Mr. Obata removes his hat to reveal a shock of thick white hair. "You must be Miss Robin? Pleasure to meet you." He bows to Birdie. "Mr. William, Mr. Tracy, and last but not least, Miss Margaret!" He bows to each ceremoniously as he says their proper names. He turns to Vivi with a wide smile. "And you are Vivian. Marta told me all about you."

Vivi looks dumbstruck, but pleased. "A pleasure to meet you, Mr. Obata."

"Please," he says, "Hiroshi. My friends call me Hiro."

Aunt Vivi blushes. Piglet giggles, and Birdie gives her the eyeball.

Piglet asks, "How do you know my *real* name, Mr. Obata?"

"Magic," Mr. Obata says with a wink toward their mother.

"Mr. Obata, I'm so glad the kids get to meet you today. I wasn't sure you would still be here."

"It is truly my pleasure. How about a tour of the yard, kids?" Mr. Obata offers.

"Yes!" The kids all say in near unison.

"We'll see you at the house after you are done," their mother says.

"Let's go, then!" Mr. Obata turns, and all four children trail him, Birdie in the lead.

4

ONE ELYSIUM STREET

AUGUST 1965

As we follow Mr. Obata down the stone path into our new yard, I see something move out of the corner of my eye. I crouch real low and see Stella peeking out from behind a rosebush in the garden! How did she know where to find me? Stella skips over and grabs my hand, giggling. "Surprise!"

"I'm sure happy to see you!" I say. She says, "Piglet, wherever you go, I'll go with you." I'm happy. When Mama told me we were moving, I didn't know if Stella would be allowed to visit.

Mr. Obata doesn't seem like a regular grown-up, and this place feels like something in one of my storybooks. Maybe there are elves and trolls here. Maybe Mr. Obata is a wicked wizard. But where is the house? And how long is this path?

Mr. Obata stops and turns to the group. "Welcome to One Elysium Street, children." He spreads his arms wide. "To your right is the Elysian Field." He indicates the expanse of perfect lawn. "This is an excellent place for playing soccer, or playing catch—"

"Or croquet!" Birdie interrupts.

"Or practicing somersaults!" I say.

Mr. Obata laughs. He doesn't sound wicked. His laugh is full and deep, the way I imagine my grandfather would laugh if I had one.

"Yes, yes," Mr. Obata continues. "It truly is a field of dreams. You can do whatever you wish to do here, and it is a *wonderful* place to sit and ponder, especially if you are worried or feeling sad."

I plan to spend a lot of time in the Elysian Field.

"To your left is the Garden of the Gods," he says, waving his hand over to the left of the path. "Every flower in this garden holds magic for you to discover in your own time. You are welcome to stroll through at your leisure, but please be mindful—don't pick any of the flowers and keep your feet on the stones."

"What if we accidentally step off?" I ask.

Mr. Obata laughs again. "Oh, well, if you step off a stone, you must hop right back on it. Otherwise the gods will get angry. The longer you stand on their land, the hotter the earth will become until it is boiling like a pot."

Willie says, "Oh, come on! That sounds like a fairy tale."

"Well, dare the gods if you must, but I beg you to be careful. They are easy to anger." Mr. Obata turns and starts walking down the path again.

My heart beats faster. Stella whispers, "This place is weird." I nod my head. I probably will avoid going into the Garden of the Gods altogether.

Birdie takes Tree by the hand. His eyes are as big as saucers.

Mr. Obata stops again at a fork in the path. Facing us, he motions with his left hand. "The path to your right is the

Righteous Path; it leads to the Bless-ed Abode, your new home."

"Are we going *there* next?" I ask, hoping so, because I know Mama and Aunt Vivi are there.

"Soon, but first, I want to show you where the left path leads. Please follow me and stay on the stones." Mr. Obata turns and starts walking.

"Stella and I are afraid, Birdie," I whisper.

"It's okay," Birdie says. "He's telling us stories so that we don't ruin his beautiful garden."

"That's what I thought," Tree says. "Piglet, you are such a sucker."

"Am not."

"Are too."

Mr. Obata turns. "Shhhh . . . listen."

Birds chirp and sing, and wind rustles the surrounding trees.

"This is the Dark Forest," Mr. Obata whispers. "There are many paths to take here, many choices to make. It's easy, *very easy*, to choose the wrong path and lose one's way."

"How lost can one get in a yard?" Tree says, and lets out a derisive chortle.

"You would be surprised." Mr. Obata turns and continues walking.

Willie is looking up at something high in a tree. "Mr. Obata, what is that?"

"That, dear boy, is the headquarters of the Y-P-S club." Mr. Obata smiles as he lowers a rope ladder using an elaborate pulley system. "This club is only for children over the age of ten."

"Cool!" Willie says, beaming at Birdie. "We have our own clubhouse!"

"Wow," I say. "I want to be in *that* club."

"Me too." Tree is pouting at the news that it isn't for him.

"Not to worry, you and Tree have your own clubhouse possibilities here in the Dark Forest."

Birdie says, "This is the most amazing yard I have ever been in!"

"Yeah," Willie agrees, "and I thought living on the golf course in Norfolk was awesome."

"Mr. Obata, can we see the other *clubhouse possibilities?*" I ask.

"Oh, little one, of course. You and your friend have been so patiently waiting!" He *sees* Stella! He really actually truly might be magic. Mr. Obata heads down a tiny stone path that veers to the right and ducks under a low-hanging frond of a giant blue spruce tree. We follow. He turns to me and says, "I had this place in mind for you and *all* of your other friends."

I pause. "Well, I *only* have one friend."

"One friend is plenty, and there will be others. You'll see."

"It's so pretty!" Under the tree there is a child-sized cottage shaped like a mushroom. The stem of the mushroom is white, and the top bright red with white speckles. I run and open the door. I step inside. It is much bigger inside than it looks on the outside, and it has furniture in it that is my size, including a table that is set for two. There are two stories, real glass windows, and the top story opens to a lookout platform.

"And now, this way." Mr. Obata beckons Tree. "See what I have in mind for you and *all* of your friends."

Stella and I pull ourselves away from *our* cottage and follow the gang around a corner to discover another magnificent tree house. This one is not as high up as Birdie and Willie's clubhouse, and it doesn't have the fancy ladder either, but it is super neat-o too. It has webbed ropes, and colorful handholds to assist in tree climbing.

"Your mother says you enjoy climbing trees and scaling walls," Mr. Obata says, beaming at Tree.

Tree is already scrambling up one of the possible routes that leads up to the tree house. He balances with ease on a tree branch to get to the platform and slides down a pole to come down. "This is awesome!"

"I'm glad you like it. I am hoping that you will hit it off with my grandson, Kai, who lives with me and helps me out a lot in the greenhouse. This is *his* favorite place to play in the Dark Forest, and he's about your age."

Tree says, "I hope we'll become *best* friends. I've never had one before."

"I hope so too," says Mr. Obata. "Well, okay then. We better get you over to the Bless-ed Abode now so that your mother doesn't start worrying."

"Oh, Marta," Vivi says. "This house . . . this place . . . well, it's magnificent, almost magical. How on earth did you find it? How can you afford it?"

"Well, that's just it, I'm *not* paying for it," Marta says. "It found me."

"What do you mean?"

"I went to the UP student services office and was looking on the housing bulletin board. There was not much on it—a few roommate positions open, but no houses. As I was standing there, hopeless, Mr. Obata appeared out of nowhere."

"He's a rather odd little man," Vivi says.

"'Excuse me, madam,' he said, 'would it be okay if I put a posting up?' And of course I stepped aside. "I was embarrassed that I was blocking his way. He put up a flyer that said: 'HOUSE SITTER WANTED—talk to Mr. Obata,' so I turned to him and said, 'Are you Mr. Obata?'"

"What a stroke of good fortune!" Vivi says.

"Yes, *and* he was delighted to find an actual adult to live on the property, a *divorced* mother with children no less. It was as if that made me seem *more* appealing. He said he had been nervous about all of the eighteen-year-olds that would apply for the job."

"How peculiar," Vivi says. "Well, I hope he doesn't have any designs on you. He's a bit *too* old, more my speed than yours."

"How old do you think he is?"

"More than sixty, maybe ten years older than I am," Vivi is eighteen years older than Marta.

"He's handsome, but I'm sure it isn't anything like that." Marta blushes. "Actually, he told me that the man who owns the house is a widower with five children of his own, a professor at UP in the English department. He's taken a teaching contract for two years back East at Princeton University."

"Oh, that *is* funny—he's gone from U-P to P-U!" Vivi says.

"Anyway, he's quite attached to this house, as his wife and he designed and built it together. He isn't ready to let go of it yet. Apparently, he is delighted to have a family like his own living here."

"How wonderful—oh, I think I hear the gang approaching," Vivi says. "They sound excited!"

BIRDIE HOLDS hands with Piglet and Tree as they head to the Bless-ed Abode. She is beyond excited about seeing their new home. It is the first time she has felt truly happy since arriving in Peakview. Not only will she get to become a crossing guard and go to the same school for two years in a row, but she'll get to live in a dream house with her *own* bedroom. She doesn't need to feel embarrassed about having friends over anymore. Maybe she'll get to have a dog!

Mr. Obata takes them down a different path from the one they came in on. Birdie, disoriented, remembers visiting the Chinese Garden once on a school field trip and thinks this yard is like that. She knows the yard is a normal-sized yard, at least it looked that way from the street, but all these mazelike paths make it feel endless.

They soon come upon another expanse of lawn with an enormous branchy tree at the center, the kind that is perfect for climbing or sitting under on a hot day, and a beautiful building made of glass at the far end.

Mr. Obata says, "We are on the back side of your new home." He waves his hand over the lawn. "This is Persephone's Couch, a wonderful place for lounging on a warm day. That tree is the Tree of Knowledge, so called because it is so old that it holds all of the world's knowledge, and over there is the greenhouse, where you will find me much of the time. I hope you will come visit."

Does Mr. Obata live in the greenhouse?

"Right now, we don't have time to go in," Mr. Obata says, as he charges down a path that goes around the lawn and past the greenhouse. Birdie tries to see what's inside but can only see blobs of color because the glass is frosted.

The house comes into view; it is almost invisible because it blends in with the environment so perfectly. It is smaller than Birdie expected. She hoped for a grand house like the ones that line Seventh Avenue, like the Governor's Mansion. Although it has two stories, it is low-slung, with a gently sloping, almost flat roof built of stone and glass. The stones are the same flat reddish ones that form the main walkways.

"How pretty," she exclaims.

"Yes, it is," says Mr. Obata, "because the *architect* designed it with *love*."

Mr. Obata leads the kids to the front door. Above the door, Birdie sees words carved into stone—"BLESSED ABODE." Mr. Obata pulls on a chain that hangs from above, and a beautiful, almost ethereal, melody rings out.

Birdie's mother opens the door. "Finally!" she says. Birdie hasn't seen her mother this happy in a long time. "Thank you, Mr. Obata—"

"Hiro," he says.

"Yes, of course, Hiro." She blushes. "You have been so generous with your time."

"It is my pleasure," he says. "You have a wonderful family. I am looking forward to getting to know all of you better."

"And we are all looking forward to getting to know you!" Aunt Vivi says.

Why is Aunt Vivi acting so weird and flirty? It's embarrassing.

Mr. Obata beams as he puts his hat on. "Well, I better get going. I'll see you on moving day, if not before."

"Absolutely!" her mother says.

"Thank you for the tour, Mr. Obata," Birdie says. "It was nice of you to show us around."

"Yeah, thank you," the other kids chime in.

* * *

THE ENTRY WAY is a spacious light-filled room with beautiful wide-planked maple floors. To the right of the door, a low curly maple bench with shelves spans the length of the room. Japanese slippers of every imaginable size line the shelves. A sign hangs over the bench: *Please trade your outdoor shoes for indoor shoes.*

"Now, an introduction to your new home! First things first," their mother says, "This is a *shoes off* household. So, whenever you come into the house you will remove your shoes, and put on your slippers. You will put your shoes in the vacant slipper slot."

"Cool," Willie says, "That's like they do in Japan! We did that when we went on our field trip to the Sakura Restaurant and to the Japanese American Museum."

"That's right, Willie. The family that owns this house is Japanese. We are guests here, and it is our job to honor their home with the same care they would give it."

"We can do that," says Birdie.

"Well," their mother says, "Let's go see each of your rooms, and the rest of the house!"

5

PACKING UP

AUGUST 1965

AFTER SHOWING US OUR ROOMS, Mama says, "It's time to go back to the apartment."

"Why can't we stay here?" I ask.

The house is magical to me, already furnished. My room is perfect, with an extra bed in case Stella wants to spend the night. One of the beds is built up real high and has a playhouse under it. There is a wooden tree in the corner that has tiny twinkling lights like a Christmas tree, and the ceiling has stars on it. Mama said they glow at night. I don't want to wait one minute to sleep in it.

"Well, we have a lot to do, sweetheart," Mama says. "We need to get everything packed and moved over. If we work hard, we might be able to move in a couple of days."

I can barely sleep that night, thinking of all of the wonderful things that Stella and I will do together in our own clubhouse. I wake up with the sun and creep out of the room. Birdie sits at the table eating a bowl of cornflakes.

She puts a finger to her lips. Then she gets a bowl and

spoon for me. I pour on the milk and sprinkle sugar over it the way Mama taught me. I smile. Birdie smiles back. I know we're smiling about the same thing.

One by one, everyone comes out to join us, first Willie, then Tree, and finally Mama. We're all talking at once.

"Okay, kids," Mama says, "let's make a plan for our move."

For the first time since my birthday, I don't feel sad. I'm not worried about where Maddie is. I'm not worried about being kidnapped. I'm not worried about being separated from Stella. I'm happy.

* * *

BEFORE BREAKFAST IS FINISHED, Aunt Vivi, out of breath, barges in with a pile of cardboard boxes. "Kids," she says, "run down and get the rest of the boxes from my car."

Did she say run? I shoot out of my seat to the front door. Tree shoves past me.

"Slow down! I don't want any broken bones today," Mama says.

"Yeah, everything is not a race," I yell.

"It is so!"

I haven't made it down to the second floor, and Tree's already at the bottom. Willie and Birdie aren't in a hurry.

When I get to Aunt Vivi's car, I find Tree standing on tippy-toe looking through the windows of her shiny blue Cadillac.

"It's locked," he says.

"Figures."

"Well, well, well," Willie says. "Lookie what I got." He dangles Aunt Vivi's keys.

"No fair," Tree says.

"Well, if you hadn't been in such a hurry, she might have given them to you," Birdie says.

"Here, Tree, you do the honors of opening the trunk."
Willie hands him the keys.

Tree inserts the key into the lock and turns it until the latch clicks open. "Like a pro," he says.

He drives me crazy, always trying to be so cool.

Willie lifts the lid, revealing a stack of flattened boxes of various sizes.

"Let's get them all out," Willie says, "then we can divvy them up between us."

They take turns pulling boxes out. I can't help, because I am not tall enough. Willie and Birdie sort them into four piles—a pile of the smallest boxes for me up to the largest boxes for Willie.

MARTA STANDS in the living room, exhausted before the day has begun, considering the floral couch she paid five dollars for at a garage sale.

"Hey, Viv," she says, "I'm not sure whether this stuff is worth keeping." The couch is stained, and the armrests are worn to threads. Try as she might, she hasn't been able to keep the kids from eating in the living room. They've ruined the cherry coffee table. Tree shattered the custom glass that protected it right after they moved into the apartment. Now it has moisture rings all over it, although she implored the kids to use coasters.

"Get rid of it! If in doubt, get rid of it," Viv says, sweeping her arm around the room. "There's always more stuff, and besides, the house has everything you could ever want."

"Yeah, I'm worried about leaving it in the same condition as we find it." Marta buries her face in her hands. "I wish I felt like I knew what I was doing."

"You're doing fine," Vivi says. "Maybe, just maybe, you'll be able to start fresh at the house, lay down new rules with the kids. Set some limits."

Set some limits. Marta bristles at the implicit criticism of her parenting skills. Vivi doesn't have children—not that she didn't want them, but she couldn't have them. She lives in a different world, a perfect world with a swimming pool, a golf course, and a perfect house that her husband, Jim, a perfect man, built for her before he keeled over from a heart attack a few years ago. She has live-in domestic help. She's rich.

"Oh, I think I'll swap out some of their more valuable furnishings for mine. I can move their beautiful stuff into the outbuilding where Mr. Obata suggested we store *our* belongings."

"As you wish," Vivi says, "but at least consider taking this opportunity to get rid of a few things, like that *horrid* couch."

The kids pile through the door with the boxes, de-escalating a potentially explosive moment between sisters. It's one thing to know something you own is awful and quite another to have someone tell you that it is.

"Okay," Marta says, "Piglet and Birdie, I would like you to work together to pack up the books. Pack them by shelf, moving from top to bottom and left to right. Use the smallest boxes for the books because they're heavy, and close the boxes by folding the top. Like this." She demonstrates crisscrossing and tucking flaps. "Birdie, you label the boxes. Write down the shelf number.

"Willie and Tree, I want you to remove all the bedding from the bunk beds and put the bedding into the laundry baskets. Then pack up all the toys in the larger cardboard boxes, tuck the flaps, and label them by whose toys they are.

When you're finished with that, come back for your next assignment."

Marta joins Vivi in the kitchen, where Vivi's already busied herself wrapping and packing glasses into the dish crates.

"Since we are only moving a few blocks, I'm not sure we need to be super careful," Marta says. "I was planning to drive this stuff over myself. Thought I would have the movers I hired move only the bigger stuff."

"That makes sense," Vivi says.

"Thanks for helping out today. I'm not sure what I would have done without you."

"Oh, it's nothing. I'm glad I can help. I'm glad you're moving someplace that will be safer and away from the sorrow of these apartments."

"Yes, it's worrisome that the police still don't have any leads on Maddie's disappearance. I'll be glad to be out of here."

Marta and Vivi work in silence for a while. Then Marta says, "Do you think her parents did it?" Whatever *it* is.

"A strong possibility," Vivi says. "If they did it, it was some sort of accident, I'd bet."

"They seem like such nice people. I have a hard time imagining."

"Yeah, but is the idea that some stranger took her more comforting?"

"I guess not."

"Not to change the subject, Marta, but I was wondering if you and the kids would like to come over to my house for dinner and a sleepover tonight since all your stuff is ready to go?"

"That's a terrific idea! We'd love that."

To Marta's surprise, the kids pull through. By the end of the day, they have the whole house packed up for the move.

When they learn that they're spending the night at their Aunt Vivi's, they're over the moon.

∽

"Aunt Vivi, can we go for a swim?" Birdie asks.

Miss Wright, Vivi's live-in helper, is starting up the poolside grill. Birdie's mom is relaxing in a lounge chair. She looks like she might be napping.

"Of course, hon," Vivi says, "but I want you big kids to keep a close eye on the little ones, okay? Don't let them creep over to the deep end."

"I promise," Birdie says. "But you know they can both swim."

"I know, but all the same, it's better to be safe."

"Who wants to go for a swim?" Birdie yells toward the house, where the others are watching television.

Moments later, they are all in the pool splashing and screaming.

Birdie and Willie take turns jumping off the diving board to see which of them can make a bigger splash.

"Can I try?" Tree asks.

"Aunt Vivi doesn't want you or Piglet in the deep end," Birdie says.

"No fair."

Piglet jumps onto Tree's back from behind. "Na, na, na-na, na na! Tree is a baby!"

Tree turns on her, grabs the top of her head, and pushes her underwater. She wriggles away from his grip and pops up.

"Mama, Tree is trying to drowned me!" she says, rousing her mother from her relaxed state.

"Drown you," she corrects. "Can't you play a nice game of Marco Polo or something?" Their mother comes and sits on the side of the pool. "Birdie and Willie, can you come and play with them?"

Miss Wright starts cooking the burgers. She is wearing a maid's uniform, black with a white collar, white trimmed sleeves, and a white apron. Must be nice to have someone like her to do all the cooking and cleaning. Birdie dreams that one day she will be like Aunt Vivi, only richer, and her husband won't die.

The fragrance of grilled hamburgers smells like the end of summer, and Birdie becomes acutely aware of her hunger. "Mom, I'm done swimming." Birdie lifts herself out of the pool, splashing her mother in the process.

"Careful there, Birdie."

"Me too." Willie says, exiting the pool on the other side of their mother.

"William!" she says. "You got me all wet." She stands up. "Okay, Piggy and Tree, it's time for the two of you to get out too."

"Shucks," says Tree. "Do we have to?" He knows the answer already and gets out of the pool without further ado.

Piglet is already sitting on the deck shivering in her towel.

"Aunt Vivi, can I help get the table set?" Birdie asks.

"Sure. We're using paper plates tonight, so not a whole lot of setting to do, but you can help me with the condiments."

Birdie loves eating at Aunt Vivi's. She always has stuff that her mother doesn't approve of, like Lay's potato chips and popsicles. Her mom doesn't like popsicles. She says that food coloring is full of poison. Birdie loves the way the blueberry pops stain her tongue and lips bright blue. So far, it hasn't hurt her one bit.

They all sit down at the table, and Miss Wright places an unadorned hamburger on a toasted bun in front of each of them, and a stack of burgers on a platter to be passed around. Tree and Willie have already eaten their first hamburger before Birdie has finished fixing hers up. She is particular about the order—mayonnaise on both buns, then yellow mustard, then the burger, then ketchup, and last, a perfect piece of iceberg lettuce. Her brothers sometimes seem like wild animals, especially when it comes to food; they are both greedy. They drive her crazy.

"You could have waited to eat that," Birdie says with an almost adult tone.

"No, I couldn't," Tree says. "I was starving to death."

"Miss Wright?" Piglet says. "Would you mind giving my friend Stella a plate?"

"Oh, I am so sorry, Princess Peggy, I didn't see her arrive."

Tree rolls his eyes. "Pig, when are you going to outgrow that invisible friend?"

Piglet squints at him. "She's more real than your friend Maddie who is probably lyin' in a grave someplace."

A silence falls over the table. Miss Wright puts a plate with a bun on the table for Stella.

"Where is Maddie tonight?" Birdie asks, a refrain she hears herself repeat regularly. "I hope she comes home soon."

Tree storms into the house. His sobbing is audible from the patio.

"Now look what you did, Piglet. That was mean," Birdie says.

Vivi says, "Yes—not kind, Margaret."

Tears well up in Piglet's eyes. "Well, he was mean to me and Stella first."

Birdie sees tears running down her mother's face. "Mom," she says, "what's wrong?"

"Oh, I guess I'm sad, sad for all of us." She dabs tears off her face with her dirty napkin. "This has been hard for

everybody, but especially Tree. I wish there were some resolution by now."

"No kidding," says Vivi. "It is stressful to see Maddie's
sweet little face peering out from the television screen every
night. I will be happy when she is found, whatever the
outcome."

Birdie gets up and crosses to her mother and gives her a
hug and a kiss on top of her head. "At least *we* are all safe
and are moving into the Bless-ed Abode!" She is careful to
break *blessed* into two syllables, the way Mr. Obata did on
their tour.

Her mother smiles. "Yes, tomorrow we'll be in our new
home at One Elysium Street, and sleeping in the Blessed
Abode." She gets up from the table and collects a few empty
plates. "Well, I better go check on Tree." She disappears
into the house.

The sun has disappeared behind a thicket of poplar
trees, casting long shadows across the yard. The cool
evening air of late summer and the weight of high expectations bear down on Birdie. She hopes she will be able to
sleep.

MARGAUX

1985

ROUND ABOUT AGAIN

SUNDAY EVENING

I emerge from reading my manuscript when Theo grunts. He's been so quiet I forgot he was here.

"What?" I say.

"Nothin', I like it so far," he says. I detect an air of surprise. "I recognize it as our childhood, but somehow everything is clearer, amplified. The familiar is stranger than I remember it, but it feels true, truer than it did then."

"Nice." I say.

"I remember saying to Mr. Sakura that I wanted to become best friends with his grandson, Kiyo. I remember when I met him for the first time, walking up to him and asking, 'You wanna be my best friend?' And he said, 'Yes, I'd like that.' We held hands and went off to play in the Dark Forest. Life was simpler then."

"Well, it was and it wasn't," I say.

"One question: Was I as terrible to you as Tree is to Piglet?"

"Sometimes worse, but honestly," I say, "I don't think of any of these characters as being people in our family. I also don't think of Tree as terrible. He is a wonderful, smart, funny, and fun little boy, and Piglet is a pain-in-the-ass little sister. Who could blame Tree? Who could blame you?"

"Maddie's disappearance, though," he says, "that's about Anna. That's close to home for me."

"I know," I say. "That singular event defined our early childhood, our entire lives, which is one of the reasons I wanted to write about it. Nothing engenders as much fear and sorrow as a missing child, especially one that is found dead years after her disappearance, not to mention a *friend*."

"Well, as you are aware, *that* case was never solved," Theo says. "But there's no statute of limitations on murder —so somebody might get caught some day."

"Some mysteries are better left unsolved, and who says it was murder?" I say.

"I'm not sure about that," he says. "Anna's parents deserve to know the truth."

"Whatever the truth is," I say. I look up at the clock. It's time to get to the Round About to meet with Kiyo and the gang. "Hey, we gotta get going, Bro."

"I bet Kiyo is gonna be surprised to see me."

"Definitely. How long has it been?"

"I saw him once just before we moved to Montana. He and his mom moved up to the mountains someplace, and he was in town visiting his grandfather."

"Was the town called Mount Hope by any chance?" I say.

"Yeah, I think so. I have no idea where that is, do you?"

"Uh-uh. That's where he still lives, I guess." I have no idea where he lives. He is a man of mystery.

When we put on our rain jackets, we look at each other and start laughing. Shit, they are the same color. Twins again.

We're quiet while we walk. As we approach the Mulberry branch, I say, "Theo, you mind stepping into the library with me for a moment? We're still a few minutes early, and I'd like to introduce you to someone."

"No problem."

Theo might need a library card to get into the Round About. I push the door open and see that it is children's story hour. Rosie sits in the storyteller's chair with children all around her on the carpeted floor. A few parents sit in chairs with children in their laps. I recognize the book—*The Giving Tree* by Shel Silverstein. It was one of my favorites as a child, although now I don't see it as such a benign tale. I reread it recently to the kids I nanny for and was horrified at how much the tree sacrificed for the boy.

She's finishing up. "And the tree was happy."

The room is quiet. That book is a lot to digest for an adult. Not without controversy either.

Rosie says, "Whaddya think of that story, kids?"

One little boy up front says, "That's a sad story." Some of the kids mumble and nod in agreement.

A small girl says, "No it isn't! It's a happy story. The tree was happy because in the end the boy still needed her."

The boy says, "I don't like the way the boy treated the tree."

Rosie's eyes land on me and Theo for a moment, acknowledging our presence. She says, "Those are both *very* good points and show me that you are good listeners. I love reading to you and can't wait to see you next week!"

The children scramble up to Rosie and give her hugs. Parents thank her. When the last one has wandered away, Rosie says, "Hello, Margaux!" To Theo, she says, "And I'm guessing, from the looks of you, that you are one of her brothers."

"Yes," I say. "Meet Theo. Theo, meet Rosie."

"Nice to meet you," he says. "Margaux mentioned you, but she didn't tell me you were a librarian. She told me that you are Top Dog at M. Des Jardins."

"Oh, I'm many things, as we all are," says Rosie.

"Theo unexpectedly dropped in on me today, and well, I was hoping he would be able to join us at the Round About, but I didn't want to presume—"

"Of course," Rosie says. "Kiyo would *never* forgive me if I didn't invite him. One moment." Rosie puts *The Giving Tree* back on the shelf and runs back to the office. When she returns, she is wearing her yellow slicker and boots. She hands a card to Theo. "Your library card, Theo."

I watch, amused, as Theo inspects his card, which I assume is identical to mine. Theo looks confused. "But—"

"But nothing, we must go now." Rosie turns toward the desk. "I'm on my way now, Dave. Don't forget to lock up," she says.

"I won't," says a man's voice from the back room.

I realize when we get to the unmarked red door that I don't have the secret knock-of-the-day anyway, so it was good that we stopped in to see Rosie. She taps. Eyes peer out. "Hiya, Rosie, identical twins tonight?"

She laughs. "Hardly."

"Cards?"

I nudge Theo. "Hand over your library card."

Theo looks confused.

"Do it," I say.

The restaurant looks entirely different tonight. Last night it was ornately furnished with jazz softly playing in the background. Tonight the place is transformed into some sort of electropop new-wave dance club. A pulsing mob is dancing under multicolored strobe lights. How on earth they could manage such a transformation in so short a time is beyond my comprehension.

"What is this place?" Theo says.

"This is the Round About." I have to almost yell to be heard over the din.

The host leads us to another red door situated opposite

the entrance and gestures us through. Kiyo and Winnie are already there, seated on the floor at a low table—Japanese style, but the table is round, not rectangular as most Japanese tables are. Like the outer room, this one is also perfectly round. When the door closes, the music disappears behind us. It feels entirely different from the other room—serene, Zen-like. I automatically slip my boots off and put them on the provided mat next to the door in line with the other shoes. Theo and Rosie do the same. We formed this habit in our Peakview house, which had been built by a famous Japanese architect.

Upon seeing us, Kiyo leaps up. "Theo! What the heck are you doing here?" His excitement at seeing his childhood best friend is palpable. I watch as they hug. Theo burrows his face into Kiyo's neck, and they both close their eyes. Their friendship is deep after all of these years. I too once had a friendship like that with Jenny, our neighbor who lived across the street from us. Would she have such joy at seeing me again? So much water under the bridge—probably not.

When they finally pull apart, Theo says, "Came to see my sister." He looks over at me. "And also to meet someone I've been pen pals with for a long time. I never dreamed that I would be seeing you too."

"Come, please take a seat," Kiyo says.

There are five cushions around the table. Rosie has stealthily claimed a seat next to Winnie. The two remaining empty pillows are on either side of Kiyo. I take the seat to his right, between Rosie and him. Theo sits between Kiyo and Winnie.

Five minimalist bowl-shaped tea vessels are lined up on the table, and an iron kettle sits in the center over a low flame. Several other items are arranged in front of Kiyo: a small bowl filled with green powder, a small scoop, a bamboo dipper, and some other bamboo tool that resembles a head scratcher.

"Theo, it is nice to meet you," Winnie says as she reaches out to shake his hand. I detect a blush, or maybe it's awkwardness. Hard to tell. Winnie tosses her straight blond hair over her shoulder. They are yin and yang in their coloring—Theo's black hair to her light blond—they make a striking pair.

"Likewise," says Theo. He gives her hand a squeeze. I see their eyes meet. "Should I be bowing?" Everybody laughs.

"Please." Kiyo gestures to the table. "Let our afternoon drink and snack begin." He smiles. "My grandfather believed that new beginnings should always begin with a tea ceremony, which he taught me to do properly. Today I'll nod to the tradition informally. Strictly speaking, we should not use a table, and certainly not a round one, but given our earlier meeting today and the Round About venue, it fits."

The server enters the room and distributes a variety of sweets around the table.

Kiyo says, "Help yourself to the delicious cookies and cakes while I prepare our tea." He takes the dipper, reaches into the kettle, and pours hot water into each cup. Then he picks up the head-scratcher thing and stirs the water around. "This is for purity," he says.

It's strange to see Kiyo as a grown man, a powerful man. I never imagined that the boy I knew would ever grow into such a graceful adult human. As a child he always was chubby and awkward. Now he has a lithe and chiseled appearance and is clearly in command. I still see the boy in him, though, an appropriate degree of humility.

Kiyo was always kind to me, gentle, unlike Theo. When Theo would pick on me, as brothers do to little sisters, Kiyo almost always came to my rescue. If he saw that I was sad, he was there to comfort me. Even then, he imbued serenity —I always felt better when he was around.

He empties the water from each cup into a larger bowl.

Next, he takes a small scoop of the green powder. "Matcha," he says as he holds it up for us to see. He places a scoop in each cup, then adds water with the dipper. Afterward, he uses the head scratcher thing to stir it. Now I understand that it is a whisk for mixing the tea.

Using two hands—one under and one on the side of the cup—he offers each of us tea with a small bow. I mirror his grasp of the cup and return his bow. I accidentally let a nervous giggle escape, but nobody acknowledges it. The others each accept his tea offering more solemnly. The tea is viscous and bright green. I take a sip. It's earthy.

"I find myself uncharacteristically speechless," Kiyo says. We all laugh and wait for him to speak. "I have longed for this reunion since the day your family moved out of the house on President Street, right after Anna—"

"Me too," I say, interrupting before his next words drop. I don't want him to say more about Anna. "I never imagined that we would all ever see each other again."

Kiyo forges ahead in spite of my efforts. "For me, the day Anna's body was discovered ended our childhood." And there the ugly thing lay among us in the middle of the round table.

Theo says, "For me, the day Anna *disappeared* felt like the end of my life. When they found her, well, I've never been able to quite get over it. I still live with the 'What if?' every day. If she had lived, would we have moved? Would I have grown old with her? Her death shortchanged me somehow."

We all sit in silence for a moment.

Kiyo says, "Yes, I am sure it must have felt that way, like your life ended then, but it didn't, did it? You are here. We are here together. If she had never disappeared, we probably wouldn't be here together now. Some things change everything."

"We had so many great times together, didn't we?" I desperately want to lighten the mood, to talk about all of the happy, magical times we had on President Street in the in-between times—between the day Anna disappeared and when they found her body—but Kiyo is hell-bent on getting straight to the crux. Why?

"Theo, we're all here now. We're here for you," Kiyo says.

Across the table I watch as Winnie places her long thin arm behind Theo's back in a comforting gesture. She is rubbing her hand across his shoulders. She's a *complete* stranger. What does she know of his pain? His loss? Theo's demeanor instantly changes from angst to calm. He starts sobbing.

When he's collected himself, he says, "I'm sorry, I didn't mean to bring the mood down. I bombed this party in more than one way!"

"Nonsense," says Winnie. "As I understand it, you were invited."

"Quite right," Rosie says. "You are an honored guest along with Margaux! We are here to celebrate you both, and Kiyo too. This is a happy day, indeed."

With that, we all fall into lively banter for the next hour and a half.

* * *

The server slips into the room to return everyone's library cards, but they are sealed in tiny red envelopes on small trays. As I pick up my envelope and slide it into my wallet, I notice there is something written on the tray. It says "Hold on tight. This ride is not for sissies."

Theo says, "Well, this has certainly been a day to remember!"

Rosie says, "And it isn't over yet."

"I am delighted to be reunited at last," Kiyo says. He

turns to me. "And, Margaux, have you made a decision yet?"

Without hesitation, I say, "Yes. I will go with you; I mean I'll go with M. Des Jardins."

"That is music to my ears," say Kiyo.

Winnie bounces up and down as she claps, and Rosie holds up her cup of tea and says, "To the magic that has brought us all together at this round table."

Rosie, Winnie, and I make plans to meet later in the week. Theo is running late for his dinner with his friend and says his good-byes. Winnie also has a dinner date planned.

Rosie says, "I need to finish a couple of tasks at the library, so I will see you later in the week, Margaux, and talk to you tomorrow, Kiyo."

Kiyo helps me on with my raincoat. When we walk out of the private room and into the main space, the Round About has again been transformed. It's a cozy piano bar now. Kiyo must see the confused expression on my face.

"Don't ask me," Kiyo says with a wink. I guess he knows more about it than he is letting on.

A man steps toward us out of the shadows, startling me—it's as if he were lying in wait. He wears a black suit, white shirt, and a narrow black tie. If he weren't wearing aviator shades, I might think he worked here. His demeanor discomfits me.

"Mr. Flores," he says, placing a hand on Kiyo's shoulder at my eye level. Part of his little finger is missing. "We need a moment with you. I'm sorry to interrupt your evening, but this is important."

I can't read the expression on Kiyo's face—he's good at hiding his feelings. He doesn't appear happy to see this man, but doesn't look surprised or upset either.

"Yes, of course." Turning to me, Kiyo says, "This will only take a couple of minutes." He follows the man over to the bar, where another man in a suit waits for them.

I study the scene, trying to imagine the conversation. I don't know Kiyo well enough to create a plausible dialog. Who are they?

Kiyo, hands in pockets, bows his departure greeting and walks toward me.

"Is everything okay?" I ask.

"Yes," Kiyo says. "Some business associates of mine." He places his hand on my back and guides me toward the exit with what I perceive as some urgency.

"See you again soon, Mr. Flores," the host says as we pass by the entry podium. "And you will need this." He hands Kiyo an oversized red umbrella.

Outside, a light rain falls. Kiyo pops the umbrella open. Around the rim of the umbrella it says "Round and Round-About We Go Again."

"May I walk you home?"

MERRY-GO-ROUND

SUNDAY NIGHT

As KIYO and I walk toward Elizabeth Street the pitter-patter of raindrops on the umbrella forms the rhythm track to a mystical song. The song retells events of yesterday and today, including Theo's sudden appearance, which feels as if it were the result of divine intervention. Most of what has happened has been wonderful, but doubts about Kiyo and my new reality are seeping in. The appearance of Kiyo's *business associates* at the *Round About* as we were departing leaves me ill at ease. Too much is changing at once.

"It's a lovely night, isn't it?" Kiyo breaks into my thoughts.

"Simply amazing," I say. "Not the weather. I quite detest rain, but tonight it doesn't bother me a bit."

"Could we take a small detour on the way to your place? There's something I would like to show you."

"Sure," I say. I had hoped Kiyo would want to extend the night into something more—dinner? I have no clue what he has in mind, but I have nothing better to do, whatever it is. If I go home I will end up reading *One Elysium Street*.

"Do you mind if I hold your hand?" he asks.

I try to look like that is the most normal thing anyone

has ever asked me. "I don't mind at all," I say. In truth, nobody has ever asked permission to hold my hand. I've been on many dates with men who have felt that they didn't need permission to shove their tongues down my throat or squeeze my breasts in a dark movie theater. Needless to say, those relationships had not turned into anything lasting.

Kiyo slips his warm dry hand into mine. I look up at him. He grins ear to ear. "What?" I say.

"I've wanted to hold your hand like this all day, and now we're doing it, and it's everything I wanted it to be."

"Me too," I say, surprising myself. I am not overly free about displaying my affections. My therapist attributes my guardedness to *childhood trauma*, but I attribute it to common sense.

"Here we are," Kiyo says. We are at the back entrance to the Elizabeth Street Garden.

"Not much of a detour," I say, disappointed. "I live on the other side—but then you already know that."

"Oh, have you spent a lot of time here?" Kiyo pretends to open an invisible gate.

"I pass it every day," I say as I step through, and he pretends to close it.

"But have you visited it?"

"Well, I have. There isn't anything here."

"Maybe you haven't looked closely enough," he says. "Come in."

We have walked perhaps twenty feet down the over-grown path. In the dim light of the evening I can make out little. I would never think to walk this path at night alone. It feels dangerous, like a place where one might get jumped.

Kiyo stops. This time he opens a real gate. Funny, I never saw a gate when I walked across the park on this path before. We go through, and as if by magic, twinkling lights appear alongside a stone path. The path leads to a patio that is covered with a stretched white canvas canopy, resembling an open-air circus tent. Underneath, I see a small table set for two. A single red rose stands in a silver bud vase. Next to it, a short white candle flickers.

"Oh, Kiyo," I say, "This is beautiful, but—"

"Shhh . . ." Kiyo touches my mouth with his finger, and leads me to the table to sit. He pulls out the chair for me. After I'm seated, he sits directly across from me.

"I hope this is not *too* much," he says, looking me directly in the eye.

My face burns. I look away. It *is* too much.

"I wanted to spend some time with you alone tonight," he says.

"This is *definitely* a lot to take in," I say. My eyes meet his for a moment.

"I know." He reaches across the table and takes my hand. "For me too, but I've learned that one must grab the brass ring when it comes within reach."

I understand what he is saying. Sounds *cliché* but also appropriate to this occasion.

A man wearing white tails appears out of nowhere. "Good evening, Mr. Flores and Ms. Andrews, I have taken the liberty of selecting a red for you tonight." He shows Kiyo the bottle, and then shows me. The label has a red rose on it, vintage 1960, the year I was born. Nagasawa Vineyards, Santa Rosa, California. I can't see the grape variety before the bottle is pulled away.

"Perfect," Kiyo says

The waiter pours a taste. Kiyo hands the glass to me, "You should do the honors."

I swish the wine around the glass, tip it to look at the color, the way my sophisticated ex-boyfriend from Brown taught me to. This is a medium dark red. "It's got legs," I say.

Kiyo laughs at my joke. I breathe in the aroma. Naming the tastes and fragrance of wine appeals to the writer in me

—notes of cherry and plum, or is it blackberry? I taste it, rolling it over my tongue. *Nice balance of fruit and tannins.* I imagine writing that in an article for *Food and Wine Magazine.* "Amazing." I say. "Cabernet?"

"Wow, you're a woman who knows her wines," Kiyo says. "This wine came from vines on what was once my maternal great grandfather's estate." His face exudes pride.

"Once?" I say.

"His is an unknown story—he was called the *Wine King of California,* responsible for much of the wine cultivation techniques that made California's wine industry what it is today. He lost it when the family was sent to a relocation camp in Idaho.

"That is a story without end. How awful to think of the impact that had on so many Americans of Japanese descent."

Kiyo goes on, "When my mother married my father, who was from a Portuguese wine-making family, his family purchased a small vineyard for them as a wedding gift—land that had been part of my great grandfather's original estate, ironically."

"What comes around goes around?"

"Well, sort of."

"Did you ever live there?"

"Yes, that's where my parents lived when I was born. I spent my early years playing hide and seek among grape vines."

"That sounds idyllic—can't imagine why one would leave such a place."

"My father was not the nicest guy—not that different a story from yours, at least from what I gather from your novel. One day my mother simply had enough of my father's drunken abuse, and she packed us up and we moved to Peakview to live with my grandfather."

"For a long time, I thought our family was the only one with problems like that," I say.

Kiyo reaches across the table, squeezes my left hand in his right. His direct gaze disarms me. "At least our mothers had the confidence, inner strength, and other resources to leave their abusers!"

"Absolutely, I am deeply grateful that my mother didn't stay with my father," I say.

"Anyway, I was around seven when we moved—that's when I met you. My mother and I lived with my grandfather for several years while my parents' divorce went through. She travelled back and forth between Peakview and Santa Rosa to keep the business going, which is why I spent so much time at your house."

"And what happened with the winery?"

"My mother ended up getting half of it in the divorce. It was part of the larger business empire she built. When she died, I sold it to my uncle, my dad's brother. I didn't want to have any part in it—too many unhappy memories. . . ."

Kiyo's pain shows in his brow. "You don't have to tell me, but I'd like to hear what happened." I reach across the table and take his left hand. Now we are holding both of each other's hands across the table.

Kiyo looks down. "He was an alcoholic, an occupational hazard, I guess." He laughs uncomfortably. "The meanest drunk you can imagine. Hated me from an early age for no reason I could understand—didn't want to see me—couldn't see me."

"Oh, Kiyo, I'm sorry. I had no idea. Where is he now?"

Kiyo lets go of my hands. "He's dead—drove off a cliff on the Pacific Coast Highway. He was drunk, of course."

"And when did you and your mother move to Mount Hope?"

Kiyo laughs. "Mount Hope isn't a real place, you know."

"What?"

"Well, it isn't a physical place, any more than this garden we are sitting in is. It's more of a *what if* you might say. An idea. It was my mother's idea of a place where we could live an idyllic life away from all of the horrors of the real world. She built it for me after they found Anna. She said she didn't want me subjected to all of the questions and speculations that would arise. There were some other things she was keeping us safe from too, but I didn't know about those, some things I am still running from."

"That's the same reason my mother gave us for leaving Peakview, wanting to get us away from speculation," I say. "I understand that, but the rest doesn't make sense to me. You say Mount Hope isn't a physical place any more than this garden is, but right now I can tell you we're in a real garden that is located across the street from my apartment. Aren't we?"

"The question is *are we?*" Kiyo says, raising an eyebrow. "How can you be sure? Will this place be here tomorrow?" He gestures to the beautiful circus tent surrounded by fairy lights and a rose garden I hadn't noticed earlier.

Maybe not. Kiyo is probably some sort of performer. That would explain everything—a master of illusion. "Okay, but I sent my manuscript to a street address with a zip code. I took it to the post office, and the post office shipped it to that address."

"That's true. That's because my mother incorporated the town of Mount Hope, and opened a post office there as part of the process. It is nothing more than a shed on our Colorado mountain property. The postmaster's only job is to know where in the world we are, and to make sure we receive all of our messages." Kiyo says.

"So, she effectively built a world for you to live in?"

"That's right. Of course, wherever we were was real for that moment. We moved all over the place, but we only had one address. Like my grandfather, who built a beautiful world for you to live in on President Street *as a shelter from the storm,* my mother knew how to plant gardens, real and metaphorical, where only barrenness stood. She did for me what her father had done for her during their internment at the Amache Internment Camp near Granada."

"Are you saying the house on President Street wasn't real?"

"No, not at all. It was real, for us, but also a world that nobody else could have imagined. One that nobody else would recognize as the wonder that we experienced. If you visited the house on President Street now, you would see what I mean."

The waiter comes back with a shared platter of pâté and a variety of French cheeses. He also serves a delightful butter lettuce salad.

"This is all a bit much," I say.

"Oh, you don't have to eat it all," Kiyo says. "It won't go to waste."

"That isn't what I mean. I'm confused. I don't know what to think."

The tray from under my library card earlier in the night comes to mind—*Hold on tight. This ride is not for sissies.* It's all a part of what is unfolding now. *Grab the brass ring.* I am on some crazy Merry-Go-Round ride.

We've finished our food. "Was that Drink and Snack?" I say.

Kiyo laughs, "That was Romantic Dinner."

"Quite," I say. "Although, it was one of the most peculiar romantic dinners I have ever been to. I am exhausted."

"Me too," Kiyo says. "Today has been a lot to take in. I hope you'll be able to embrace this new part of your world."

We get up and walk down the path and through the little gate. When I look back, everything has vanished, but Kiyo is still here. There's a lot more to Kiyo's story than he's told me, no doubt. Everything is too perfect. If I walk this path with him, will I discover some ugly truth behind all of the beauty? His enigmatic personality propels me toward him, not away. In the past, if I had met a man like him I would have run away and never looked back. Am I holding onto a childhood fantasy?

We walk in silence to my front door. He leans over and kisses me lightly on the cheek. "I'll be back soon. Be careful, okay?"

"I always am," I say. "Goodnight, Kiyo Flores." I kiss him lightly on the lips. We hug for a moment before parting ways.

RED ENVELOPES

LATE SUNDAY TO MONDAY

BE CAREFUL. What a strange thing for Kiyo to have said. Maybe I'm reading more into it than I should. People often say "Be good, take care" when saying goodbye, but *be careful* rings of warning, like he knows that danger lurks.

Kiyo's kiss is still burning when I get up to my apartment. By New York standards it's early, ten o'clock, but I need to be at my nanny job by seven in the morning.

As I open the door, my heart beats faster, remembering Theo's startling surprise earlier. To my relief, Theo is stretched out on his back on the couch.

"Hey, Sis," he says. "This has been a super weird day."

"Yeah, well, that makes for two of us. How'd things with your friend go?"

"Fantastic!" he says. "But discombobulating. I thought my friend was a guy named Fred, so imagine my shock to learn that her name's Winnifred—*your* Winnie!"

"Oh my, that's huge. And exactly how long have you been corresponding?"

"For five years."

"Forgive me for saying so, but writing to a pen pal seems childish. How'd that happen?"

"When I was at school in Boulder, one of my classmates said that he had a friend named Fred from prep school days that he thought I would get along with. He gave me the address and suggested that I write. He said Fred and I would fit together like two Lego pieces. So, one night, I wrote Fred a rambling ten-page letter while high on shrooms. I spilled my guts out about my inability to love, told him all my secrets, including about Anna. I included a couple of my more obscure poems. I figured he'd think I was a total nut job and never write back."

"But Fred did write back, and although you thought she was a man, you kept writing."

"I fell in love with him," he says. "I felt confused—I was always certain about my sexual orientation. Only recently did I decide to meet him in person. After all, I reasoned that we don't get to choose who we love, and I had begun to embrace it."

"And Winnie? Did she know she was meeting *you*?"

"She figured out who I was after reading your novel, but before that, no. She thought I was a woman! She thought I might be a lesbian with all of the talk about Anna."

"What? Why?" I say.

"I used my middle name. Actually, I signed my letters *Ash*. When Fred asked me what it was short for, I told him the truth—Ashley. I didn't think it through."

"This has all the trappings of a Shakespeare comedy," I say. "So of course she divulged all of her secrets to you too?"

"Well, yes . . . she did."

"Do tell!"

"They wouldn't be secrets if I told you, would they? And how would you like it if I told all of your secrets? Besides, you are the *last* person I would tell. You'd write them all down and put 'em in one of your novels, the way you do."

That stings. "Okay, be that way."

Then Theo says, "Anyway, it is weird. We had a pretty good laugh over the confusion, and a lovely dinner. And at the end of it all, we know that we love each other, and we want to try and make a go of something."

"You say that with such certainty—you met in person only a couple of hours ago."

"It is more certain than anything else that has ever happened in my life."

"I didn't take you for such a romantic."

"Not to change the subject, but hey, I think they might have mixed up our library cards at the Round About earlier," Theo says. He pulls his red envelope out of his pocket and hands it to me.

I open the envelope and see the same card that Rosie issued to me—the one that reads "Knowledge Is Power." I say, "How do you know this isn't *your* card? Doesn't have my name on it or anything."

"Because *my* card said 'The Truth Will Set You Free.'"

I assumed our cards were identical. I pull out the red envelope from my bag. Sure enough, the cards were switched. "Hmm . . . do you think it was intentional?"

"Good question. Doesn't matter, I'd like to have *my* card back. It's your get-out-of-jail-free card, because it made me realize that eventually if people know the truth about what happened to Anna, it is going to be better for everybody involved."

* * *

THE NEXT MORNING I wake up early. I'm trying to be quiet as I make coffee, but I awaken Theo anyway.

The blankets on the couch come down, revealing his sleepy face. "Gonna take a quick shower," he says. He gets up and stumbles into the bathroom, wearing only his boxer shorts and carrying his clothes.

When he comes back out five minutes later, he's fully dressed. "Well, I'm gonna head back to Paloma's today. I promised to spend the day with her to talk about your book." He lays his hand on the manuscript on the counter. "Can I take this with me on the train? I'd like to finish reading it before talking to her."

"Of course. I have another copy *and* the original."

"I'll return this one," Theo says. "I know how expensive it can get to make copies these days."

"Yeah, thanks," I say. "I appreciate that."

"Have you considered buying one of those new home computers?" Theo's always been a big fan of new technology. He ran out and bought a Commodore computer right away and was the only person I knew in high school who used a programmable calculator rather than a slide rule —nutty.

"Nope. I like my typewriter. I like paper."

"Well, you still have to print it out on paper."

"I like to feel the imprint of the type on the back side of the typing paper. I know that sounds weird, but I hate the way computer printing looks and feels; it's soulless."

"If you use a daisy wheel printer, you can feel the imprint on the back side and it looks exactly like a typewriter typed it," Theo says.

"Maybe someday."

"Down the road a few years you'll wonder how you endured all the pain of typing and editing without a computer. We're in the midst of a revolution. It's better to jump on the ride now than to be left behind," he says.

"That's what people say. Okay, I'll think about it," I say. "But right now, I need to get to work."

"Okay, I'll be back in a couple of days. I promised to see Winnie again before heading back to Colorado."

"You going to stay here?"

"Probably not," Theo says. "Winnie wants me to stay at her place." He grins.

"Theo has a girlfriend!" I say in a singsong voice.

"Shut up, brat. And you better not tell a soul."

"Cross my heart."

THE ROW

MONDAY MORNING

I STEP out into the dim gray of early morning. Not a soul on the street. I cross to the other side. I *have* to see what Elizabeth Street Garden looks like in daylight. Standing at the entrance, I look down the overgrown path and contemplate the wisdom of walking through here alone at such an empty hour, but I decide to do it anyway. At most I will encounter some hobo who has hunkered down for the night, at worst a mugger or a rapist. My heart pounds with fear of what *this* decision will bring, but I can't say the terror is greater than the walk I took with Kiyo last night. Last night was the more foolhardy decision. The world is full of perils. I have written a novel about that. Kiyo Flores is a dangerous man—of that, I am sure. No doubt, he will break my heart.

The sight line of the path, surrounded by weeds and brush, opens straight over to the Little Italy Restoration Apartment building on the south side and to the brick walls of another building on the north side of the park. Leafy vines cover the wall on the north, with yellow and orange leaves standing in stark relief against the brick. I fail to discover the gate we went through, and there is no stone path, patio, white canvas circus tent, nor a rose garden.

Perhaps Kiyo spiked Drink and Snack earlier in the evening. What a ridiculous thought—but no more ludicrous than the idea that there was a beautiful place here last night where I had a romantic dinner with Kiyo Flores.

I exit onto Mott Street and walk north, winding my way up to Washington Square North to my nanny job. As I walk, I replay events. I imagine Theo's take on my book. I imagine his conversation with Paloma when he returns to her house. If only I could stand witness.

* * *

I'VE BEEN a nanny since my undergrad days at Brown, where I concentrated in creative writing. They have *concentrations* at Brown, not majors or minors like normal schools. It's loosey-goosey. Students design their own programs of study and have an option to take courses pass-fail, which is why Paloma lords her Yale degree over mine. Yale is *more* rigorous, she says.

My academic advisor knew I was on financial aid and recommended I try to find a nannying position—said it was good money and a great way to find pockets of time for studying and writing. What she didn't tell me was it also provides a writer with rich interpersonal material. Nothing like observing the dysfunction of other people's families to give greater appreciation of the intricacies of one's own.

The Harris family lives a luxe life in one of the only privately owned townhomes on The Row on Washington Square North, so called for the row of nearly identical, historical red-brick marble-trimmed homes that line the street. Most have been converted into apartments—faculty housing for NYU professors—but theirs has been in the family since the turn of the century. How fortunate that I get paid to spend my days in this beautiful spot.

I climb the stairs to the landing and ring the bell.

Mariana, the housekeeper, opens the door. "Oi, Margaux! It's about time you got here." She's miffed.

I glance at my Swatch. Two minutes late. "I'm not *that* late, am I?"

"No, but I have to get to an appointment this morning. Remember? I asked you to come early?" Mariana lives in. She fills the gaps in the morning between the time Mrs. Harris leaves for her office and the time I arrive.

"Oh, I'm sorry, a lot happened over the weekend—"

"No matter. I gotta get going. The kids are eating breakfast. Mrs. Harris left you the activities list for the week. Mr. Harris is out of town, so she's hoping you can take up some slack."

Take up some slack usually means staying later into the night. I'm not eager to do that with Theo coming back into town and getting together with Winnie and Rosie later in the week. I wish Mrs. Harris were more considerate of my time. Paying me entitles her to my life? I was clear with her when I started—my weekends and nights were untouchable, and yet she constantly tests my boundaries.

"Okay, thanks for the warning," I say.

"*Não é nada!*" she says in Portuguese. "See you later."

I take off my shoes and put on the slippers I keep in my bag, hang up my coat, and head to the kitchen at the back of the first floor. The twins, Katie and John, who are seven, sit at the island counter. Katie has her nose in a book. She looks up. "Hi, Margie!" John nods. His mouth is full of cereal. I love them; they're a lot like Theo and me at that age—best friends and enemies at the same time. Difference is, they *are* twins.

"Hey, guys," I say. "You almost ready to head out to school?"

John grins. "You forgot?"

"Forgot what?" I say.

"We don't have school today!" Katie says. "Remember?

You're supposed to take us over to Aunt Judy's. We're going to the aquarium, and after that she said us and our cousins might get to go on the Ferris wheel."

I refrain from correcting Katie's grammar. She hates that.

"I wanna go on the merry-go-round," John says.

"That's cuz yer a fraidy-cat," Katie says.

"Am not. I like the merry-go-round better," he says.

"Okay, okay," I say. "It's all coming back." Today is a light day—deliver the kids and be here when they get home. The week already looks better. I'll have the day to myself to finish reading *Elysium Street*. I might squeeze in some writing time. "I'm supposed to deliver you to your aunt before nine. Do you have everything you need for the day in your knapsacks?"

"Like what?" John says.

"I dunno—a hat, gloves, umbrella?" I say. "Never hurts to be prepared." I look at Katie. "And you might want to bring your book! I know I would if I were you. We'll leave in about thirty minutes."

* * *

MRS. HARRIS ARRANGED for us to use her car service to go up to her sister's place on the Upper East Side. I hate doing it, though, because it takes longer than going on the subway. You have to call them, wait for them to arrive, and then there's the traffic on the surface roads to contend with. She believes the kids will be safer in a car. Possibly, but I'm not convinced.

The driver barrels down the FDR, which is congested, as usual. He weaves in and out, like he's in a crazy hurry. This car is older than the usual cars that come from the service. It rides like a boat, with noxious fumes to boot.

"I think I'm gonna throw up," John says.

"Don't be gross," Katie says.

"I'm serious."

The driver lurches right to get off the parkway. He stops abruptly on a side street, but it's too late—John is actively vomiting all over the back of the front seat.

"Jesus H. Christ," the driver says, looking back. "Git da fuck outta my *caw*." Must be from the Bronx. "Now I'm gonna hafta have da whole damn ting cleaned. That's gonna cost yous extra."

"I'm sorry," I say. "He's a kid, and you were driving—"

"Jus' git da fuck out." He's red in the face, eyeing me with a menacing look—deranged—I know better than to fight back.

"Okay, okay." I grab John and Katie's hands and we get out. I check the back seat to make sure we have everything. "Thanks a lot . . . ," I say. I want to follow up with *asshole*, but I don't. I sense the danger of this man. I know men like him. Stay calm. Instead, I say "Have a nice day," and slam the door harder than I intended. The car squeals as he tears away from the curb. I'm rattled.

John is crying.

Katie says, "I'm scared."

"You don't have to be afraid, sweetheart," I say. "He's not a nice man, but he's gone." I wish we had taken the subway. We'd be there by now. "Come on," I say. "We'll walk from here."

It is already eight thirty. Where are we? We walk west. The avenue blocks always seem endless. Finally we reach Second Avenue. I scan the block for a pay phone. Now I can see that we are on Fifty-Sixth Street. If we keep walking west, we should run into someplace from where I can call Judy. I'd take the subway, but I promised Mrs. Harris never to do that with the kids. She has an irrational fear of the third rail and of all the germs. So many people live in fear of all the wrong things.

I pull out a kerchief from my bag and wipe John's tears away, and the vomit on the corner of his mouth. "I'm sorry," he says. "I get car sick."

"It's okay, babe," I say. "I do too. Someday you'll know how to keep it all in." That isn't necessarily a good thing; it is the truth.

As we continue walking, the hairs on my neck prickle. Are we being followed? I glance back and see a man wearing a black coat and carrying an umbrella. That isn't unusual in New York.

Katie takes John's hand in hers, and the three of us cross the street. I glance behind again. The man has disappeared.

We're walking for a while longer when John says, "Look! Look at that shiny building ahead."

Sure enough, it's Trump Tower in its brand-sparkling-new splendor. I'd been reading about the young real-estate mogul, Donald Trump, and how he was taking the city by storm. It's an ugly building built by an ugly man, probably a man with a small dick.

"Can we go there?" John asks.

"It's farther than it looks, but sure." I know we can get hot chocolate and find a pay phone there. Judy is going to be worried.

The kids have picked up their pace now that they have a destination in sight. I have to run-walk to keep up with them. When we arrive at Trump Tower, I'm a sweaty mess. In my casual attire with two kids in tow, I stand out among the mix of well-clad shoppers and tourists in the mall. I quickly locate the pay phone, Judy's number, and a quarter.

"Hello?" Judy says.

"Hi, Judy. Margaux here." I tell her what happened.

"I was starting to wonder," she says. "What an awful man. You should report him to the car service. My sister is going to be upset when she hears about this."

"Uh, maybe we should keep it between us?"

120

"Not so sure about that. That man should lose his job."

"Well, I don't disagree . . ." All the same, I hope she doesn't tell Mrs. Harris. Sometimes parents are better off not knowing about the *real* dangers their children face day to day. If my mother had known half of the shit we did as kids, she never would have let us out of the house again.

"How about I swing by there and pick the kids up?"

"That works," I say.

"At the pick-up area in twenty minutes or so?"

"Sounds good." Phew.

* * *

THE HANDOFF at Trump Tower goes without a hitch. I'm free at last. I find the nearest subway station and head downtown to my place. I'm looking forward to the relative peace and quiet of my apartment. When I get there, Theo is gone, but he left me a note:

> *Dear Sis,*
>
> *Thanks for everything. I should be back in town on Wednesday. I'll let you know how things go with Paloma. I probably won't tell her too much about all of the weirdness with Kiyo. You know how she is.*
>
> *Hugs,*
> *Theo*

I pull out the *Elysium Street* manuscript, curl up in my reading chair, and begin where I left off.

ONE ELYSIUM STREET

CHAPTER 6 THROUGH 10

6

BEANIE JONES

SEPTEMBER 1965

THE FIRST NIGHT in our new house I'm lying in my bed in my new bedroom, happy that Stella is here to keep me company. I gave her the high bed. She likes it. I'm afraid without Birdie and the boys, but excited at the same time. I've never had my own room. Mama bought me brand-new matching quilts for the beds—one side has colorful polka dots, and the other side is solid white. When she made the beds, she put the white side up for some reason. I turned them over to show the polka dots instead. I'm afraid to sleep under something that's all white. It reminds me of ghosts, of death. Whenever they show dead people on television, they are always under a white sheet. I don't want to be dead. Maddie might be sleeping someplace under a white sheet.

* * *

WE'VE BEEN in the new house for almost a week, and everything is out of the boxes. We live here.

It's the Saturday before school starts. Morning sun streams in my window, waking me and Stella. She climbs down, and we hold hands and walk real quiet-like down the long hallway past Birdie's bedroom in case she's still sleeping. The boys chose the rooms down in the basement, and Mama's room is on the other side of the house. Excited chatter spills out from the kitchen. Tree and Willie are sitting in what Mama calls the breakfast nook, an area in the big kitchen that has a built-in round table and a wooden bench. It's large enough for the whole family. Stella and I slip in next to Willie. I don't want to sit next to Tree in case he decides to punch me for some reason. Compared to the kitchen we had in the apartment, this one is humongous.

"Good morning!" Mama's voice surprises me as she comes out a door on the other end of the kitchen, where there is a little room she calls the pantry, something that makes her happy. She's carrying the new Farberware table griddle Aunt Vivi gave us as a housewarming gift. "Who wants pancakes?"

"Duh," says Tree, "who doesn't?"

"I do!" I say. "And Stella does too."

Tree rolls his eyes.

"Good!" she says. She sets the griddle down and plugs it into the electric outlet in the middle of the table. I never saw a plug in the middle of a table before. "Today, you guys are going to learn how to flip your own pancakes."

"Yay!" I say.

"Well, you might need help, Piglet. It's a long reach," Mama says.

"Yeah, squirt," Tree says. "Leave it to the big boys." He puffs up his chest.

"I didn't say she couldn't do it," Mama says. "Willie, you might need to help her. We want to make sure nobody gets burned."

Birdie comes into the kitchen. "Hiya," she says. She's already dressed, unlike the rest of us, who're still in our pajamas. She goes over to the fridge and pulls out the milk, pours a glass, and guzzles it down. "Mom, don't forget, I'm going to crossing-guard training this morning over at school."

"I didn't forget," Mama says. "You said you wanted to walk with Catrina. Are you sure? I can drive you guys if you want."

"Nah, we wanna walk."

"Well, I want you girls to be careful, no talking to strangers."

Mama says that a lot lately, ever since Maddie disappeared.

Birdie lets out a sigh. "Mother, don't worry, we can take care of ourselves."

"I know, but be careful."

* * *

AFTER BREAKFAST, Stella and I get dressed and go outside. Today it is real pretty outside. It still feels like summer. I want to practice my somersaults and cartwheels in the Elysian Field. Mr. Obata cut the grass yesterday, and it feels like a velvet carpet under my bare feet. Stella and I have a somersault race to see who can get across the lawn the fastest. We tie every time.

On the other side of the bushes, a man's voice catches my attention. I hold still, hoping it's not the kidnapper— maybe he's watching us through the gaps in the bushes and waiting for the right time to snatch us.

"Good job! You did it perfectly," the man's voice says. Is he talking to me? I sneak over to the iron gate but can't see anything. Mama says I can't leave the yard without Willie or

Birdie, but Stella and I got to see what is going on. I stand on my tippy-toes and unlatch the gate.

A man and a girl out in the middle of the street are facing each other. The man is holding a large red ball. He tosses it gently to the girl and she catches it.

"Yes! That's the way," he says. "You got it!" I wish I had a daddy like that. The girl jumps up and down with excitement and squeals. What's she so excited about? Any dope can catch a ball that big.

Stella and I sit down on the step and watch. The man catches a glimpse of us and calls out, "Hello! You must be our new neighbor."

He takes the girl's hand, and now she's looking at me and Stella too. "Oh no, they are coming over to talk to us," I whisper to Stella.

"You must be Margaret," he says. "Mr. Obata told us that a girl the same age as Beanie was moving in."

"Beanie?" I say. "That's a weird name." The girl hides her face in the man's leg.

"Oh, her real name is Beatrice. We call her Beanie because she's so tiny, like a bean."

The gate swings open. It's Tree. "Piglet, Mom is looking for you."

The little girl's face lights up. "Piglet? That's a dumb name." I don't like her. She's mean. "Where's your friend Winnie-the-Pooh?" Beanie says.

"Well," I say, "at least I'm not fat like you." I don't know why I said that. She isn't fat. I'm mad that she made fun of my name. I like her matching polka-dotted top and shorts. I wish I had pretty clothes like that instead of Birdie's and Willie's old hand-me-downs.

Tree scoffs. "Come on, Pig, you're not supposed to be outside of the yard alone."

"I'd love a chance to meet your mother. Is she home

right now?" Beanie's dad says to Tree. Beanie and I are busy glaring at each other. Stella is making ugly faces at her.

"Yeah, sure," Tree says. "Come on in."

We all go through the gate, and Tree latches it behind us.

"Beanie," the man says, "why don't you stay here and play with Margaret while I go talk to her mother. Stay in the yard."

Beanie looks like she might cry. "Okay," she says.

Stella and Beanie and I stand there staring at each other in silence for a moment. "You know how to do a somersault?" I say.

She shakes her head.

"You wanna learn?" I ask.

She nods.

Marta cleans up the last of the morning dishes, thinking about what a wonderful choice Viv made in her gift of the griddle. She's the one who noticed the outlet in the middle of the table and knew from her travels to Japan that it's for an electric grill.

"Mom?" Tree calls from the entryway. "We have a visitor!"

"Okay, be there in a minute."

Who could it be? Luckily she's already dressed. She checks herself in the bathroom mirror and lets her wavy shoulder-length dark hair out of the ponytail she put in earlier for cooking. At thirty-eight, her hair is already beginning to gray.

A nice-looking clean-cut man stands in the entryway. Looks a bit younger than she is, maybe by ten years.

"Hi," he says, "I'm the neighbor from across the street. Neil, Neil Jones." He extends his hand to shake.

"How nice to meet you!" Marta says as she takes his hand. His grip is firm but his hand is clammy. Amazing how much information gets transferred in such a simple social act. "I've been meaning to stop over to introduce myself, but as you might imagine, I've been pretty busy unpacking and trying to get things set up before school starts."

"No worries at all," he says. "Barbara, the wife, and I have been meaning to welcome you to the neighborhood properly."

The way he says *the wife* makes Marta's skin crawl.

"We understand that it must be tough to be in your situation."

"Oh, yes, it is tough to be new in the neighborhood." Marta smiles. "As a military wife, however—"

"I was thinking of your situation as a *single mother*," he says. "That must be difficult."

Marta laughs. "Well, it's a lot easier than being married to my ex-husband," she says. "And I'm far from alone, as you can see. I also have family here in Peakview—my mother and sister—and they give me a lot of help."

"Oh, I'm sure."

Marta hears his condescension.

"Anyway, I suspect we'll be seeing quite a bit of each other as our daughters, Margaret and Beatrice, will be in kindergarten together."

"Oh, how nice!" Marta says. "Is Beatrice in morning or afternoon?"

"Afternoon, I think the wife said."

"Oh, what a shame. Pi—Margaret will be in the morning class." Thank God Marta won't have to interact daily with the Joneses. If she's lucky, Barbara will be more to her taste than her husband. "I'm certain that Beatrice and Margaret will become fast friends. She's welcome to come over to play anytime. As you can see, our yard is fully enclosed and safe."

"Safety is of paramount importance to Babs and me, especially after what happened with the Smith girl—"

"Maddie . . . yes, her disappearance has had quite an impact on our family. She was my son's school friend and one of our neighbors."

"Well, you can rest assured here, as I am one of *Peakview's finest*, been on the force for about ten years now. I didn't work on the Smith case, but I'm aware of many of the details." Abruptly, he changes the subject. "You have a delightful property here, one might say *magical* . . . There's a certain *oriental* aesthetic to the landscaping, don't you think?"

"Yes, Mr. Obata is of Japanese descent, as are the owners, so it would stand to reason."

"The owner, Professor Ito, is Japanese, but his wife who died *was* a N—Black." He says it as if it is somehow scandalous. "Apparently, in California, where they came from, they let anybody marry everybody. I wouldn't be surprised if they start letting men marry men in the not-so-distant future."

Marta lost for words, worries that she may have been too welcoming of the Jones's daughter. "Well, I don't know about that," she says finally. "It was nice to meet you, Mr. Jones. I'm looking forward to meeting your wife, but I was readying to go to visit my mother. I'm sure you understand?"

"Of course. I should be going anyway. I left Beanie outside playing with your daughter. They were off to a bit of a rocky start, so I thought maybe they could work it out."

"Welp, that was a *big* nothing," Birdie says as she and

Catrina walk home from the elementary school after their crossing-guard training.

The instructors handed out safety vests and sashes, showed them where the stop signs are stored, and taught them the basic principles of being a crossing guard. There was no talk of what an honor it is to be conferred responsibility for the well-being of their fellow students.

"Yeah," says Catrina. "At least they could have given us a badge or something."

As they cross the bridge over the highway, a car slows down, and the driver sticks his head out the window and yells, "Hey, wanna give me a blow job?" He doesn't wait for an answer—starts laughing and keeps on going.

"That was weird," Birdie says.

"Yeah, what does that mean?"

"I'm not sure, but I don't plan to ask my mother about it," Birdie says.

Catrina laughs. "No kidding."

"She is so freaky these days about letting me go *anyplace* without adult supervision."

"Yeah, my mom too."

They walk in silence to the other end of the bridge. Birdie says, "Have you seen Mr. and Mrs. Smith lately?"

"No, my mom says they're hiding from newspaper reporters. Everybody thinks they had something to do with Maddie's disappearance."

"Didn't you babysit her?" Birdie asks.

"Yeah, I did. Such a sweet girl. Mrs. Smith is real nice, but Mr. Smith gives me the creeps."

"How so?"

"I dunno." Catrina's quiet. She looks sad. "He always insisted on walking me home after babysitting and would find a reason to touch me, like reach out and pat my butt. I told him not to do that, and he said it was a 'love pat.' What could I say?"

"My foot! Did you tell your mom or Mrs. Smith?"

"I told my mom, but she said that is how some men are. It doesn't mean he's a creeper or a murderer."

"Well, it's hard to think he would hurt his own little girl, isn't it? And besides, if he'd done something like that to Maddie, Mrs. Smith would have probably figured it out by now, don't you think?"

"Yeah, maybe so," Catrina says.

7

MRS. FRIEND

SEPTEMBER 1965

I WAKE up before daylight on the first day of school and whisper, "Stella?" She doesn't answer. I say it louder. "Stella?"

She pops her head over the rail of the top bunk. I can barely make out her shape. "Why are you bothering me?"

"I'm excited . . . I'm scared."

"Don't be scared," she says.

"I wish you could come with me, but Mama says guests aren't allowed at school."

"I'll be here when you come home. And besides you're gonna make a big splash in kindergarten, like that new band Willie listens to on the transistor."

"Ew. The Beetles? Such a gross name. Besides, everyone knows beetles don't make music—crickets do." I giggle at my own joke.

"Yeah, but are crickets gonna be on the *Ed Sullivan Show* next Sunday?"

That's all Willie talks about lately. "Good point," I say and fall back asleep.

* * *

Mama drives us to school for the first day, all except Birdie who went with Catrina. After this we'll walk like all of the other neighborhood kids. She wants me to know the correct route, the *safest route*.

"Tree, I want you to stay with your sister at *all* times. Do you understand?"

"Yeah, sure," he says. I know he couldn't care less, and he won't stay with me. I can take care of myself anyway.

She drops us off at the front of the school. "Okay, Piglet, when you're finished today, meet me right here, okay? I'll be here to pick you up."

"Okay," I say. I can tell Mama is scared too. "I'll meet you right here," I say.

Tree takes my hand. "She'll be okay, Mom. I promise. I'll keep her safe. I'll make sure she is here at lunchtime."

"You're a good boy," Mama says. "Have a great first day of school, and I hope you both make lots of friends."

As soon as we walk through the front door, Tree drops my hand. "You're on your own now. There's your classroom —classroom A." He points at a door. I know my letters more or less from an alphabet book at home, and I can see that shape by the door. "Yer lucky, you got Mrs. Friend as your teacher. She's real nice."

Mrs. Friend? That's a silly name. I wish Stella were here so I could tell her. She would have something funny to say. "Thanks," I say. "I'll try to be brave." Tree disappears down the hall.

A tall lady stands in the open doorway.

"Hello, sweetheart," the lady says. She has long, skinny

feet and wears pointy high heels. She bends down so that her face is closer to me than her feet. Most grown-ups don't do that. She smells good, like roses, and she's real pretty with golden-blond hair piled high on her head. She looks like a movie star. Mama says that style of hair is called a beehive. I hope no bees are in Mrs. Friend's hairdo. I'm *afraid* of bees.

"Hi," I say.

"What's your name?" she asks.

"Margaret Anderson," I say. My voice barely comes out, my heart is beating real fast.

"That's a pretty name! I'm your teacher, Mrs. Friend."

"I think that's a *funny* name," I say.

Mrs. Friend laughs. "Yes, it is, but at least it's a happy name! Do you know how to spell your name?"

"Yes," I say. "*P-I-G-G-Y.*"

"Oh, you go by Peggy? That's a good nickname for Margaret."

"No, my name is Margaret!" Doesn't she know how to spell? Tree taught me how to spell my name yesterday.

AFTER DROPPING the kids off at school, Marta heads over to the university. Today is the first day of her senior year at UP. She doesn't have to stick around campus. Other than a trip to the registrar to pick up her schedule, she only has a meeting with her academic advisor, Dr. James. His office door is closed when she arrives, so she takes a seat in the hallway.

Marta can't believe how fast her time at university has gone. When she started as a freshman at age thirty-five,

Doug told her she would flunk out. He undoubtedly hoped so. He wanted to think she couldn't survive without him. Two years have passed since their divorce was finalized, and she is still here. Thank God he is in the military. Marta knows Doug never would have paid the child support required by law otherwise; the Navy garnished his wages. Without the child support and a full scholarship, she would not have been able to make it this far.

The last time she saw Doug was shortly after his mother's funeral in Denver in sixty-three. He came over to the house where they lived then, drunk, and was angry, yelling obscenities. She sent the kids to their bedrooms and locked the door to keep him out. He accused her of embezzling the child support. Doug imagined the money he sent went directly to the children, like an allowance. He gives Kit an allowance equal to one-fifth of the child support now. Apparently he asked Kit what Marta spent *all that money* on? What does he imagine child support is? Does he have the faintest clue about how much it costs to raise children?

He also accused her of ruining his life, his career. The abuse claims Marta levied in the divorce papers triggered the Navy to require a psych evaluation. Doug said no one would ever promote him after that. Turned out not to be the case—he was promoted only months later and sent on assignment to Rota, Spain, as chief surgeon. Oh, how she ruined his life. And already he has remarried. Married their next-door neighbor from the base in Norfolk, Darla, a woman who'd always had her eye on him.

Dr. James's door opens, and a young female student comes out. "Thank you, Professor!" she says. "You're the best!" She's pandering and he's eating it up.

Marta stands, and Dr. James drops his flattered face upon seeing her. "Mrs. Anderson, please come in."

She likes Dr. James. They are on a first-name basis. The

formality is an act for others in the biology department, with prying eyes ready to spread any tidbit they can about any antics or sexual misconduct on the part of faculty with students. He's smart, funny, everything she would like in a man if she liked men, but she prefers the company of women. She has only ever had one romantic relationship with a woman, and that hadn't ended particularly well.

Dr. James closes the door to his office behind her.

"Hello," Marta says. "It's good to see you, Bob!" Early on, they discovered that they had gone to high school together briefly at Peakview East—that was during the war. They had several friends in common but didn't know each other, because Bob enlisted shortly after Marta arrived at the school.

"Likewise," he says. He settles into his desk chair. "So, Marta, tell me, have you had a chance to think about what we talked about last spring?"

"You mean graduate school?" Marta has thought about it. Has been wondering about it. "Yes, I think I would like to continue on in school, maybe pursue medicine."

"Are you thinking of nursing?"

"No, I'm thinking of becoming a doctor."

Bob presses his fingertips together and holds them up in front of his lips as if considering what Marta has said. "That's not realistic, I mean at your age. You are *more than smart enough* but . . ."

Marta purses her lips and takes a deep breath through her nose to tamp down the fury rising like magma within her. When she first told Doug she wanted to go to college, way back when they were first married, he said, *A woman as pretty as you doesn't need to go to college.* She wrote and edited most of his papers while he was in medical school. She read all the same books he did. Other than practice, she has a solid foundation to become a doctor. "Well, I've wondered about that, not to mention my responsibilities with the kids, but *damn it*, I don't want to wind up as a waitress in a truck stop trying to make ends meet when I'm in my sixties."

"Have you considered teaching?" he says.

"Yes, I've considered that . . . but I want to have an impact."

"Ouch!" Bob says. "I've always felt that I've made an impact through teaching *and* research."

"I'm sorry," I say. "I didn't mean it the way it came out. Of course teachers make a huge difference, and absolutely research does too."

"Well, maybe consider research? Which brings me to my next question. I'm looking for a lab assistant. The pay is good, and it will be part-time—you set your own hours— you'd be running experiments for me and helping me write papers. You interested?"

"Not sure if I can say no!" Marta's full-tuition scholarship and monthly stipend for defraying room-and-board costs help, but the kids get more expensive with each passing year and the child support doesn't cover costs. It would be nice to have money for a babysitter, piano lessons, new shoes. Things are looking up.

"Good, I hoped you would say that."

After wrapping up the meeting with her advisor and visiting the registrar's office, it's already time to pick up Piglet from school. This half-day kindergarten thing is going to be tough to juggle. She needs to find a dependable sitter, especially if she is going to be working and going to classes.

Maybe the Joneses know of one, although she is hesitant to ask them given her feelings about Neil, but it might provide a good opportunity for her to meet "the wife," Barbara.

She gets to the school right on time. Mrs. Friend leads a train of kids, paired and holding hands. They gather in a circle under the flagpole. Piglet sees Marta and runs over to her teacher and gives her a hug. Tears fill Marta's eyes.

🕊

BIRDIE, Catrina, and the rest of the sixth graders are out on the playground when morning kindergarten gets out. Birdie sees her mother drive up but pretends she doesn't.

From afar, she watches Piglet run over to hug her teacher and then scamper over to the car. Piglet is lucky. She doesn't know what she lost in the divorce. She was a baby when it all happened. To Birdie, Piglet lives in a perpetual state of joy, lost in her fanciful thoughts. She never does any chores and has no responsibilities whatsoever.

And Tree—he's right there with Piglet in how spoiled he is. Mother is so worried she is going to turn him into a mama's boy that she gets him things to compensate, like a ten-speed bike and a real guitar, when Willie and she practically have nothing. Tree isn't interested in playing guitar; Birdie covets it.

In truth, Maddie Smith's disappearance was an unexpected gift, because Mother stopped leaning so hard on Birdie and Willie to watch the younger kids. Finally Aunt Vivi and Grandma Mimi started helping out like they should've been doing all along.

"Hey, Birdie," Catrina says. "A penny for your thoughts?"

"Oh, nothin', I was watching Piglet and thinking how cute she is."

"Yeah, cute as a button," Catrina says. "She could be a Mouseketeer."

"Maybe—she's weird, though," says Birdie. Sometimes Birdie wishes Piglet would disappear like Maddie.

When Marta turns onto Elysium Street with Piglet in the back seat, Barbara Jones is in her driveway, getting out of her shiny Town and Country station wagon. Now might be the perfect opportunity to introduce herself.

"Piglet, have you met Beanie's mom yet?" Marta asks.

"Yeah, I met her yesterday. She's real nice, and pretty too."

"I can see that!" Barbara is built like Twiggy, long limbed and skinny. She's wearing black pedal pushers, loafers, and a sleeveless pink and white gingham top. Her dishwater-blond hair is cut in a pixie. She's cool compared to Marta—androgynous in a sexy way. "You want to introduce me?"

"Yes sirree!" Piglet jumps out of the car and races toward Mrs. Jones. "Hi, Mrs. Jones! Did you take Beanie to school already?"

"Oh, hello, Margaret. Yes, I did! We got there early because she was so excited. She was hoping she might see you in passing." Mrs. Jones looks toward Marta. "And you must be Margaret's mother, Marta. Neil said he met you on Saturday, but he didn't tell me—"

Marta senses Barbara's eyes taking her in—something feels flirtatious about her gaze. Maybe Marta is wishing for something—*silly.* "What? Didn't tell you what?"

"That you are pretty—probably didn't want me to get jealous."

Marta blushes. "You've got to be kidding! I look like an old heifer."

"Oh, honey! I can see that I need to get to work on building up your self-esteem. How about you and Margaret come on into the house with me, and I'll pour us some ice-cold drinks. We can sit for a spell on the back porch and get to know each other while Margaret explores the yard."

"What a lovely idea," Marta says. She and Piglet follow Barbara inside. Marta senses the possibility of friendship. Barbara's effusive warmth and welcome puzzle her—Neil seems a poor match.

8

SUPERMAN SAVES THE DAY

APRIL 1966

I WALK to school with Tree and Kai, Mr. Obata's grandson, every day. Turns out Mr. Obata doesn't live in the green-house or in a green house, like Birdie thought. He lives up the street from us on the corner of President and Ash in a white house with a magical garden of his own.

Kai and his mom live with Mr. Obata, but she travels a lot for work, so he spends a lot of time at our house. His parents are divorced, like mine. I'm not sure where his dad is. Kai says he doesn't know either, but he says he doesn't miss him a bit. Wonder why. I like having Kai around. He makes Tree nicer, and Kai is real kind to me and Stella too.

Usually we stick together like glue, but today on our walk to school, Kai and Tree left me in the dust when some older kids told them about a dare-double-dare. They've stopped on the highway bridge up ahead and are yelling something. When I get closer, I can make out what they are saying.

Tree says, "Hold on! Help is on the way." Then he

climbs over the bridge railing. Why is he doing that? That's not safe! I run to catch up. My heart pounds.

Kai yells, "We need a rope!"

Kai and the other boys are taking off their jackets and shirts and tying them together to make a rope. I watch as Tree moves cautiously toward a bigger boy who is dangling from the bridge. I don't know him.

The boy yells, "I can't hold on." He's whimpering something pitiful.

Down below, the cars have stopped. The sound of approaching sirens comes from above and below. They won't be here soon enough.

Tree looks up at us. "Throw the rope down," he yells. I can tell he's scared. I've never seen him afraid of anything. One of the bigger boys lowers the rope they assembled from their clothes. Tree, both feet stable on the bar the boy is hanging from, holds on above with one hand and guides the rope toward the boy. Looks like he's done this before. "Grab the rope!" he says.

"I can't."

"You have to. There are five guys up top holding the other end. They'll pull you up, and I'll help too. You can do this." Tree sounds almost grown up to me.

The boy manages to grab on. The other boys pull from above. They have raised him high enough that Tree can grab the boy's belt with one hand. "Okay, there you go. Put your feet up on the bar where my feet are and grab on to the bar where my hand is." I've never seen Tree like this before. Brave. He's a hero, like Superman. I puff up with pride.

The boy does as told. Now he and Tree are both clinging to the railing. Onlookers from the cars below clap and cheer.

"Okay," Tree says. "Follow me." Tree sidesteps over to the closest end of the bridge, where he is able to easily get over the top railing to safety. "You're doing great," he says to the boy. It's like him and me on the balcony at the Apartments. The difference is he's saving someone instead of running away.

A fire truck arrives, closely followed by an ambulance and the KTVP-2 live-reporting people. I recognize the lady from the reports on TV about Maddie.

A firefighter, carrying a rope, leaps into action to help. He looks over the railing, "Where's the boy?" His face looks worried. The people on the ground point at the group of boys on the far end of the bridge.

I say, "My brother and his friends saved him."

The firefighter breaks into a smile. "That is the best news I've heard all week." He picks me up and carries me over to the group of celebrating boys. "Which of you belongs to this little one?" The man sets me down.

Tree steps forward. "Uh, she's my little sister."

I run over to Tree and give him a big hug. "That was stupid," I say. "I'm glad you're okay. What would I have told Mama?"

"You better not tell Mom a thing," Tree says. He ruffles my hair, and then we see the TV reporters approaching.

The firefighter steps between us and the reporters. "You're going to have to wait to get this story until a time when their parents can be with them, and that won't be until after we've had a chance to talk to them. Feel free to talk to the witnesses below, though." Turning to us, he says, "Kids, come with me. We're going to give you a lift to school and have a chat with your principal about the events of this morning."

"Mrs. Friend is going to be upset if I am late," I say. I don't want to "have a chat with the principal." He scares me.

"Oh, I think she'll understand today," the firefighter says.

* * *

I LOVE KINDERGARTEN. I can write my name now—*M-a-r-g-a-r-e-t*—I learned how to write capital and small letters too. When I realized the mean trick that Tree played on me by teaching me to spell Piggy instead of my real name, I was embarrassed and mad, but Mrs. Friend never mentioned it. She asked me if I wanted to be called by a nickname. I said, "No sirree. Just plain old Margaret."

I have my own Crayola crayons, eight of them. Mrs. Friend gave each student a felt roll with a spot for every crayon as a welcome gift—mine is purple, my favorite color. I haven't made a lot of friends at school yet like Mr. Obata said I would, but I don't care. Stella comes to visit me when I'm on recess; so far nobody has noticed. Beanie is my bestest friend besides Stella, but they don't know each other. Stella's jealous of Beanie, so she only comes around when I'm not with her. I miss her sometimes.

9

THINGS CHANGE

APRIL 1966

BIRDIE STANDS on her usual corner for crossing-guard duty. *What are all of those sirens? Why has it been so long since any kids have come?* She glances at her Micky Mouse Timex watch, a birthday gift from Aunt Vivi. Still ten minutes left of guard duty. *What is going on? Why haven't Kai, Tree, or Piglet shown up yet?* Something isn't right. Worry creeps in. A fire truck, one of those big hook-and-ladder trucks with its lights on, is headed her way. As it passes through the intersection, she sees Tree and Piglet waving at her from inside the cabin of the truck.

Her heart pounds. *What? No fair!* How'd they end up getting a ride to school in a fire truck? Nothing like that has ever happened to her, except for maybe when she was three and got lost on the boardwalk in Virginia and got to ride in a police car. She doesn't remember that.

A small crowd of children approach her corner, finally. "What's going on?" she asks one of the older kids.

"Oh, nothing, some idiot tried to cross the highway bridge on the outside of the railing."

Tree! He *is* an idiot.

Then the kid says, "Your brother saved him. He would've died if your brother didn't go out there and save him."

"Really?"

"Yep, we saw it with our own eyes. He's a hero. A true-life superhero."

Great. Birdie might as well put on an invisibility cloak. When will her turn to shine come? When will people see how wonderful she is? When will she get to ride in the cab of a fire truck? Every day she feels a little more invisible.

* * *

AT SCHOOL that day the only thing anybody talks about is how her little brother saved the day. It doesn't matter that he likely set the example of crossing on the outside railing in the first place. He's been practicing that trick since kindergarten, an old pro by now, has done it dozens of times—she knows because she has seen him do it. He probably is the one that dared the bigger kid to give it a go, the same way he's always getting Piglet to take chances. Last week he convinced Piglet to jump off the roof of the Blessed Abode with an umbrella, said she would fly like Mary Poppins. She didn't. Fortunately, the only thing that got broken was the umbrella, though Piglet ended up with some nasty scratches from the juniper bush she landed in. One of these days he's going to get her, or somebody else, killed, and that would ruin him.

The school year has been a *big* disappointment. It was supposed to be the year when she would become class president, the year she'd become popular. The opposite is happening. The other day, one of the boys in gym class passed her during laps and said, *You look like a fat cow.* She is a fat cow. Her body is changing in multiple unpleasant ways. She's stinky and has coarse black hairs growing under her arms and down below too. She's a freak of nature and might end up in the circus as either the fat lady or the bearded lady, or maybe even the fat bearded lady.

Her eyes swell with tears at the thought of being in the circus. She goes into the girl's room to cry, and when she pulls down her underpants, she sees blood. She thinks she might be dying and goes to the nurse's office.

The phone rings about a half hour after the kids leave for school that morning. Marta startles at the sound, which breaks the silence of the blissfully empty house.

It's probably Barbara. Turns out she and Barbara have a lot in common beyond daughters of the same age. Like Marta, Barbara is highly intelligent, a fact reflected in her superior sense of humor. She also has Southern roots and a love of straight bourbon.

Marta once voiced her concern over Barbara's day drinking, but Barbara shooed her worries away, *Don't be silly. I'm a Southern girl—and we can handle our liquor.*

They spend a lot of time together going for leisurely walks when Neil is at work and hanging out in each other's kitchens after the kids have gone to bed. They talk about books, kids, pets, husbands, and love—a lot about love, something Barbara claims not to feel for Neil.

Barbara flirts with Marta, and they hold hands and kiss each other goodbye on the lips—when nobody's looking—but there is nothing more, to Marta's disappointment. She feels like she has fallen in love, but Barbara's mixed signals confuse her.

"Hello there," she says in a tone of voice reserved for familiars.

"Hello, is this Mrs. Anderson?" a man's voice says.

Her demeanor shifts. "Yes, it is, may I ask who's calling?"

"Principal Walters from Peakview Elementary—we met the night of the parent teacher conferences."

"Of course." Marta's heart races. Has something happened to Tree or Piglet?

"I'm calling to let you know that your kids are fine—"

"Why wouldn't they be? What happened?"

"Well, there was an *incident* on the way to school this morning with one of the older boys—"

"A bully?"

"No, nothing like that. I don't want to alarm you, but your son saved a boy who was dangling from the highway bridge. He literally put his own life in danger to save the other boy. Extraordinary! I wanted to prepare you, because it is going to be all over the news tonight and in the newspaper too. We didn't let any of the kids talk to the reporters, though, so you can expect a call or a visit from them sometime later today."

Marta catches her breath. How could a small boy possibly save someone dangling from a bridge? "My son? Tree, I mean Trace? He's okay? And Pig—I mean Margaret, she's okay too?"

"Yes, both are more than fine. Birdie, on the other hand, well, she's having a rough time. Nurse Miller had a talk with her about her *condition*, and provided her with some sanitary supplies, well, you know what I mean."

"Of course . . . poor thing!" Marta hadn't thought to talk to Birdie about periods—she's only eleven! Marta was sixteen when her period started, and she figured they had lots of time ahead.

"Anyway, she wants to come home. She's upset."

"Yes, I will come pick her up."

Marta calls in to work. She had planned to go in this afternoon, but with all that is going on, perhaps it's better to stick close to home.

* * *

THE VISITORS' parking lot at the school is full, so Marta parks on the street. A crowd is gathered in front by the flag-pole around something or someone. As she nears the entrance, she recognizes the news reporter, Holly Riggs, from KTVP-2.

At The Apartments, Marta managed to avoid the reporter when she was asking residents to talk about Maddie's disappearance. Reporters were always trying to get residents to implicate the Smiths or some other poor bastard who people thought was weird. None of it led to anything except for speculation. Until they find Maddie, there will be no answers. It's already coming up on a year.

Marta easily slips by the group and through the front door without notice. In the office, Birdie sits in a chair, face tear-stained and blotchy.

"Aw, sweetie, I'm so sorry." Marta wraps her arms around Birdie's growing body, and Birdie starts sobbing all over again. "Shhhh . . . ," Marta says. "Everything is going to be okay."

* * *

WHEN THEY GET HOME, Marta gives Birdie an aspirin and helps her into a hot bath. She'd noticed the breast buds but missed the bigger picture. It *is* rare to see her older children nude.

"We can talk later," Marta says. "You should rest this afternoon. I have set some supplies over on the counter for you—pads, safety pins, some clean panties. I'll go to the drugstore later to pick up some nicer things for you." By *nicer things*, she means a sanitary belt and some tampons, although she doubts Birdie will be willing to try those.

Birdie says, "I don't want this. I wish I were a boy."

"Nobody wants this," Marta says. Nobody in their right mind would choose to be a woman. "You'll get used to it, and it happens to all girls, so you won't be alone."

The doorbell rings. "Call me if you need anything." Marta goes to answer the door.

Hiro Obata stands in front of Holly Riggs, the news reporter that she saw earlier at the school.

Hiro says, "Marta, I'm so sorry, I tried to stop them from bothering you—"

"It's okay," Marta says. "I know what this is about, and it'll be okay." Hiro is trying to protect her, but she doesn't have anything to hide, and nothing to tell.

The reporter says, "I have a few questions for you about your sons."

"Sons?" Was Willie there too for some reason? He left the house much earlier with Birdie and friends.

The reporter turns to Hiro. "Isn't Kai Nunes your son?"

"No, he's my grandson. He lives with me, though. Is he in trouble?"

Of course, Trace and Kai were together on the way to school. Marta hadn't thought to ask Principal Walters about the other kids.

"No, you haven't heard yet?" the reporter says. "Your grandson and your son"—she looks at each of them in turn —"along with some other boys, rescued one of their schoolmates from certain death on their way to school this morning. By all accounts, Kai and Trace were in charge of the rescue. We'd like to interview them together for the evening news, if you two will give permission."

Hiro and Marta look at each other. Hiro says, "I guess

it's alright with me. Marta, what do you think? I'll go along with whatever you decide."

Marta hesitates a moment before answering. "I guess it would be okay, but I'd like to have a list of the questions you plan to ask in advance." She's worried they might ask questions about Maddie. Tree is finally less anxious, and Marta wants to keep it that way. But reporters are always digging. They must know by now that Tree and Maddie were classmates.

"Yes, of course, that can be arranged," Holly says. "If it works for you, we were thinking around four at the KTVP-2 studio? It'll be on the live evening news, so that will give us time for reviewing questions and getting ready."

"That should be okay," Marta says. "Hiro, does that work for you?"

"Should be fine."

Marta glances at her watch. "I'm sorry. I need to go pick up my youngest daughter right now. You'll have to excuse us."

"See you at four, then," Holly Riggs says.

As soon as they leave, Marta calls Barbara.

"Oh, hello, Barbara, so glad that I caught you before you left to take Beanie to school. Would you mind picking up Piglet today?"

"No problem at all," she says. "Is everything okay?"

"Yeah, it's okay. Birdie got her first period and I had to bring her home, and then some other crazy stuff you'll be hearing about, no doubt. I'll tell you when you get here."

After settling that, Marta calls the elementary school to tell them that Barbara will be picking up Piglet, and that she'll pick up Tree and Kai later this afternoon. She'll stop at the drugstore on the way.

BIRDIE, Willie, and me go over to the Jones's to watch the evening news on their new RCA color television. I'm mad that I didn't get to go to the station. After all, I *was* there on the bridge too. I saw the whole thing happen from beginning to end. I heard the dare-double-dare, whatever that means.

After a couple of other boring news stories, the news announcer says, "Earlier today, drivers on Central Mountain Highway were surprised to see a child dangling from the Avenue A overpass. Motorists stopped and got out of their cars, helpless. You can imagine their surprise when they saw a small boy come over the railing and, along with a group of boys on top of the bridge, perform a daring rescue. Our own Holly Riggs was there at the scene and is here in the studio now with the two boys who orchestrated this heroic feat. Holly?"

"Yes, I'm here with Tracy Anderson and Kai Nunes, the second grade boys who performed the daring rescue."

The camera zooms in on Tree and Kai. They are smiling big. Kai wears a striped tie, white shirt and gray jacket, and Tree has on a navy blazer with a white oxford-cloth shirt and no tie.

"Tell me, Tracy, since you're the one who climbed to the outside of the railing, were you scared?"

"No, not for myself. I'm an expert climber. I knew I could do it. I was scared that the boy might not be able to hold on."

I *know* Tree was scared—he's fibbing. He always wants to look tough, maybe because he is smaller than the other boys in his grade.

"And you, Kai, what was your role?"

Kai says, "Well, I had the idea to make a rope out of our

clothes. I'm good at tying knots. I learned how to do different knots in Cub Scouts."

"Do either of you know why that boy was out there?"

Kai and Tree shake their heads. Tree says, "We heard it was some crazy dare."

Holly Riggs says, "Now I want to welcome in the boy who you saved, who thankfully is alive to tell us his side of the story. Let's welcome Tom O'Brien."

Kai and Tree look surprised as Tom comes on set.

"Tom, what on earth were you thinking when you went out there on that overpass?"

"Well, it was a stupid dare from one of my buddies. He told me he saw one of the little kids cross over the highway on the outside and bet me that I didn't have the guts to do it. It was stupid."

Holly Riggs says, "Interesting, and do you know who that kid was?"

Tom points at Tree. I know Tree is gonna be in a heap of trouble when he gets home, and by the look on his face, he knows it too. Kai squirms.

"Tracy, is it true that you crossed on the outside of the overpass?"

"Well," Tree says, "I only did it once, and I did it because one of the bigger kids dared *me* to."

Birdie, Willie, and I don't say anything, but we make eye contact. He's lying. He's crossed that overpass a lot more times than once! He's worried about how mad Mama will be.

"Well, folks, fortunately for these boys, this story has a happy ending today. Tom, do you have anything you want to say?"

"Yeah, don't ever try a stunt like I tried today. I'm real sorry I did what I done, but I'm glad Trace and Kai figured out how to save me. Thanks, guys."

Tree and Kai look extremely uncomfortable. In turn they say "Yer welcome." And "Glad it worked out."

"Next up, we are going to talk to city planners about how we can make our highway overpasses safer for children. In the meantime, parents, please talk to your children about safety on their walks back and forth to school."

10

DOORBELL IN THE NIGHT

MAY 1966

SUMMER VACATION IS ALMOST HERE, and today is my sixth birthday. Mama bought real invitations and said, because I am turning six, I could invite six people, not including my brothers, sister, grandma, and aunt. My list had Beanie, Kai, and Stella on it, of course. I also invited Catrina and Rob and Mrs. Friend. Mama asked if it was okay for her to invite Barbara. Of course, what a silly question.

Outside, Mr. Obata is working on setting up the Elysian Field for the party. He puts up a real pretty white shade tent with a long folding table under it where we will put the food. He also brings out a bunch of folding chairs for people to sit on. Mrs. Wright, Aunt Vivi's cook, is coming over to grill the food. She also made a cake. Aunt Vivi visits us a lot more lately. I like having her around.

Mama, Birdie, and Rob have been busy putting together party favors in brown paper bags—bubbles, party horns, and candy. Mama said we're going to make our own party hats out of newspaper, and we'll have a paper-plane contest to see who can make the best airplane. It's a paper-themed birthday party, I guess. Kai and Tree are folding origami animals and flowers to stick on the party bags. Kai knows how to make a lot of different shapes. The paper is pretty and colorful.

"Kai, can you teach me and Stella to make something?"

"Sure," he says. "Let's see. You guys want to make an animal or a flower?"

"Can you make a rose?" I ask. "The Garden of the Gods is full of them, and they're my favorite flower. I love the yellow ones the best!"

"Did you know that different-colored roses have different meanings?" Mr. Obata says. "And yellow roses represent friendship. Perfect for today."

"Yes, and grandfather taught me how to make an origami rose when I was about your age," says Kai.

Mr. Obata adds, "That *was* two years ago, Margaret. You're catching up to Kai and your brother."

I giggle at Mr. Obata's joke. I *am* more grown up, but I know I will never catch up.

"Pick your paper," Kai says. "You should pick a bigger square—easier to fold when you are learning."

It so happens that there is a pretty piece of pale-yellow paper. The two sides of the paper are different, one side darker than the other. The darker side has some sort of pretty pattern on it.

"Okay, Margie." Kai's nickname for me. He *never* calls me Piglet, Pig, or Piggy. I'm grateful for that. "To begin, we'll fold the paper diagonally by matching up the corners, like this." He folds the paper and shows me the perfectly matched edge. "You have to be careful and get the edges to match, and you have to press the fold with your nail, like this." He shows how he uses his thumbnail to make the fold flat.

"Like this?" I say. I hold my triangle up to him.

"Yes, just like that."

I follow his instructions exactly, and after about ten minutes I have made something resembling a rose. "Mine's not as good as yours," I say, handing it to him.

"Is it for me?" he says.

"Sure, if you want it!"

"I think it's beautiful and will keep it always. You'll get better with practice." He hands me the bright-red rose he made. It's perfect.

"Thank you!" I say. Then I turn. "Mr. Obata, look what Kai gave me. What does *this* color mean?"

"A single red rose is for love and devotion," he says. "Sweet."

Kai's face reddens.

"Oh, I like that," I say. "I hope we'll be friends forever."

"I think we will," says Kai.

* * *

AROUND TWO IN THE AFTERNOON, the rest of the guests arrive. Stella is late, maybe because Beanie and Barbara arrived early. Aunt Vivi and Mrs. Wright come sweeping in, arms full of groceries, a cake, several presents. Grandma Mimi arrives on Aunt Vivi's heels.

"Ah, Vivian!" Mr. Obata greets Aunt Vivi warmly. He acts silly, kneeling down in front of her and lifting her hand to his lips to kiss it.

"Oh, Hiro!" Aunt Vivi blushes. When Mr. Obata stands up, she plants a kiss right on his lips and gives him a hug!

I catch Mama rolling her eyes at Aunt Vivi.

I saw Aunt Vivi down the street one day at Mr. Obata's house. Later that day I asked what she was doing there, and she said he was giving her some pointers on gardening. Maybe. Grown-ups are weird. I think they like each other.

Right away, as usual, Rob, Catrina, Willie, and Birdie

disappear into the Dark Forest, no doubt having a meeting at the Y-P-S club. They don't do much of anything up there. Tree, Kai, and I have spied on them many times. Sometimes we hear them talking and giggling, playing games like cards, but mostly things are strangely quiet.

One day when Stella and I were spying on them, we heard Birdie say, "I know, let's play truth or dare!"

"Okay," Willie said. "Let's draw pine needles to see who gets to go first."

"I get to go first!" Catrina said. "Birdie, truth or dare?"

"Dare?" Birdie said.

"I dare you to give Rob a French kiss."

I have no idea what that is, but I thought it sounded like it might be a nice candy of some sort, like a special Hershey's Kiss.

But then I heard Birdie say, "Eww! No way am I letting him stick his tongue down my throat."

"Come on, Birdie, yer the one who picked this game," Willie said.

How gross would that be to have Rob or anyone stick their tongue down my throat? I gagged at the thought. They probably knew I was spying on them and were trying to gross me out. Stella and I didn't stick around.

Beanie and I are hanging on the iron gate, waiting for the last guest to arrive—Mrs. Friend. "Think she's coming?" I say.

"Maybe not," Beanie says. "I bet she forgot."

"That's mean," I say. "Beanie-Meanie-Big-Fat-Greenie."

"Ah, c'mon, Piggy-wig, she forgot me too."

"I'm sorry," I say.

"Me too," she says. "And besides, who cares? She's a silly grown-up."

We hug and run back to the party. That's how Beanie and I are. We fight, and then we hug and become best friends again.

Even with the absence of Stella and Mrs. Friend, this year's party is way better than last year's. For one thing nobody goes missing, nobody cries, worries, or feels sad. We make fun party hats, blow bubbles, and fly "flying Os" in the Elysian Field—Mr. Obata teaches us to make those, of course. And Kai Nunes made a red rose for me that I plan to keep forever.

Birdie has too much fun with Rob, Catrina, and Willie to be annoyed by the attention the adults give Piglet during the party or to be jealous about the presents she gets. Since moving to One Elysium Street, everything has changed. The Y-P-S club has an exclusive membership, and kids at school have heard about it.

Willie, Catrina, and Rob have all brought different classmates to club meetings, and word has got around that Birdie and Willie are rich spoiled brats. Nothing could be further from the truth, but let people think what they want. That might have something to do with why she hasn't made more friends at school, on account of being thought of as stuck-up. But being stuck-up has its perks too. People want to be like you—they're jealous of *you*, which is better than being jealous of them.

Tomorrow's a school day, so after Catrina goes home, Birdie goes to her room to finish her homework. She has one last book report to write, and then she'll be finished with elementary school. She must finish the book first—*Alice's Adventures in Wonderland*. She climbs into her cozy reading chair. It's a weird story. She can't make heads or tails of it. Why did the author write this book?

When she finishes reading, she heads to her desk, carefully places her lined notebook paper at an angle in front of her, and begins writing. She writes in pen, shaping each cursive letter with great care, and stops to admire her own penmanship and terrific spelling.

Robin Anderson
May 30, 1966
Book Report—Alice in Wonderland by Lewis Carroll

Alice is a girl who lived a long time ago who is really bored. One day, she sees a talking rabbit wearing clothes and follows the rabbit down a rabbit hole and ends up in a creepy place called Wonderland. It's like nothing she's ever seen before, with lots of weird stuff happening.

Along the way Alice meets atot a lot of crazy characters. There's a grumpy caterpillar, a smiling cat that can disappear, a guy called the Mad Hatter who is really into tea parties, and the Queen of Hearts who is really bossy and keeps shouting "Off with their heads!" about almost everything.

The rules in Wonderland are super weird and keep changing. Alice grows really big and then really small just by eating or drinking different things. It's like a nightmare where nothing makes sense. She plays a strange game of croquet with flamingos and hedgehogs and gets into all sorts of trouble.

Alice tries to make sense of everything, but it's just really confusing, and it was confusing to me too. She keeps asking questions but doesn't get any answers. It's like everyone is talking in riddles.

In the end, Alice finds herself in a court-room with the Queen of Hearts, and things get really scary, and then she suddenly wakes up, realizing it was all just a dream.

Personally, I don't like this book. It isn't meaningful. I like books that are more about real life that actually mean something that I can understand. I would only recommend this book for people who like nonsense. I won't be reading the sequel to this book!

After she finishes writing, she rereads it, admiring her work. Only one cross-out. She'll get an A for sure. She puts her pj's on, crawls under her snuggly comforter, and is dropping off when the sound of the door chime startles her awake.

Who could that be at this hour? She gets up and pads down the hallway. The living room light has come on, and Mother, Willie, and Tree are standing there debating whether or not to open the door. Birdie goes into the darkened dining room and peeks out a window with a clear view to the front door.

The only thing she sees out there is a large silver dog. His fur glitters under the porch light, like some magical creature. He jumps up and bites the knotted rope handle of the chime and it rings out again, reverberating throughout the house.

"Mom! Guys!" she yells. "It's a dog!"

Mother opens the door. "Oh my! It's a German Weimaraner, a beautiful young one at that. Someone is probably worried about you," she says to the dog as she bends down to check for a collar. There isn't one. The dog wags what it has of a tail and licks her face. "Oh, ick. Don't do that. Okay, okay, you can come in."

By now Piglet has come into the room. She's terrified of dogs, so she hangs back.

Birdie kneels and hugs it like a long-lost friend. "It's a boy!" she says. "I can see its *thingy*."

"Penis," Mother says. "You should always use the correct word unless you don't know it. But yes, I too can see that he is male."

"Can we keep it?" Tree asks.

"Please? I promise to take care of him," Birdie says.

Willie says, "I promise to help Birdie take care of it."

Piglet remains silent on the matter.

"Well, we need to try to find his owner before making any decision. This is a valuable hunting dog. Somebody is undoubtedly looking for him."

Birdie says, "Well, I hope we don't ever find the owner."

"Okay, Birdie, the dog can stay in your room tonight, until we figure out what to do with him."

Birdie does a happy dance. That little prayer she said in the Garden of the Gods earlier in the day worked.

MARGAUX

1985

GOSSIP GAL
MONDAY AFTERNOON

I WAKE up when a warm ray of sunlight crosses my closed eyes. I was dreaming about living on President Street. It was the night Leadbelly, the first of many of our family dogs, showed up. *Shit!* I fell asleep reading my own novel; it must be the most fucking boring story ever! Judy said she would have the kids back by four. It's now three thirty, so I have to hurry to get over to The Row before they do.

Breathless and a sweaty mess, I ring the doorbell and peel off my jacket. Clearly I dressed too warmly for the day. Finally, Mariana opens the door. "I was wondering when you were going to get here," she says.

"Well, lucky me. I take your relief as a sign that I arrived before they did!"

"*Não me importa,*" she says. "I don't care if you get fired." Mariana can be such a bitch, but I like her no-bullshit attitude.

As I hang up my jacket, a black Lincoln pulls up in front of the townhouse. Judy gets out and stands next to the car, watching to make sure the kids get inside safely. I wave at her and smile. It must have taken them a long time to get from Coney Island, where the aquarium is, to here. Glad I wasn't responsible for any of that.

Katie and John scramble up the stairs, happy to be home. Spending time with their cousins isn't their favorite thing. Judy is surprisingly down to earth, nothing like her sister, but her kids are hard to take. They, like many affluent children, suffer from a sense of superiority and entitlement.

* * *

AN HOUR LATER, I'm sitting in the kitchen at the counter with the twins when the phone rings. Mariana answers it in the living room.

"Harris residence, may I ask who's calling?" She says this without a trace of an accent.

"Oh, of course, Mrs. Harris . . . one moment."

Mariana pops her head in. "It's for you."

"Thanks," I say. I go to the pantry area, where there is a mounted wall phone, and pick up the receiver. The receiver clicks as Mariana hangs up the other end. "Hello?"

"Hi, Margie, I hate to do this to you, but I need to go out with a business acquaintance for a somewhat late dinner, and I was wondering if you could stay on until I get home? It might be late, around midnight or so?"

"Yeah, that's fine," I say. "Mariana forewarned me about this week. I need to have Wednesday through Friday evenings to myself, though, as my brother is in town, and my literary agent—"

"Oh? You have a literary agent?" Mrs. Harris sounds surprised—and interested. She has never expressed curiosity about my life before.

"Yeah, I do."

"May I ask who?"

"Sure. I doubt you have ever heard of them—M. Des—"

"Jardins!" she says. "Now *that* is impressive."

"You *know* them?"

"Of course, everybody who is anybody knows about them in literary circles. They last represented Dorothy Parker fifty years ago, and they recently have made a splashy reentry into the world of publishing about town. Kiyo Flores, Mihana Sakura's grandson, is taking up where his grandmother left off—reconvening a Vicious Circle, I hear. Apparently, they already have some hot up-and-coming young writers on their prospective list."

"And what do you do again, Mrs. Harris?" I hadn't thought to ask. She hasn't ever volunteered information about herself. She has talked plenty about her husband, a successful trader on Wall Street, but never anything about her own work.

"Oh, I used to be a journalist," she says. "Now I'm a gossip columnist at the *New York Post*."

Holy shit! "Are you *the* Gossip Gal?"

"I hate that title," she says. "Makes my job sound so cheap, tawdry, but that wouldn't be entirely wrong."

I detect regret in her voice. "I thought the Gossip Gal's name was Nanci Heart," I say.

"Well, I hope you are good at keeping secrets," she says. "Nellie Harris is Nanci Heart."

"I do a decent job of secret-keeping—it runs in my family," I say. Mostly I can keep a secret. I can't freakin' believe that I am nannying for the Gossip Gal, one of the most sharp-tongued and witty news writers I have ever read. She's uncovered countless scandals among New York elites and celebrities. She especially loves revealing financial fraud and deeply hidden secrets of politicians, but her real gift is in her sense of humor about it all.

"Good, a good writer is always discreet," she says. "Okay then, I'll see you later tonight."

* * *

AFTER THE TWINS have finished their homework, I let them
watch a movie. The Harrises have a new video player
connected to the big TV in the game room, and they rent all
kinds of movies from a place in Midtown called Video
Shack. The kids pick one called *The Secret of NIMH*, an
animated film. I slip it into the video player, but of course it
needs to be rewound. I push the button and it begins
whirring and winding.

"I'm gonna go make us some popcorn," I say. "John,
when it finishes rewinding, go ahead and push the play
button."

"No prob," he says.

The twins have been busy setting up their movie-
watching nest in the corner of the large sectional. Theo and
I used to do the same thing.

The movie soundtrack signals that the kids have started
it up. Pop, pop . . . pop, the last kernels explode. I drizzle
melted butter over the top and add a sprinkle of salt. My
mouth waters from the fragrance.

"Popcorn!" I say as I walk into the room. The twins are
snuggled together; they look like they are already half
asleep. I settle in next to them, pull the one remaining lap
robe off the back of the couch, and rest my feet on the
coffee table.

The story is weird. Mrs. Brisby, a widowed field mouse,
seeks help from some rats to save her ill son and their home.
The rats, as it turns out, are mutants with human-level intel-
ligence due to scientific experiments at the National Institute
of Mental Health (NIMH), hence the name of the movie.
They help Mrs. Brisby on her quest. The animation is cool,
but creepy and dark. Not sure how appropriate it is for
seven-year-olds, but no matter, they didn't make it to the
halfway point.

I jiggle Katie and John awake. "Come on, sleepy heads. Time to go brush your teeth and go to bed."

"Aw, shucks," John says. "Can't we stay up longer?"

"Nope. Tomorrow *is* a school day, and you both are pretty tired after all the earlier excitement."

After I get them into bed, I go back to the game room and turn the television to NBC. Oh good, it's the new *Alfred Hitchcock Presents*. I'd heard it was being brought back, but since I don't have a TV, I haven't been able to catch any of the episodes. This one is called "Wake Me When I'm Dead." Not classic Hitchcock, but okay, got the psychological part right. At a quarter past eleven, as I'm watching the news, a car door outside slams.

I peek out the draped window to see if Mrs. Harris has arrived home. She has, but she's not alone—she's with a man who is *not* Mr. Harris, and they're kissing. I drop the drape, turn off the TV, and go out to the kitchen to finish cleaning up. She comes in about five minutes later. *A good writer is always discreet.* Maybe she isn't a good writer. It's none of my business.

She's obviously tipsy. "Hello there," she says. "Sorry I'm so late." She drops her handbag on a table in the hallway and takes off her coat, leaving it on a chair back.

"That's okay." I cross over to the coat closet to retrieve my things. "You told me you'd be out until midnight, and so you're home early."

"I asked the driver to wait for you," she says. "Don't worry, it isn't the same one you had this morning. He's been fired."

"I guess Judy told you. I thought she would. That was not the best situation," I said.

"You handled it. All's well that ends well, right?"

"I guess so, and with that, I will say good night." I head out the door and into the waiting town car. "202 Elizabeth Street," I say. A moment later we are stopped at a light on

Waverly. A man, Mrs. Harris's lover, passes the car on the sidewalk, headed toward her place with a bottle of wine and a single rose in hand. Who is he?

DREAM WALKING
TUESDAY MORNING

THE NEXT MORNING when I arrive at The Row, Mrs. Harris has already departed. Mariana greets me with her usual demeanor. I can't tell what she thinks of me, or if she thinks of me at all.

"Good morning," I say.

"If you say so," Mariana says. "It's another day to me."

"Yeah . . . ," I say as I put my things away and swap my shoes.

Mariana says, "Why you always do that? You know the Mrs. doesn't care one way or another."

"I know. It's the way I was brought up."

"You Japanese or something? You don't look Japanese to me."

"Well, maybe part of me deep inside is Japanese," I say. "It's a long story."

"Hmm, well we both got things to do, but maybe sometime you can tell me about it."

"Yeah, sometime."

Mariana doesn't strike me as the reading type. If she is, maybe someday she'll read my book and figure out who is who. Everyone who knows me is going to think they know who I am and where I come from, but they won't.

I walk into the kitchen, where the kids are finishing up their breakfasts. They don't acknowledge my entrance. "Heya!" I say.

Katie looks up from her book. She's reading one of the Laura Ingalls Wilder books—*Farmer Boy*. I thought that book was super boring. I wanted to know more about Laura and Mary's dramas, not some dumb boy named Almanzo whose only concern in life was whether he got his own horse. "Hi," she says, and goes back to reading.

I guess Katie likes the book better than I did. In retrospect, I understand the author's desire to delve more deeply into the boyhood life of the man she would eventually marry. What is it about him that she loved? Almanzo is boring but earnest—too good to be true or interesting. He's *nothing* like Kiyo, a man of mystery. I can't stop wondering about him, if there is the possibility of something, but then I remember he doesn't live here. Maybe he isn't real. What are the chances that someone from your childhood appears back in your life and is the perfect match? *Next to nothing.*

"John," I say, to make conversation. I grab a glass out of the cupboard. "How'd you sleep last night?"

"Uh, good. Why?"

"Just wondering."

"Well, there was this one weird thing . . . ," he says. He's not the most talkative child, so his continuation surprises me. "I woke up and heard some voices, so I came out to see what was going on. My uncle Chad was here in the kitchen in his underwear."

"Your mom's brother?"

"Nope, my dad's."

"Maybe a dream?" I say. Now I have my answer as to the *who*. Mr. Harris's brother is having a fling with Mrs. Harris. Everybody has a secret.

"Yeah, I guess it was," he says. "When I asked my mom what he was doing here this morning, she said I must have been dream walking. She told me it's a problem some children have."

"Yeah, I was a dream walker too." I fill my glass with tap water. "I saw a lot of things during the day and at night that nobody is supposed to see."

"Kind of scares me."

"Yeah, me too." I go over to him and give him a hug. "Don't worry too much about it, though. Someday you'll be able to make sense of those things." Although I doubt he'll ever fully understand how his uncle could do such a thing to his father.

* * *

"John! Katie! Time to leave for school," I yell. Walking the twins to school is the most important part of my job until two thirty, when I pick them up and ferry them to various after-school lessons. They have one after-school activity for every day of the week—swimming, piano, choir, tennis, and ballet, in that order. Everything is in walking distance. After we get home, I give them a snack, and then the twins do their homework. Mr. and Mrs. Harris usually get home before seven, by which time Mariana's husband, Pedro, their part-time personal chef, has made dinner for the family. I usually leave as soon as Mr. and Mrs. Harris arrive.

"Give that back!" Katie screams. Katie chases John down the stairs. "Margie, tell John to give me back my book!"

John is laughing and holding Katie's book in the air above his head. She is trying to grab it.

"Come on, John, please give her the book. We need to leave *now*."

John bops Katie on the head softly with *Farmer Boy*. "I

was playing . . . All you ever do is read." He hands her the book.

The kids put on their coats. It's chilly outside. Their dark duffle coats match the color of their school uniforms. I grab their umbrellas. We will need them.

"If you read more, you wouldn't be so dumb," Katie says.

John looks hurt. "Well, I think you're the stupid one."

I drag them out the door and down the steps. "Both of you, stop this right now. You're equally smart and wonderful people. Not everybody is good at or likes to read, John, and that's okay. And Katie, John is good at things that you don't like to do. He is excellent at drawing, for example."

What I know that Katie doesn't know is that John has a learning disability. Reading does not come as naturally to him as it does for her. Mr. and Mrs. Harris have asked me not to mention his learning disability to anyone, including Katie. I'm not sure about that decision on their part, but they're the parents.

A light drizzle falls. As we reach the sidewalk, my eye catches sight of a man standing down the way and across the street under an umbrella. He's Asian, smoking a cigarette—doesn't appear to notice us. Could it be the same man I saw yesterday? Unlikely.

"Okay, while we walk to school, let's play a game my mother used to make my brother Theo and me play. It's called Just Be Nice. I want you to take turns saying something that you like about each other." I glance back over my shoulder, heart beating, but the sidewalk is empty behind us. I must be getting paranoid. "Whoever has the most nice things to say wins, but they have to be true—you must believe what you are saying."

That works to settle things down. They each take turns saying something they like about the other one, and we walk all five blocks to the Grace Church School without incident. By design, the competition ends in a tie.

* * *

I DECIDE to go over to Caffè Reggio after dropping the kids off. I often go there to write in my journal or read. Today, I'll read a few more chapters from *One Elysium Street*. I need to finish my review before meeting with Theo. So far, I've only marked a few minor changes. There is nothing damning, nothing to suggest our family had anything to do with Anna's disappearance all those years ago. It's highly improbable anyone would make that connection.

I luck out and get a primo table in a nook next to one of the windows. As I settle in, I catch a glimpse of Mrs. Harris across the room. She's sitting at an out-of-the-way corner table alone, studying a document. If she has seen me, she pretends she hasn't. She's beautiful in the way that wealthy women are—perfectly coiffed, well dressed. Her auburn hair falls softly around her face without being in her eyes. Reminds me of my first-grade teacher.

The man from the other night who I now know to be Mr. Harris's brother, Chad—joins her at the table and reaches across to briefly hold her hand. She passes the document over to him. I can't see his face. While he looks it over, Mrs. Harris gazes down at her hand. Is she looking at her wedding band? Yes, now she is twirling it on her finger.

"What can I get for you today?"

I didn't notice the waiter's arrival because I was so preoccupied with Mrs. Harris's indiscretions. "I'll have a cappuccino and one of those delicious almond cookies," I say.

After the waiter leaves, I pull out my manuscript and open it to chapter eleven.

ONE ELYSIUM STREET

CHAPTERS 11 AND 12

11

KEEPING UP WITH THE JONESES

MAY-JUNE 1966

BIRDIE TAKES the dog into her room with a bowl of water. Her mother said she would buy some dog food tomorrow and ask Barbara in the morning about getting some of theirs to tide us over. Birdie shows him the rug on the floor next to her.

"Sit," she says, pointing at the rug. He sits! "Down," she says, firmly signaling with a flat hand, the way Mr. Jones taught her to do with Dottie. He lies down! Either she is a genius or he is well trained.

Birdie has wanted a dog for as long as she can remember. Since moving to One Elysium Street, she has spent significant time with the Jones's dog Dottie, a Dalmatian that they rescued from the fire department. The Peakview Fire Department kept her as a mascot and a companion animal to be used when visiting schools, but she bit a child at a school event, and the department was considering putting her down. Mr. Jones, a dog lover, caught wind of it because Barbara was volunteering that day in the classroom where the child was allegedly bitten. She told Neil that Dottie had not *bitten* but *snapped* at one of the children who was pulling on one of her ears. *Who could blame her?* she said. *Everyone should get a second chance, even a dog that bites a child.* And Neil agreed.

Mr. Jones worked with Dottie on training exercises, and now she is impervious to children. He demonstrated to Birdie how Beanie could pull, jab, hit, or lightly kick Dottie without getting a reaction. He showed Birdie how he does training exercises with her. He said, *Dogs are a lot like people. They respond to positive reinforcement. You can train any dog, any person, including yourself, no matter how damaged they are, to change their behavior by using positive reinforcement techniques.*

Birdie put this to the test by training Dottie to do tricks that she had never been taught—roll over, beg, shake hands, and turn circles on her hind legs. It worked every time. She also used it on her little brother and sister to help rid them of some of their more annoying-to-her behaviors. She helped Piglet stop sucking her fingers, and she got Tree to stop eating his boogers. Through all of this, Birdie and Mr. Jones have become quite close. He is like a father to her. She can't wait to work with him on training this dog, whatever his name will be.

The dog lies comfortably on the floor while Birdie climbs under her covers. Her bed is a Japanese-style bed that her mother told her is called a futon. It sits on a low wooden frame. She hangs one hand from the bed and strokes the dog's silvery fur. Where did he come from? What should she name him? Will he become friends with Dottie? She drifts off to sleep with her hand on the dog's belly.

In the morning she finds the dog stretched out next to her on the bed. "You tricked me!" she says. "And here I thought you were a good dog." He looks at her with his striking bluish-green eyes and gives his stub of a tail a wiggle, then licks her face. "Yucky. I love you too."

She gets up and hurriedly puts on her school clothes so that she can let the dog out to go to the bathroom. How *did* he get into the yard in the first place? Was the gate left unlatched? Maybe there's a hole in one of the fences. She'll ask Mr. Obata if he can check.

When she opens her bedroom door, the dog patters out of her room like he owns the house, like he has been in it before. He goes directly into the kitchen, where her mother is preparing a mix of kibble and canned dog food. "I called Barbara first thing," she said. "Also, I'll ask Mr. Obata if he can watch the dog today while you are at school. If not, Barbara said she's happy to."

"Wow, thank you, Mom," Birdie says. Her mother must like the dog too. That's good. If the owners don't show up, that means she probably will let Birdie keep it.

"Birdie, I don't want you to get too attached to him. We need to make a sincere effort at finding his owner before deciding he belongs to us."

"Okay, Mom, but can I name him at least? I don't like calling him Dog or Boy. He needs a *real* name."

"Sure. Well . . . since he appears to be a purebred Weimaraner, we should give him a name that reflects his breed in some way, like a German name or, alternatively, one that reflects something about him physically. Tonight I'll help you come up with a name worthy of his beautiful soul."

The dog gobbles up the bowl of food in less than a minute, then runs over to the back door and barks once. His bark is big and gruff, scary. Birdie goes and opens the door to let him out. He immediately runs toward the Tree of Knowledge, hikes his leg, and pees on it. *Uh-oh, Mr. Obata isn't going to like that.* Next, he goes out into the middle of Persephone's Couch and lays down a gigantic pile of steaming poop.

Birdie's mother comes out of the house. "How are you going to clean that up?" she asks.

"The Jones's have this cool pooper-scooper thingy. Maybe we could get one of those?"

"Maybe. And how are you going to pay for that?" her mother asks.

"Babysitting money? I've been babysitting for Beanie a lot lately and have saved."

"Okay, but right now you need to go find Mr. Obata and ask him if he has a shovel or something you can use to clean it up. He isn't going to like it much if this dog ruins his beautiful landscaping."

Birdie goes to the greenhouse, but Mr. Obata isn't there. He doesn't seem to be anywhere in the yard either. She fortunately discovers a gardening trowel in a bucket by the greenhouse and uses it to scoop the poop, carefully replacing the tool where she found it when she is done.

THE FIRST SCHOOL year on Elysium Street has worked out much better than Marta could have imagined. She has arranged her schedule so that she can be home when the older kids get home from school, and Barbara picks Piglet up from school on most days since she must bring Beanie for afternoon kindergarten anyway. When Piglet gets home, Mr. Obata spends the afternoon with her. He enlists her help around the grounds.

Marta's morning routine consists of getting up at four or five in the morning to do any studying that needs to be done, and at around seven she makes the kids a hot breakfast. Breakfast is the most important meal of the day, as the saying goes. She doesn't believe that, but the world does, and she wants to be a good mother. After breakfast she sends the kids off to school in two waves.

Birdie, Willie, Catrina, and Rob always take off together about a half an hour before the younger kids. Piglet, Tree, and Kai all walk together. After the whole drama with Tree and Kai on the highway bridge the previous month, Marta reminds them daily of their duty to keep Piglet safe, emphasizing that it is their responsibility to set a good example for the younger kids. She thinks this approach is working; at least there haven't been any reports to the contrary. Piglet would tell her if anything happened, because she is guileless. The older kids think she's a tattletale, and there might be some truth to that, but mostly she is innocent in relaying information, talking about the events of the days as if they are normal. She doesn't mean to get the other kids in trouble, but sometimes she does because they are doing things they shouldn't be doing.

* * *

BEFORE LEAVING for her work at the lab, Marta seeks out Mr. Obata. She needs to make sure that he is okay with hosting the dog, if only for a day. She finds him in the greenhouse where he tends to his beautiful orchids.

"Good morning, Hiro," she says.

"Hello, Marta! You're the person I wanted to see."

"I bet," she says. "You were probably wondering about that large dog who pooped on your lawn this morning!"

"Yes, about that—"

"I'm so sorry. We had quite some excitement in the middle of the night last night. Our doorbell rang, and when we answered it, he was standing there."

"Well—"

"We're trying to find the owners. We don't plan on keeping it."

"Oh, I am sorry to hear that," Mr. Obata says. "I know

the owner of this dog personally—he's the owner of this house!"

"What is his dog doing here, then? Why didn't they take him to Princeton?" Marta asks. "What *horrible* person leaves the family dog behind?"

"Ahhh . . . ," Mr. Obata says, "don't be so quick to judge. Leadbelly came home of his own accord. It's a mystery—"

"His name is Leadbelly? What a perfect name for him!"

"Quite. The Ito's were big jazz fans, and well, as you can see, he's the color of lead. I was shocked to see him when he showed up at my house last night. He rang *my* doorbell. When I answered the door, he jumped up on me and licked my face with the joy of finding a long-lost friend. I don't have a good house for a dog or an enclosed yard, so I walked him down here and let him in the gate. I fed him before bringing him over and left water outside for him by the greenhouse, but I guess he wanted to come *all the way* home!"

"That is remarkable!" Marta says.

"It's a minor miracle. Professor Ito was driving from Peakview to Princeton with his five children and the dog in their brand-new Volvo Amazon Estate—a nice family car. Anyway, they stopped for a meal in Council Bluffs, Iowa. It was a sweltering day, so Professor Ito opened all the windows, including the one in the back compartment, where Leadbelly was. Normally, Leadbelly would stay put when told—he's well behaved. When the family returned to the car and found him gone, they thought perhaps he had been stolen. Many hunters prize these dogs for duck hunting, and they're expensive."

"Oh, how terrible," Marta says.

"Yes, the family was heartbroken. After Mrs. Ito's death, to lose their family pet that way . . . They spent several days in the Council Bluffs area looking for him—

checked the pounds, put up signs around town, and went door to door."

"That still doesn't explain how he ended up here."

"No, that is a question we may never know the answer to. Perhaps he escaped a captor, or maybe he jumped out of the car of his own accord. I favor the dog-stealing theory because of his missing collar. Either way, he found his way. I called Mr. Ito this morning, and he was overwhelmed with joy at the news. After ten months since he went missing, they had given up hope. Anyway, he wonders if your family would be willing to care for Leadbelly until their return? He says he knows it is a lot to ask, but—"

"Of course we will take care of him. We will love him as our own. Oh, Birdie is going to be so delighted. Thank you, Hiro! Thank you!" Marta can't contain herself and gives Mr. Obata a big hug. "And, do you mind keeping an eye on him today?"

"It would be my pleasure," he says. "Oh, one more thing, I noticed that Birdie used my trowel to pick up the dog waste this morning. Would you mind telling her that she will find a pooper-scooper is in the tool shed? She can use the big plastic bucket with the tight lid by the greenhouse to dispose what she picks up."

"I'll do that!"

Dogs scare the bejeebers out of me. I want to like them, but they don't like me.

One day at The Apartments, we were all playing roll-down-the-hill on a grassy slope, and there was this giant dog, taller than me, that looked like Lassie. It had long flowing hair and a big pink tongue and real sharp teeth. It lunged at me, and in terror I started running. It chased me, nipping at my clothes and heels. I ran as fast as I could—felt like my heart was going to jump right out of my body. Ran for my life all the way upstairs to our apartment, and the dog followed me inside all the way to the kitchen, where Mama was cooking. She shooed that dog right out, then told me *Never run from a dog—stand your ground*. She said *That dog was just trying to play. If he wanted to eat you, he would have. You can't outrun a dog, silly*. I'm still convinced it wanted to eat me.

When Mrs. Jones and I arrive home from school, I explode out of her station wagon as soon as she parks. I can hardly wait to see the dog, although I'm afraid of it. I hope he's still here; I hope that Mama didn't find the owners or take him to the pound.

"Bye, Mrs. Jones—Barbara." I keep forgetting to call her Barbara like she told me to. I'm supposed to call grown-ups by their last name. "Thanks for bringing me home."

"You're welcome, Piglet. Tell Mr. Obata I'll stop by in a bit."

I run across the street and open the gate. I don't see the dog, or anybody. Where *is* Mr. Obata?

I find him in the Garden of the Gods cutting back the rosebushes.

"Hi, Mr. Obata," I say.

When he looks up, he smiles big. "Well hello, Margaret! How was school today?"

"Pretty good," I say. "But I was eager to get home to play . . . Why are you killing the roses?" I ask.

"Oh, I'm not killing them. I'm deadheading them." Snip-snip. The dried-up rose blossoms fall to the ground. "Getting rid of the old blossoms provides energy for the new ones; it's the circle of life, you see."

He shows me how he carefully cuts back each branch that is finished blooming to the first leaf cluster with five leaves.

"Five is an important number in Japanese culture," he

says. "It's a symbol of being complete, the five senses—seeing, hearing, smelling, tasting, and touching. Roses are all about the senses, and all about five. You know a flower is likely a member of the rose family if it has five petals."

"I guess I am a member of the rose family since there are five kids in my family."

Mr. Obata laughs. "I know you are as precious as a rose." He stands up and gives me a squeeze. After that, I decide that five is my lucky number.

"I have a special surprise for you, a friend I want you to meet." He takes my hand, and we walk around to the back of the house, near the greenhouse. The dog is stretched out on Persephone's Couch in the shade of the Tree of Knowledge. When he sees us, he stands up.

Mr. Obata says, "Leadbelly, come." The dog walks calmly over to us. "Leadbelly, meet Margaret. Margaret, meet Leadbelly."

Leadbelly holds his right front paw up in the air.

"I think he wants to shake your hand!" Mr. Obata says.

"Okay." I reach my hand out and hold his paw softly, but only for a quick second. He puts his paw back on the ground. He smiles.

"Is Leadbelly *your* dog?"

"No, but he's an old friend. He belongs to the family that lives in this house."

"Us? Our family?"

"For the time being, yes. His owners are the ones who own this house, and they have asked if your family can take care of him until they get back. Would you like to pet him?"

I nod. "I'm scared."

"I thought you might be," Mr. Obata says. He makes some hand signals to Leadbelly. Leadbelly comes over and lies down in front of me and then rolls over on his back.

"He wants you to pet his tummy. That means he trusts you."

I squat and carefully reach over to touch his tummy. It's soft and warm.

"You see, nothing to fear with him. He will be your steadfast friend and protector."

"I love him already," I say.

"Good, and of course, be considerate of him. Don't pull on his ears or tail or hit him. The nicest dog will bite a person if they are unkind."

"Oh, I would never hurt a flea," I say.

"I don't think you would," he says.

12

HEAT OF SUMMER

JULY 1966

BIRDIE STRETCHES her bare legs out in front of her and slathers on coconut oil. Her skin has turned a golden brown. One of the perks of living at One Elysium Street is that her mother can afford a summer family membership at the Broadmoor Swim Club, an outdoor pool that is a few blocks from the house. Catrina's and Rob's families belong to it too. Every morning, Catrina, Rob, Willie, and she leave the house together, like grown-ups, to spend luxurious days alternately baking in the Colorado sun and dipping in the unheated pool.

The pool is enormous, perfectly round, and surrounded by a man-made sand beach. They could rent beach umbrellas, but they never do, because none of them has a dollar to spare. Why would you *ever* want to sit in the shade anyway?

Today, Birdie and Catrina arrive sooner than the boys. Her mother and Barbara will come later with the younger kids. She and Catrina find the perfect spot with the shortest swim to the island, where there is a diving platform, a high and a low diving board, and two slides. The island is off-center in the pool to accommodate the need for deeper water for the diving boards and a graded shallower side for the slides and younger swimmers.

"Don't you think Rob is dreamy?" Birdie asks Catrina.

"Not at all!" Catrina says. "You took that French-kissing dare too much to heart."

"Well, it was much more than I thought it would be, that's for sure."

"Like how?" Catrina asks.

"I felt all tingly and weird, but weird in a good way. I thought it was gonna be gross, and at first it was, but then something happened . . ."

"Hmm . . . when that dare came back to me with Willie, I thought it was disgusting," Catrina says. "It made me wanna gag."

"Maybe Rob knew what he was doing, and Willie didn't. I bet Willie never kissed a girl before kissing you."

"Truth is, I never kissed a boy before kissing him, and I am pretty sure I'll never do it again!" Catrina says. "Race you to the island!"

* * *

ROB AND WILLIE arrive around eleven. Birdie gives them a wave, hoping that they'll come sit with Catrina and her, but either they don't see her or they are pretending not to. They dump their towels on the sand, run into the shallow side of the pool, and dive under in tandem. The pool is crowded now, and she can't see them. Just as she begins to worry, they finally reappear near the island and climb up the ladder to the diving platform.

Catrina says, "Boys are dumb."

"How so?" Birdie says.

"They're always doing dumb and dangerous things."

"I think they're braver than girls."

"I am pretty sure they are stupid—all those hits to their heads playing football and wrestling," Catrina says.

Rob does a swan dive from the platform. Birdie's heart skips a beat. He makes it look easy. Willie does a cannonball. His only goal is to make as big a splash as he can. Show-off.

Birdie says, "Well, my brother is no great catch, I'll give you that, but Rob's dive was spectacular!"

Marta and Barbara load the car with towels and inflatable pool toys for the kids.

"Everybody in!" It's the usual collection of six- and eight-year-olds—Piglet, Beanie, Tree, and Kai.

Marta is enjoying this summer more than any time she can remember since leaving Doug, more than any time in her life. Things have turned a corner. For the first time, she lives without fear for her children's safety or for her own safety. The wounds left from years of Doug's abuse have finally begun to heal. She and Barbara spend as much time as possible together, usually in the company of kids so as not to look suspicious.

Barbara pushes all four kids into the back seat of the station wagon. "No standing, and *no* fighting," she says.

Marta takes her brimmed hat off when she gets into the passenger seat. She should have driven. Barbara is the worst driver of anybody she knows, and she's already started drinking today, but it is only a few blocks, and Barbara's Town and Country station wagon is newer and more spacious than her Ford Falcon and has air-conditioning.

On their way to the swim club, they pass The Apartments on their left. Seeing them causes a lump to form in Marta's throat. Maddie has never been found. Have the

Smiths moved? Are they still looking for their daughter? Marta's eyes well up.

"You okay?" Barbara asks.

"Yeah, was thinking about our last summer here . . ."

"Yeah, that must have been hard."

They stop at the railroad crossing. There are only two trains a day, but the schedule is unpredictable.

"All clear," Marta says. "Sorry, don't mean to be a back-seat driver. I can't go over these tracks without remembering that young couple who was killed here a couple of years ago."

"I guess this little part of Peakview is filled with ghosts," Barbara says.

They come to a stop sign on the other side of the tracks before crossing Vista Boulevard and go three more blocks to the swim club. The parking lot is full, but they manage to find a spot on the outer perimeter.

"Leave the windows open a crack," Barbara says. "It's so hot today." Her station wagon has electric windows and locks—a real luxury.

"Okay, kids, you need to stick close to us as we cross the lot. Let's make a people chain."

Piglet grabs on to one of Barbara's hands, and Beanie grabs Piglet's hand; Marta takes Barbara's free hand with the boys on the outside, and they make their way through the lot like a string of geese. The mamas fly point. Barbara looks her in the eye and gives the back of Marta's hand a thumb stroke.

At the gate, they show their membership cards to the attendant. "You've made it just in time today—the pool is near capacity," she says.

"Oh good," Marta says, "I would hate to wait today in this heat!"

The kids start to run as soon as they get through the gate.

"Kids, no running!"

They slow down momentarily and slowly regain speed the farther away they get from Barbara and Marta, who lag —they hold hands for an extra few seconds, squeeze, and let go.

Beanie and I head for the horsey swings at the playground near the pool. I take the gray one with a purple saddle, and Beanie takes the next one, which is white with a red saddle.

"Hey, Beanie, bet I can go higher than you."

"We'll see about that."

We both pump as hard as we can. We're swinging perfectly in time with each other.

"Let's call it a tie. I'm getting hot," I say.

"Me too. Let's go get in the water."

We slow our swings to a stop and run through the sand and into the shallow end. I accidentally splash Beanie right in the face.

"Ouch," she says. "That was mean!" Beanie rubs her eyes, acting like a crybaby.

"That didn't hurt, did it? I did it by accident."

Beanie lets out a huge laugh as she swings her arm through the water and soaks me.

"Let's see if we can find Tree and Kai. Maybe we can play a game of Marco Polo or something," she says.

Beanie is a better swimmer than I am. She takes lessons at the YMCA and is thinking of joining the Tadpole swim team. You have to be able to tread water and do the crawl with alternate side breathing for the whole length of the pool. I only know how to dog-paddle.

"Well, only if we stay in the shallow," I say.

"Sure," says Beanie.

We look around and spot the boys sitting on the edge of the island.

"Kai! Tree!" Beanie yells, but they can't hear her. "Wait a second, I'll be right back." Beanie dives underwater, and I watch her wiggly body swim away toward the island. She pops up on the other side of the deep-end rope. Now she has their attention. Looks like they're not interested in playing with us. Beanie dives underwater again, and I wait for her to pop up near me. I wait. It is taking way too long. I start getting scared.

"Mama! Barbara!" I scream. Barbara and Mama have their backs to the pool—Barbara is putting suntan lotion on Mama. "Lifeguard! Anybody! My friend is in trouble." I dog-paddle as fast as I can to the deep-end rope. My heart is pounding. I hold on to the rope, looking for signs of Beanie, but I can't see her anywhere. It's like she sunk to the bottom. "Kai! Help!" I scream. Kai looks up and jumps in. He's a good swimmer. Tree follows.

When Kai gets to me, he puts his arm around me. "You'll be okay, Margie," he says.

"No, it's Beanie! I think she might have drowned."

Kai and Tree look all around. The lifeguard blows her whistle. "Kids, get off the rope!"

Kai signals her for help. She climbs down from her chair and makes her way out to us.

"What's the problem?"

"My friend disappeared," I say. My voice is quivery from the cold water. "I think she's in trouble."

The lifeguard blows her whistle again. "Everybody out of the pool!" she yells. Kids are groaning. The lifeguard yells, "All hands on deck! Possible swimmer down."

There are at least eight lifeguards in the water and several others above, all looking for a submerged swimmer.

After a few minutes, the head lifeguard, using a horn, yells, "All clear. Swimmers may return to the water."

By now, Kai, Tree, and I are on the beach with Barbara and Mama, who didn't notice the commotion. "Beanie's missing!" I'm crying now.

"What are you talking about?" Barbara says. "She's right there." She points toward the snack bar. "She went to get a snow cone."

I spot Beanie walking toward us with a blue snow cone. My panic turns to anger. How could Beanie leave me like that? Why'd she do that?

Beanie looks oblivious to the stir her little disappearing trick caused.

"Beanie Jones," I say, "I hate you. You're the meanest girl I ever met."

Where is Stella when I need her? Come to think of it, I haven't seen her for a long time, since before my birthday. She's vanished—maybe I hurt her feelings or something. I didn't mean to. I got busy with Beanie and all my other friends. Stella would not have disappeared on me the way I did on her, or the way Beanie did on me. Hope she isn't lost forever.

MARGAUX

1985

KEEPING SECRETS
TUESDAY CONTINUED

"Can I get you anything else?" the waiter asks. I look up from my reading.

"Yes, I'll have another cappuccino, please." They hate when people linger for too long without ordering anything. I don't blame them.

Mrs. Harris and the *wrong* Mr. Harris, her brother-in-law, have left. Did they notice me sitting here? If they did, would they care? As far as Mrs. Harris is concerned, I don't know anything. And after all, she and her brother-in-law *could* have legitimate business with each other. And I have every right to sit and have coffee. Mrs. Harris knows I am a writer now, a serious writer, and one that the renowned M. Des Jardins agency is going to represent.

I've only read two chapters so far. I need to read a few more. It occurred to me while I was reading chapter twelve, Heat of Summer, that Paloma's problem has nothing to do with my portrayal of Theo in the character of Tree and everything to do with how I've drawn Birdie and Marta. As she often does, she projects. Paloma must think that I'm revealing too much about her true feelings and motivations. On my part, it's all conjecture, fiction, and I can't see why she would take it so seriously. Paloma has always been extremely conflicted about our mother's sexuality. She convinced herself that Roz, the neighbor that our mother fell in love with on President Street—and my best friend Jenny's mother—was simply a *very good friend*. If that were the case, then our mother had a revolving door of "good friends" after Roz died, friends who spent a lot of time in our various houses for periods of time and then vanished out of our lives for no apparent reason. I saw things that Paloma didn't see. Things I knew I wasn't supposed to see. I can keep a secret or two. I'm expert at it.

ONE ELYSIUM STREET

CHAPTERS 13 TO 15

13

GETTING SAVED

JULY TO AUGUST 1966

It's Sunday at the end of July, and I'm the first one out to the kitchen nook for breakfast. Mama has made her coffee and is mixing up pancake batter. The griddle is warming up in the middle of the table. Mama taught me that the secret to cooking pancakes is to get the griddle hot. She showed me how to test it with a drop of water from my finger. If the water hops and disappears, the griddle is ready for pancakes. I learned the hard way that if you're not patient and try to cook a pancake before the griddle is hot, the pancake is not going to turn out at all; it will turn out white, wrinkled, and raw, or worse, a big mess. If it is too hot, the outside will be burned and the inside raw. Pancakes are tricky business.

I hate Sundays because Beanie goes to church, and it feels like she's there all day. After church her family goes out for brunch at the Pancake House. One time we were driving by the Pancake House and I asked Mama why we never go there, and she said, *The lions were too big.* I said, *I didn't know lions liked pancakes. Lines,* she said, *as in too many people.* Everybody still teases me about that.

"Mama," I say, "Barbara asked me if I want to go to vacation Bible school with Beanie this week. She told me to ask you."

"Yeah, she told me she was going to invite you guys. It's okay with me," she says. "I always liked going to Sunday school and vacation Bible school when I was growing up. I had perfect attendance, and they gave me a pin shaped like a cross! Maybe you'll get one of those."

"How come we don't go to church like the Joneses?"

"Well, honey, that's a good question with a complicated answer. The short answer is that I don't believe in God and Jesus in the same way most churchgoers do, but I'm not you. Barbara convinced me that you kids should have a choice in the matter, which is why I told her to ask you guys directly."

"What do people do at church?"

"They sing songs, say prayers, and in Sunday school, people learn about the Bible."

"What's the Bible?"

"It's a big book full of stories from the olden times that teach people things about how God supposedly wants us to live our lives."

"What is God?"

"God is the biggest question of all. How did we get here? Why are we here? What started it all?"

"So God is science?"

Mama told me that her science work is about answering those kinds of questions.

She laughs. "Well, maybe."

"Is there only one God? Mr. Obata says there are many different gods. Some are nice and some are not."

Mama says, "That depends on what you believe."

"And who is Jesus?"

"Possibly the son of God, depending on what you

believe. Some people believe that we are all the sons and daughters of God. Some people believe that we are *all* God."

"I'm confused," I say. "But *what* is God?"

"Well, all I can tell you is that God isn't an old man with a beard that you can talk to like you can talk to your granddad."

"That's good, since I don't have a granddad," I say. "And what about the Lord? Is the Lord the same as God? Beanie told me she prays to the Lord every night when she goes to bed, like this." I get off the bench and down on my knees with my hands pressed together in front of my lips and recite the prayer Beanie taught me.

Now I lay me down to sleep,
I pray the Lord my soul to keep;
If I should die before I wake,
I pray the Lord my soul to take.

Tree drags in from the basement stairs wearing his pajamas. I'm still down on my knees. He says, "What're you prayin' about?"

I jump up. "I was showing Mama how Beanie prays every night."

"That's stupid," he says. "I never get down on my knees when I pray."

"You pray? What prayer do you say?"

"I say different things. I don't think of it as praying. It's more thinking and hoping. Believe it or not, I pray for you— also Mom, Birdie, Willie, and Kit. I pray that God will keep us all safe. That none of us is going to go missing like Maddie did."

* * *

UNLIKE CHURCH, which is on Sundays and Wednesday nights, vacation Bible school is all week, and weirdly, it takes place in a church that looks like a big old haunted house. The house is creepy, built of dark stones. Beanie calls their church the House of Miracles.

Barbara parks the car, and the three of us pile out. Birdie and Willie were not the *least bit* interested in attending vacation Bible school or church, and Kai was not invited for some reason. I asked Mr. Jones why not, and he said, *Those people have their own religion.* I asked, *Which people?* He said *Orientals*, whatever that is. I stopped asking. He sounded grumpy.

A big cloth sign hangs across the front porch of the House of Miracles, "VACATION BIBLE SCHOOL August 1 thru August 12"—two whole weeks.

Bible school is like real school, but at real school we start every day with the Pledge, and at vacation Bible school we say the Pledge and then we say the Lord's Prayer. Beanie helped me memorize it after our first day. I was real embarrassed that I was the *only* one other than Tree who didn't know it. But I like the part about *Howard be thy name* and the part at the end where we say *forever and ever, amen,* because then we get to do the fun stuff—like singing and crafts. We made some cool things like a cross made of burnt matchsticks and the city of Bethlehem from carved Ivory soap bars. That's where Baby Jesus was born. My favorite song is a song called "Into My Heart." We sing that song during the daily "alter call." That's when you can go up and get saved by Jesus. I go up to get saved every day. I keep waiting to be saved. I say the words, but nothing changes. Maybe it takes time.

* * *

210

TODAY IS OUR LAST DAY. Maybe next year I can try to get saved again. I want to be saved. Our prize for perfect attendance is a tiny Bible, like something made for a doll, not a person. The words are so small I can't read them, and if I could, I don't think I would.

MARTA SHOULD HAVE THOUGHT of sending the kids to vacation Bible school on her own—free childcare, and you *know* your kids are safe because they're in a church, or that is how it is supposed to be. Last year, her mother told her about a married couple down in Mobile, Sister Joy and Brother Dobbs, leaders in a charismatic branch of the Pentecostal Church who were convicted of the rapes and murders of several young children. *Could anything like that ever happen here? Maybe. We are never completely safe.*

One day when the kids are at vacation Bible school, Barbara comes over for coffee after dropping them off, and before Marta has to be at the lab.

Marta says, "Thanks for suggesting vacation Bible school for the kids. You know, I had a pretty negative experience with religion in my own upbringing, and well, Doug wasn't religious."

"Yeah, funny how it all works out. Neil is the religious one in our family. As you know, I was raised Episcopalian— we're more about ritual than Jesus. His people are Holy Roller types—speaking in tongues, the whole business. I never imagined I would go to a church like the House of Miracles. My mother would be turning over in her grave right now if she knew."

Marta laughs. "Well, it worked out great for me with my job this summer, and Tree and Piglet are having fun."

"Yes, I've noticed that! For Beanie, it's a blast to have her best friend in the whole wide world there with her." Barbara's eyes meet Marta's briefly. "They are pretty cute together, aren't they?" She reaches across the table and puts her hand on top of Marta's. Marta pulls away.

"Yes, they're cute," Marta says.

"Did I do something wrong?"

"Barbara, I care about you deeply, I do, but we can't go on pretending like nothing is going on between us."

"Well, what is going on?"

Her tone irritates Marta. "You tell me . . . You're quite affectionate—looking for opportunities when we're alone to hold hands, to give me foot massages, to kiss my lips good-bye. I don't know what to think. How far are you willing to take it? I don't know what it means."

"You know how things are with Neil. I don't have the same freedom as you," she says. "Why can't we let things be what they are without calling *it* anything? I love the time we spend together. I love you, our friendship."

"I understand how scary this is. I'm afraid too, but I need to know if it's going anywhere. This eternal flirtation between us is torturous."

Barbara says, "For me too, and if I could change things, I would. It isn't the time."

"You must see how I might feel that you're stringing me along."

"That is not what's going on, and you know it," Barbara says. "I love you. I can't imagine my life without you in it."

"After every time we are together, when you go home, I imagine you having sex with your husband. I wonder what you think about when you're doing that?"

Barbara sits in silence. She wraps both hands around her coffee mug. "I'm scared, that's what I'm thinking. Do you think I want to fuck him? If Neil begins to suspect what's going on, he's liable to kill one or both of us. We need to keep our children safe. Every bone in my body knows that my feelings for you are *wrong*. They're wrong in the eyes of society, and they are wrong in the eyes of *God*."

"Oh, so you think God thinks screwing your racist, cop-with-guns, wife-beating husband is right? That is a god I don't ever want to meet."

"Well, I thought you of all people would have a greater appreciation for what's at stake for me and Beanie—what's at stake for you."

Barbara and Marta have shared their histories. This is one of the things they have in common. The difference is Marta had the strength to leave. She knows that Neil has beaten Barbara many times; he once hit her in the face so hard she thought she might lose an eye. That was before Beanie came along. Since then, he's been less violent, but he's shoved her to the ground a couple of times, physically and emotionally tortured her, held her in a choke hold, all the while saying how much he adores her. He told her if she *ever* had an affair, he would kill her and her lover. To be cuckolded for a woman might send him right over the edge.

"I see your point," Marta concedes. Being openly in a same-sex relationship is an impossibility, even in these modern times. Maybe someday that will change.

They sit quietly for a few moments, both looking down at their cups of coffee as if they were the most engaging objects in the world.

"Did I tell you that Neil is getting a promotion of sorts? He's been made a detective, homicide division. They're putting him on the Smith case, of all things."

14

DANGEROUS WORLD

FALL 1966

THE PHONE RINGS. Marta hears Piglet answer, "Anderson residence, Margaret speaking. May I ask who's calling?" Piglet learned to answer the phone like that from Beanie, who learned it from her mother. For Marta, a simple hello suffices.

Piglet comes running. "Mama! Mama! Kit is on the phone."

Marta hurries into the kitchen and picks up the handset. "Kit?"

"Yeah, Mother, it's me." His voice is deep, dark, and distant. "I'm ready to come home. Would that be okay?"

Marta chokes up. "Yes, it is more than okay! We have an apartment upstairs for you where you will have some privacy." She hoped he might want to come home, maybe for college—maybe he'll change his mind about not going, especially with the draft and all.

"Well, that's good cuz Dad handed me a ticket to Denver yesterday. He doesn't want me here anymore. I'll be home tomorrow night." The hurt in Kit's voice is painful to hear.

"What time does your plane come in?"

"Around nine thirty."

"I'll be there to pick you up."

"Okay," he says.

"I love you, Kit-Kat."

"Okay," he says. Marta hears his reticence about coming home loud and clear.

"See you tomorrow!"

"Okay, bye," he says.

The line goes silent, but Marta holds the receiver in disbelief. She finally puts the handset in its cradle, and then she cries.

Marta's capacity to deal with Kit's anger after the divorce came to a head when he took her car out and crashed it before he had a driver's license and then got busted for stealing someone else's car for a joyride. She could hardly blame him after what he had seen at home and felt he had to do. But it was either send him to live with Doug and his new wife or allow him to go to juvenile hall.

How long had he been with his father? She sent him after their divorce had been finalized, which was about two years after she left Doug, and he had already remarried. Kit was barely sixteen. It must have been early sixty-three, so before Doug's mother died. Hard to believe that more than three years had passed. Sending him to live with her abuser was the only option, but possibly the worst choice she ever made in her life.

Marta spends most of the next day getting Kit's apartment cleaned and organized. Professor Ito designed the quarters for his mother-in-law, who lived with them for a time when their children were young. It has served as a guest room since then. In addition to its own bathroom, it has an efficiency kitchen with a small sink, a two-burner stove, and a compact refrigerator. That'll do for Kit since he'll probably eat with the family, or who knows? Maybe he has other plans.

Marta doesn't have any expectations. In the eyes of the world, a nineteen-year-old is an adult. They can vote and serve as fodder in senseless wars, like the war that turned Doug into the violent-minded mess he became. Turns out killing people, even when you are doing it from an airplane, like Doug did as a strafing pilot, messes people up. Marta is terrified that Kit will be drafted and sent to Vietnam.

* * *

AT STAPLETON, Marta waits anxiously for the flight arriving from Spain via Dulles at gate four. She feels unsure of herself. Passengers begin streaming into the waiting area. Every young man she sees she thinks might be him. Will she recognize him? Of course, that's ridiculous. She's seen photos of him that Doug's wife thoughtfully sent in the Christmas cards. Doug's wife is a decent person, at least, always sends gifts to the children for their birthdays and Christmas. Doug, left to his own devices, would never have done that. Marta hopes she has treated Kit well. Being a stepparent is not easy under the best of circumstances, but the kid she sent to them was a sullen, know-it-all, teenage mess.

And then Kit appears—much taller than she expected; he had always been quite small for his age and was about her height when she last saw him. He's more gangly too, but she recognizes the way he walks, his James Dean affectation. As a small boy, he always had to copy some cool guy. He's wearing aviator sunglasses and a black leather jacket. His hair is long—he looks like Paul in the Beatles. No wonder Doug wanted him to leave. He must have been an embarrassment on the base. Doug likes life in the military because it dictates all the rules—how to wear one's hair being one.

When Kit sees Marta, he breaks into a smile and hurries a bit more quickly toward her. She awkwardly reaches out, not knowing whether to shake his hand or hug him. She has to look up into his face; he's at least six inches taller than she is.

He makes the move and hugs her so hard he picks her up off the ground. He smells of leather and cigarettes. Does he smoke? She quit her three-pack-a-day habit around the time he left.

"Oh, Mother," he says. "You have no idea how happy I am to see you."

They are still hugging each other. Marta is afraid to let go. "Me too. I didn't know if I ever would." She starts crying.

"Aw, come on, don't do that."

"I'm so sorry I sent you away."

"Don't be. It's okay. I needed a kick in the butt. You didn't deserve all that stuff I was doing."

* * *

THE DAY after Kit gets home, Marta decides to have a party in his honor. She invites Vivi, her mother, Mr. Obata, and the Joneses—even Neil, for appearances. She hopes he doesn't come. She plans to grill steak, a real luxury. Before the guests arrive, she sets the steaks to marinate up where there is no chance of Leadbelly getting them, as he did the last time she had a dinner party.

Everybody congregates in the kitchen while she cooks. The adults enjoy various alcoholic beverages, and as a special treat the children get to have Coca-Cola. Kit steps out on the back patio to smoke a *fag*, as he calls them.

Within thirty seconds he comes back into the house. Marta can see by his expression that something is wrong.

"Why, that was a quick smoke."

"Uh, yeah, Mother, you need to come out and see something," he says quietly. "Maybe bring Mr. Obata too."

Marta goes over to Mr. Obata, who is giving Barbara gardening tips.

"Barbara, do you mind if I borrow Hiro for a second?"

"Not at all," she says.

The three of them step out onto the back patio. Kit points to a dark figure on the opposite side of the patio, a rather large woman with long disheveled hair. She wears some sort of smock or apron and holds a large carving knife. Oblivious to their presence, the woman scrapes at the grill with the knife for bits of burnt-on skin and fat and then licks it off. But for her heavy stature, one might think she were starving.

Mr. Obata signals that they should all go back inside.

Once inside, he locks the door and says, "That could put a crimp on your grilling plans!"

"Do you *really* think we're in danger?" Marta says.

"Did you see that knife?" Kit says. "That's enough to scare me."

"Maybe we should call the police," Marta says.

Mr. Obata shifts his eyes toward Neil, who is having some sort of contentious conversation with Vivi and Mimi in the dining room. Knowing her mother, Marta suspects they are talking politics.

"Aren't we in the presence of *one of Peakview's finest?*" Mr. Obata says.

"Right." Marta hates the idea of giving Neil a moment of attention, but under the circumstances . . .

She approaches the group. Politics it is.

Marta's mother and sister are both Democrats from the South, and clearly Neil assumed they would be on *his* side of civil rights issues. The country has become a divided mess with desegregation. Marta is thrilled to break up the miniature civil war taking place in her own home. "Excuse me, Neil, I hate to break up this lovefest, and I know you are off duty, but we have an armed trespasser in our yard and are wondering what we should do?"

"Oh my," says Mimi, "are the kids all accounted for?"

"Good question," Marta says. "Why don't you and Vivi go find out where they all are and tell them to stay put until we get things settled."

Marta goes back to the kitchen with Neil and sees that Kit has the window over the sink open.

"What are you doing?" she asks.

"Oh, I gave her a cigarette and a slice of bread."

"What are you thinking? She might be a murderer! Close that window now."

Kit closes the window and locks it. "I don't think so. I was watching her. She was talking to herself or to some invisible person out there. I think she might be a crazy person."

Marta had forgotten what a big heart Kit has. When he was little, before the other kids came along, they took him to New York City. He wanted to give every beggar a penny, and he had a pocket full of them.

Neil peers out the window. "May I use your phone?" he says. "I need to call this in, I'm afraid, given the proximity of this event with the Smith case and the fact that I'm off-duty."

Marta hadn't considered a connection to the Smith case, but it makes sense, and Neil would know as a newly minted detective working on it.

"Of course. Thank you, Neil." She points out the phone on the wall. Reprehensible as she finds him, she's glad he showed up.

Vivi and Mimi come back with news that all kids are safe and accounted for.

When Neil hangs up, he says, "Well, they're sending a squad car over."

"That's a relief!" Marta says.

Five minutes later, five squad cars show up. Marta stands in the dining room with the window cracked to hear what the group of officers are saying. Mr. Obata goes out to tell them about the areas of the yard. Marta hears him say, "Be mindful of the gardens, please." Such a sweet man.

"A lot of hiding places here," one cop comments.

Another jokes, "And good places to bury a body."

Marta doesn't like the implication.

"Yes, indeed," says Mr. Obata. "Be careful in the woods. It is easy to lose one's way."

The officers laugh. Marta knows that Hiro Obata is serious. She, herself, has been lost a time or two in the Dark Forest before finding her way back to the Righteous Path. Officers fan out in the yard.

A short while later, the doorbell rings. It's Neil; he's been out with the other officers. "We found her. She was asleep in the little mushroom playhouse. In the meantime, I also found out that she is a patient over at the Dutch Reform Psychiatric Hospital, which, if you didn't know already, is a stone's throw from here."

Marta didn't know that. Perhaps they should have moved a bit farther away. Danger lurks in every corner of this neighborhood.

15

SCARED STIFF

SEPTEMBER 1966 TO AUGUST 1967

FIRST GRADE IS BETTER than kindergarten was. Beanie and I are in the same class—with the same teacher Tree had, Miss Pancake. Everybody loves her the most, and not because her name is our favorite food. Miss Pancake is the nicest and prettiest teacher at Peakview Elementary.

We all settle into our circle of little desk chairs around Miss Pancake, who is seated in her larger chair front and center. She wears a knee-length red-and-black wool skirt, a sweater vest, and a white blouse. Her knees tilt to the side with ankles crossed. Her hair is perfectly combed. I love the way it sweeps across her forehead and curls around her face. Not a hair out of place, and she wears pretty red lipstick. I'm in love with her, as much as a girl can be in love with a girl.

I'm fidgeting. "Miss Pancake, Miss Pancake! What's your first name?" I ask. Somebody asks her this every day—it's an unwritten rule. We keep track from one day to the next who gets to ask the question, and today it's my turn.

"Blueberry," she says—she sounds a little like my grandma Mimi, only she's from Texas, not Alabama. We all laugh—it's the *best* joke. We know her real name is Virginia. The grown-ups call her Ginger—we think that's funny too.

"Okay, settle down, children. I *do* have something important to tell you about my name today," Miss Pancake says with her most serious voice.

We're all ears—and eyes. "I'm getting married over the Christmas holiday, and when I come back, I will no longer be Miss Pancake. My new name will be Mrs. Jacob Armstrong." She stands up and writes it in her perfect penmanship on the blackboard. "It's okay if you forget between now and when school starts again, but I want you to know that when I am called Mrs. Armstrong, I will be the same person as Miss Pancake."

My heart sinks. I'm the only one to raise my hand. I wave it wildly in the air.

"Margaret?"

"Why can't you keep your last name? It's such a good name."

"Well, that's an excellent question, hug-bug." She calls me that owing to the fact that I always give her big hugs. I'm her pet. "It's *tradition*. It's the way things have always been done. When my mother married my father, she took my father's name. One day when you get married, you'll take your husband's name."

"I'm never taking any old husband's name," I say.

Miss Pancake laughs. "Someday you might feel differently about that."

I doubt it. I'm *never* going to get married. I'm going to be Margaret Anderson *forever and ever, amen.* When Miss Pancake becomes Mrs. Armstrong she is *not* going to be the same person, I know it.

* * *

COME SPRING, with the warmer weather, Kai, Tree, Beanie, and I play outside a lot more. Mr. Jones told us once that if we waved and yelled hello to the train engineers when they were coming through, they might throw us candy. *They did that when I was a boy,* he said.

"Hey, guys," Tree says. "I think the train is coming." We all hold still to listen. The whistle blows at the crossing down by The Apartments. "Let's see if they'll throw us candy like Beanie's dad said."

We run into the field between the dead-end marker for Elysium Street and the tracks. All four of us jump up and down like Mexican jumping beans, waving our hands above our heads. We scream "Hello! Hello! Candy! Candy!" as loud as we can.

Sure enough, a head pops out the window of the engine car. The man throws a bunch of things toward us. We scramble for the candy like it's fallen from a birthday piñata, but we have to look hard for it with all the weeds in the field.

"Got one," Kai says. "Only thing is I don't think it's candy."

The rumbling train drowns out Kai's voice, so I run over to him. He's holding something white.

"It looks like chalk," he says.

"Weird," I say. Tree and Beanie also find some white things. "Wonder what we're supposed to do with that?"

"Dunno," says Tree. "Wish it were candy. Guess they don't give that away like in the olden times."

"I got an idea," I say. "Maybe we could use it to draw a hopscotch on the sidewalk."

"That's dumb," Tree says.

Kai says, "I have another idea. We could make our own four-square game at the end of the street, like the ones we have at school, then all four of us can play—boys against girls."

"No way," Beanie says. "You guys'll clobber us. How about Tree and I make a team, and Kai and Piglet make a team?"

* * *

ONE DAY, closer to summer, when Birdie's and Willie's friends are over, the familiar rumble and sound of the whistle in the distance alert us that the train will soon pass by.

Rob says, "Penny squashing time!"

We all follow the big kids out of the yard and over to the tracks. Willie and Rob put a penny on the track for each of us. My heart is beating hard because I'm afraid they aren't going to move out of the way fast enough. The train is blowing its whistle like crazy. "*Hurry*, you guys!" I scream.

Kai comes over and takes my hand. "Everything is going to be okay, Margie. Those guys have done this before." He's right, of course. The boys get away from the tracks with plenty of time to spare. After the train passes, we all run over to collect our smooth, flat pennies. I pull my hand away quickly when I get burned.

"Pig, wait a sec," Willie says. "They're hot because there is a lot of friction between the wheel and the track." As if that means anything to me. It's magic.

"BIRDIE, you mind babysitting Tree and Piglet tonight?" her mother asks.

"Moooom!" Birdie says. "I told Catrina I was gonna spend the night with her."

Her mother assumes she's always available. She's officially a teenager now. She has a life. Rob asked her to go steady. He gave her a ring, a gumball machine prize, but she only wears it around him. It's embarrassing, and she hasn't told anyone. Willie knows, but he's not one to blab.

"I'm sorry. You never mentioned you were going to Catrina's tonight, and I have an important function I need to go to over at the university. It can't be helped."

"Maybe Mr. Obata, or the Joneses?" Birdie says.

"Sorry. Hiro is going out with Aunt Vivi tonight, and Barbara and Neil are leaving for Disneyland tomorrow and are busy packing. Don't ask about Kit. He's not home."

"Why can't Willie do it?"

"He's spending the night at Rob's. Difference is, he asked for permission days ago."

"That is no fair," Birdie says. "You like the boys more than you like me. You treat me like your personal slave!" She storms off to her room and slams the door. She wants to see Rob tonight. Catrina too, but mostly Rob.

An hour later, she's still sulking in her room when she hears her mother calling down the hall, "Birdie, I'm heading out. I turned on the oven, and as a special treat I bought you guys chicken potpies."

"Okaaay, Mother," Birdie says.

"Be good!" her mother calls.

As soon as Birdie hears the door close, she sprints to the phone in the kitchen to call Catrina.

"Hey, Catrina, I can't spend the night tonight, but I was thinking I might come over to The Apartments to hang out with you and the guys. What do you think?" She figures she'll be gone for an hour and back before her mom gets home. She'll threaten Piglet and Tree with something to make them keep her secret.

Catrina tells her to meet them at the playground after dinner. She and the guys will be there.

Birdie places the potpies in the oven and sets the timer.

Tree is in the basement playing the guitar he got last Christmas, and Piglet is in her room talking to herself or Stella, not that it's a meaningful distinction.

When the timer goes off, she calls, "Hey, Tree and Piglet, time for dinner!"

Piglet bursts into the kitchen. "Yay! Chicken potpie!"

Birdie covers her ears at the shrillness of Piglet's squeal. Lately, Piglet and Tree have been getting on her nerves.

Chicken potpies are the closest thing they ever have to TV dinners. Their mother is against frozen foods, except for a few frozen vegetables like Green Giant baby peas and Birds Eye chopped spinach. TV dinners are absolutely out of the question. Birdie has tried hard to convince her to buy TV dinners for babysitting nights, but her mother always says no.

Birdie has to call for Tree a second time. He's been focused on learning to play a song. He and Kai started a band called the Unicorns, and they're going to perform at a talent show over at the Y.

As soon as they finish eating, Birdie says, "Hey, guys, I have to run over to Catrina's to return a shirt I borrowed from her and wondered if you would be okay staying here by yourselves for about fifteen minutes or so?"

Tree says, "Sure, we're not babies, you know."

"Maybe you could play a game of checkers with me?" Piglet says to Tree. Birdie can see that Tree isn't all that keen on the idea of playing checkers with Piglet. Who could blame him?

"That's a great idea," says Birdie. "Maybe you guys could hang out down in the game room while I'm gone. It'll probably be the safest place given what was in the paper this morning."

"What was in the paper?" Tree asks.

"Apparently, the Hatchet Lady is on the loose, the

Butcher Lady's sister. She lives up at Red Rocks but has been coming into Peakview to snatch kids. She's already chopped up a couple of kids and fed them to her dogs." Birdie and Willie named the crazy woman in their yard last summer "the Butcher Lady" and made up a series of scary stories about her to tell Tree and Piglet. "If you stay downstairs while I'm gone, I'm sure everything'll be fine, and I'll lock all the doors." Her attempt at scaring them is working.

"Okay," Tree says. "But you better hurry back."

"I will," she says. "Besides, Leadbelly will protect you guys. Take him downstairs with you."

TREE and I go downstairs to the game room with Leadbelly following right behind. It's a big open room that sits between the boys' bedrooms. There's a ping-pong table, a card table, and shelves full of books and games to play. I like the games of Life, Parcheesi, Chinese checkers, and checkers. Tree likes Go, Stratego, and chess, but I don't know how to play those, so we usually play checkers. Mama says this room is for the whole family, but it isn't *really*. It belongs to the boys.

Kai and Tree built a cool blanket fort under the ping-pong table, with big pillows to sit on and white sparkly Christmas lights strung underneath. On really cold and hot days, he and Kai hang out playing Go all day, and sometimes all night. They call it their "bat cave." Tree doesn't usually let me in, so today is special.

He gets the checkers set off the shelf, and we crawl under the table. Magical. We are encapsulated in our own little world—a fairy-tale cocoon.

Tree says, "You can go first since you're the youngest."

"That's okay, you can go first since you're the dumbest."

"Very funny," he says, and he picks up two checkers. "How about this: in one hand I have a black checker, and the other hand a red. Pick a hand, and if you get the black one you go first." He's holding his fists out in front, waiting for me to pick.

I point to each hand alternately and recite:

> *Eeny, meeny, miny, moe*
> *Catch a piggy by the toe*
> *If she hollers let her go!*
> *Eeny, meeny, miny, moe*
> *My mother told me to pick the very best one, and*
> *You are not it.*

Tree opens his hand to reveal a black checker. "You go first."

"Wait, I want to see the checker in your other hand."

"I already put it back," he says. "Besides, why wouldn't you want to go first?"

"I don't know," I say. "I figure if you want me to, it must not be the best thing for me."

"Let's play, Pig!"

I put the black pieces on the black squares like Willie taught me.

"What're you waiting for? It's your turn," Tree says.

I can tell he's losing patience. I move my first piece.

Before long, he has beaten me five times in a row.

"I hate this game!" I say.

"It was your idea," says Tree. He looks at his Timex. "Huh, wonder why Birdie isn't back yet? She said she'd be back in fifteen minutes. It's already been an hour."

"I hope the Hatchet Lady didn't get her," I say.

"Yeah, or somebody worse," Tree says.

"What could be worse? She sounds bad."

A loud bang comes from upstairs. Leadbelly lets out a single echoing bark and wags his tail.

"Shhhh . . . you dumb dog," Tree says. "Some guard dog you are."

My heart pounds loud in my ears. I'm shaking.

Tree turns off the lights under the table. Now it's pitch-black. Heavy footsteps land on the wood floor above. Clomp, clomp, clomp—they are headed our way.

"Who is it?" I whisper.

"I don't know, but I don't like it."

Whoever it is has now opened the door at the top of the basement stairs. The light flashes on and off. Slow, lumbering steps boom as they descend into the game room. We are too afraid to lift the blanket to peek. Leadbelly is useless!

Suddenly, a face appears lit up by a flashlight from underneath. I pee my pants a little.

"Suckers!" Birdie's voice rings out.

I start crying. "I'm gonna tell Mama on you, Birdie. That is the meanest thing you ever did."

* * *

THAT SUMMER IS full of fun and pranks. We play out in the field by the train tracks almost every day. We collect a whole bucket of chalk and smash every coin we have.

One day Beanie and I see Kai and Tree digging a hole with Mr. Obata's shovels.

"What are you guys doing?" Beanie asks.

"Building an underground fort—a bomb shelter," Kai says.

"What gave you an idea like that?" I say.

"I was telling Kai how I built one up the track by The Apartments with some other kids when I was in first grade.

We didn't do a good job, cuz a few days after we built it, it caved in. Lucky we weren't in it."

Kai says, "So we came up with a plan to reinforce the walls and roof with plywood so that wouldn't happen again."

"Sounds cool. Can we help?" Beanie asks.

"Yeah, you want to take turns digging?"

* * *

WE SPEND the next several days working on the fort. It's hard work. Mr. Jones comes over to check our work and make sure it's safe, and he cuts some two-by-fours to add bracing in the corners and the middle. He suggests we add a skylight, and he has the perfect piece of clear plastic in his workshop. When it's done, we have a pretty cool underground fort that all four of us can sit in with room to spare.

One day we are all playing cards, and this teenager we call Bully-Boy, who Tree and I know from The Apartments, pops his head in the entrance.

"Okay if I join you?" he says.

"Sure," Tree says.

It's not okay with me, but I don't say so. At The Apartments he is always mean to kids at the playground, which is why we gave him that silly nickname. He scares me.

Bully-Boy joins our circle, sits next to me in front of the opening. We play a couple of rounds of gin rummy. He's being nice. He reaches over and strokes my hair. "You sure are a pretty little thing."

I'm not sure what to say, so I say, "Thanks."

After another hand of gin rummy, he says, "You wanna see something cool?"

"Sure, why not?" Kai says.

He pulls something out of his pocket. He holds it up,

pushes a button, and a silver blade pops up. The knife flashes in the sunlight streaming through the skylight.

Bully-Boy's face changes from nice to mean. "You don't think I'm interested in playing cards, do you?"

Tree says, "You're trying to scare us, right?"

"No, I'm serious. You better do exactly what I say, or I'm gonna cut you into ribbons."

"We don't have any money," I say.

"Yeah, we smashed all our coins already," Beanie says.

I want to scream, but I don't. "You seem like a good guy—"

"I don't want your fucking money. I want to watch you guys *do it.*"

"Do what?" I say.

"You know, sexy stuff." Bully-Boy is rubbing his crotch now. Maybe he needs to pee.

We can't get out of the fort, because he's blocking the way. Beanie is whimpering, and Kai and Tree look terrified.

He unzips his pants and sticks his penis out. It doesn't look like any penis I've ever seen. Kai's and Tree's look like small droopy fingers compared to this one, which is big and sticking straight out.

He points his knife at me. "You—I want you to suck my dick—give me a blow job, rug rat. Do as I say, or I'll cut you."

I'm crying, but I move to do what he says. He smells sweaty and sour, and when I move toward him, I gag from his odor. He pushes me away.

"Stupid girl," he says. "I have a better idea. All of you, take off your clothes."

"Why are you doing this?" Kai asks.

"Because why not? It's fun watching you little worms squirm," he says.

Bully-Boy is meaner than he used to be on the playground.

We all take off our clothes. We've seen each other naked before, so it's no big deal.

The bully sits glaring at us. He's licking his chapped lips. "Okay, you two"—he points at me and Kai—"I want to see you fuck. And you two also." He points at Beanie and Tree.

I don't know what *fuck* is, but apparently Kai does. "Go ahead and lie down," he whispers to me. "Trust me." I lie down flat. He gets on top of me, his bare body warm against mine. I'm safe.

"Okay, *fuck!*" Bully-Boy yells. "What's wrong with you morons? You gotta stick it into her slit and pull it out and put it in."

I can't see what Beanie and Tree are doing, but Kai is bouncing his hips up and down. I don't get why someone would want us to do this.

Bully-Boy backs out of the fort. "Stay there doing that for ten more minutes. If you breathe a word of this to anyone, I am gonna come back and kill you and your whole family—you'll end up like Maddie Smith."

As he walks away, he's laughing. We don't wait for ten minutes, only long enough that we can't see him anymore. We hurry up and get our clothes on.

"Okay, that was the weirdest thing ever," Tree says. "You guys all okay?"

"Yeah," I say. "I'm scared."

Beanie says, "I want to get out of here and never come back."

"Me too, Beanie," Kai says.

"How about we tear the fort down?" Tree says.

We all spring into action, ripping the roof off first.

"What should we do?" Kai asks. "I mean about that guy? Should we tell the police? Maybe he's the one who killed Maddie."

"Bully-Boy?" Tree says. "I doubt it. We should let it go.

After all, none of us got hurt. You heard what he said about killing us . . ."

"Yeah, and my dad, I'm not sure what he would do," says Beanie. "He might take it out on me and my mom. He says women ask for what they get."

"And Mama—she would be real upset and worry, and not let us do anything fun ever again," I say. "Let's pinky swear not to tell anybody about this day."

We interlock pinkies.

MARGAUX

1985

GRATEFUL

TUESDAY, MIDDAY

"Margaux!"

I look up and see Winnie standing there. "Hi! What are you doing here?"

"What else? Getting a cup of coffee. May I join you?"

"Of course, have a seat."

Winnie tosses her long blond hair to one side before sitting down—it's so long she would sit on it otherwise. Her eyes land on the manuscript. "Looks like you are working."

"Yeah, I'm trying to read through the story with an eye to preserving our family's privacy. My sister, Paloma, has expressed concerns about my portrayal of the Theo counterpart."

"Oh, I don't think you need to worry." Winnie speaks as if she knows Theo better than I do. Maybe she does since they have been writing to each other for the past five years. After he graduated from high school, instead of heading straight to college, Theo got a job working for an outdoor tour company that operated treks in Tibet. When he came back a year later, he had become Buddhist and a strict vegetarian. He finished his undergrad studies quickly. As soon as he could he enrolled at the Naropa Institute, an off-beat

Tibetan Buddhist school in Boulder where he got an MFA in poetry, of all things. After that, I felt like I didn't know him anymore. He definitely was not the boy who had taunted and tortured me as a child—an anti-Buddha.

"I've come to the same conclusion about Theo," I say. "And he told me as much. Do I *really* need to worry about Paloma, though, or my mother?"

"Has your mother read the manuscript?"

"Paloma said she sent it to her—without my permission, I might add—but my mother hasn't said anything to me about it yet."

"Why don't you ask her?" Winnie says.

"I will," I say. "Tomorrow night I'm hoping to get together with you and Theo to talk about the story in more detail. Would that work?"

Winnie blushes. "Yes, I think that would be fine. Meet at the Round About at six for a snack and a drink?" She winks.

"Perfect," I say. I stack the manuscript. "Three more chapters to read."

"And what do you think about it so far?" Winnie asks.

"Well, I finished reading the part where the younger kids get molested by the teenage boy. It dredges up a lot of emotions to read what I wrote. Makes me question if in real life we kids made the right decision in not telling the adults the whole story, once we finally told them."

"I understand why you would wonder about that, and also why you would not have told them."

"What happened to the kid—Bully-Boy, as we called him? Did he have something to do with Anna's disappearance? Did he go on to hurt other children because we didn't report him to the police?"

"Yeah, those questions crossed my mind as well."

"On the other hand, if we had told them the whole story, our mother and Kiyo's grandfather would probably have freaked out, and who knows what Jenny's dad would have done? The police and the press would have had a heyday with it. As it was, the four of us viewed the whole event as a weird thing that happened one day in the field. We knew the guy was mean, but because we weren't *really* injured . . ."

Winnie looks at me with soft eyes, like she understands. "Is it possible that you were more injured than you realized?"

"What do you mean?"

"Oh, you know, trust issues . . . things like that."

Of course she is right. Our parents would have been horrified, but they would have protected us.

"I guess we'll never know the what-if of that story."

"Probably not," Winnie says. She finishes her coffee. "On a different note, I'm starving. Wanna go get some lunch?"

* * *

WINNIE, like Theo, is a Buddhist and a vegetarian. She suggests a place called Quantum Leap.

As we wait for a table, I say, "Theo has never shared much about his spiritual life with me. I didn't know that Buddhists are vegetarians."

"Not all Buddhists are," Winnie says. "It isn't prescribed. There are many different Buddhist sects and lots of expressions of Buddhist philosophy within particular practices. In general, Buddhists abstain from taking life—I'm vegetarian because I want to achieve empathy and compassion for all living beings."

"That makes a lot of sense. How did you become a Buddhist?"

"I guess you could say I was born that way." Winnie laughs. "My parents were beatniks, then hippies—both writers—so you see, I've come by my profession the old-fashioned way, and my religion too, although I don't think of Buddhism as a religion."

"You write?"

"Of course," Winnie says. "And I read a lot, which is how I've come to be Rosie's assistant. Most writers need a job, and this is as good as it gets."

"No kidding. At least if your writing doesn't make money, you won't be stuck in a dead-end job like I am for the rest of your life."

The host comes to the podium. "Right this way." He smells of patchouli oil, a fragrance that throws me back to the days when my oldest brother, Keith, still lived at the house on President Street.

We settle into our seats.

"Theo told me the wild mixed-up story about how the two of you met."

Winnie laughs. "Wasn't that something?"

"How is it that neither of you figured it out over such a long time of corresponding?" I ask. "Why didn't you send each other photos or something?"

"It was against our pen-pal rules."

"Rules?"

"Yeah, when Theo—Ash—first wrote to me, she sent me this crazy long letter. It was all over the place, and she told me about many of the secrets that are in your book. Anyway, I wasn't entirely sure about the whole thing. I was afraid she might be a nut job, so I set a few rules."

"Like what?"

"For one, no photos, mainly because I want to judge the writer by their words not by their face, and I want equal treatment. Once people know you are a pretty blond woman, they treat you like you're an idiot; they expect you to be dumb."

"I see what you mean, but I always wanted to be a blond —Piglet is a blond, and she's smart."

"That is one of the reasons I like her so much."

"Well, I wanted her to be the opposite of me," I say, half fishing for a compliment.

Winnie laughs. "I like you too, and can see why Theo feels so close to you."

"Any other rules?"

"No phone calls, because long distance is too expensive. Had to be a strictly letter-based relationship. Letters also afford more thoughtful interactions, in my opinion."

"That must have been difficult to abide by after you two fell in love."

"Not really," Winnie says. "We both enjoyed the suspense. The slow unfolding of ourselves."

"Anything else?"

"We would never lie," Winnie says. "When Ash told me she was coming to New York last week, I was nervous. Of course, by then I knew *she* was *he*, after reading your manuscript and being assigned by Kiyo and Rosie to help make some magic. I knew he didn't know who I was, though. Mostly I felt bad, because I set up the rule about no lying. I *had* to lie about being me at the Round About. I didn't want to spoil Kiyo's reunion with Theo. It was unbelievably difficult. The whole time I wanted to drape myself all over him."

"Well, I'm sure Theo forgave you immediately when you met up later."

"Oh yes, and then some. We're overjoyed with who each other turned out to be. He said his attraction to me at the Round About was immediate. The mystery of how our mutual friend came to set us up remains. We'll have to talk to him about that someday. We have our suspicions."

"Yeah, me too. Like maybe a certain magic maker was involved!"

Before long, it's coming up on two in the afternoon. "Oh my," I say, "I need to get moving. I have a job nannying the children of no other than the Gossip Gal from the *Post*!"

"Oh, be careful," Winnie says. "That woman is dangerous, if you ask me."

"What do you mean?"

"She seeks out secrets and uses them to kill people— figuratively, of course. If I were you, I'd hold my cards close."

"I hope I haven't divulged too much already. I mentioned that M. Des Jardins is representing me, and suddenly I jumped a few leaps in her estimation."

"You would be of interest to her. She submitted a manuscript to us, and we turned her down. Once upon a time she was a promising journalist, but that was before she went to the *Post*."

"Hmm . . . maybe I need to start looking for a different job?" I say.

"Not a bad idea. She might try to dig up dirt about M. Des Jardins. We've heard through our grapevine that she has been poking around for information about Kiyo. If she discovers that you and he are childhood friends, there is no telling where her sensationalist mind will take her."

* * *

I GET over to Grace Church School with barely a minute to spare. The kids have piano lessons with Mrs. Tuzova today, and she doesn't tolerate tardiness. I wave at the twins as soon as they explode out the door.

"Hi, Margie!" Katie yells. John nods.

Katie is chatty, as usual. "You know what we did today?"

"No, what?"

"We went on a field trip to a fire station!"

"What was the coolest thing you saw there?"

John perks up. "The hook-and-ladder truck!"

Katie says, "I liked the pole. They let us slide down it."

"My brother Theo had a firehouse pole as a method for getting down from his tree house," I say. "I loved sliding down it too."

"Wow!" says John. "A tree house! That's cool."

"Yeah, we were lucky," I say. We *were* lucky. With all the sad events that took place while we lived on President Street, we were fortunate because we had Mr. Sakura's magical thinking on our side.

It's a ten-minute walk to Mrs. Tuzova's apartment on Saint Marks Place. The sun is out, but a bank of fog is rolling in. When we arrive at the building, John pushes the button under the name Tuzova, and she buzzes us in. We climb four flights and knock.

Multiple deadlocks click open, one after another. The first time I brought the kids here, Mrs. Tuzova joked, *I'm worried about thieves breaking in and stealing my Steinway.* No chance of that ever happening. How'd a grand piano get up to her apartment in the first place?

She opens the door with her characteristic greeting, cigarette in hand. "Come," she says, and quickly closes the door and locks it behind us.

She's lived in this place for fifty years. It reeks of stale tobacco. The walls, once white, are a brownish yellow and crowded with photos of her Russian relatives and of her as a child prodigy in Saint Petersburg. One time I asked her how she ended up in New York, and all she said was, *Escaped the Red Terror. They took everything we had, but they couldn't take this.* She placed both hands over her heart.

The piano fills most of what passes for a living room, and other than a couple of extra folding chairs, there's little furniture. I get the impression that Mrs. Tuzova doesn't see many people besides her students.

She's all business when it comes to the lesson. Cigarette hanging out of her mouth, she points at Katie. "Sit."

Katie obediently sits on the piano bench. John and I sit in the two folding chairs, out of the way against the wall of photos.

"Begin," Mrs. Tuzova says. As Katie plays her memorized warm-up scales, Mrs. Tuzova lights another cigarette. The first one still burns in an ashtray on a plant stand next to the piano.

When Mrs. Tuzova pokes her thumb in the center of Katie's back, an ash from her dangling cigarette drops to the floor. Katie straightens up without a break in her scales. Mrs. Tuzova taps the eraser of a pencil on the piano and says, "*One*-and-two-and-*three*-and-four-and! *One*-and-two-and-*three*-and-four-and!" She emphasizes the first and third beats.

Katie finishes her scales, and Mrs. Tuzova says, "Your piece."

Katie and John have been practicing and memorizing a simplified piece by Nikolai Rimsky-Korsakov called "The Young Prince and the Young Princess" from *Scheherazade* for their upcoming recital. I can't help but think that Mrs. Tuzova chose this for the twins with a sense of irony. Katie plods through the music mechanically.

"Feeling!" Mrs. Tuzova says.

Katie makes some adjustments. She closes her eyes. She sways, lifts her hands gently from the keys. She knows what it looks like, but she doesn't know how to feel music. She's trying. When she finishes, Mrs. Tuzova says, "Needs more work." She lights another cigarette and turns to John. "You."

Katie and John switch places, a familiar dance. John, perfect posture, begins running through his scales. They're flawless to my ear. His hands float effortlessly above the keys.

"Definition!" Mrs. Tuzova barks. He instantly plays each note more distinctly. Mrs. Tuzova scares me, but the kids love her, and I can tell she loves them. She knows they are smart; she wants them to be better, to work harder, to be more disciplined. Of the two, John is clearly superior, but she never draws any direct comparisons.

After John finishes playing through the recital piece, she says, "Could've been worse." John looks pleased with himself.

Mrs. Tuzova looks at her watch. "Time." She goes to the door, unlocks the series of dead bolts, and swings it open. "Young lady," she says to me, "keep the children safe. I have a bad feeling today."

She has a bad feeling every day.

Nonetheless, Mrs. Tuzova's warning takes root in my imagination. When we come out onto the street, I scan the area. Drizzle falls, and shapes of umbrella-covered people, clad in dark clothing, move along the sidewalk in both directions—another dreary day in Lower Manhattan.

On our walk home, Katie asks, "Did your mom make you take piano lessons?"

"Our mother could never afford things like piano lessons," I say. Now that we're adults, it is one of my mother's biggest regrets. She and Keith scraped together the money for a guitar for Theo, but she couldn't afford lessons to go with it. She once rented a spinet piano so that Paloma could learn to play, but that didn't last long. Maybe we had to move again. Maybe Paloma lost interest.

Katie falls silent for a moment. "I wish we didn't have money for piano lessons," she says.

"Be grateful for what you have, sweet girl. One day, I promise you that you'll be happy you learned to play the piano. It may end up being your greatest joy in life."

* * *

IT IS SCARCELY FOUR O'CLOCK, and the streetlamps have already turned on. My heart quickens as we approach The

Row. The man we saw when we left the house in the morning now leans on a lamppost on the corner.

"Hey, kids, last one home is a rotten egg!" I say.

We all race across the street, past the man, and up the row house stairs. Out of breath, we ring the buzzer, and Mariana opens the door. "There you are!" she says. She closes the door behind us and locks it, as usual. We're safe.

The kids strip off their damp duffle coats. Mariana takes them and hangs them on the coat rack to dry and places the umbrellas we were using in the stand. We all remove our shoes.

"Okay, you two, to the kitchen, and don't forget your homework."

A plate of molasses cookies, still warm, sits on the counter with two glasses of milk. Pedro is busy prepping ingredients for dinner.

"Margaux, Mrs. Harris is in the study. She'd like to have a word with you. I'll stay with the kids," Mariana says. "I hope things are okay."

"Thanks, Mariana." My heart thumps. This can't be good. In the year that I have been working here, never once has Mrs. Harris requested a conversation, let alone been home this early. Hard to know which unpalatable conversation she wants to have.

I make my way to Mrs. Harris's study. The French doors are splayed open; Mrs. Harris sits behind a heavy old desk, typing away on a home computer. The keys of the keyboard are noisy, but not in a pleasant way like my typewriter. She looks up. "Come in," she says. "And have a seat."

OLD FRIENDS

TUESDAY EVENING

"GIVE ME ONE MINUTE. I am finishing a thought," Mrs. Harris says.

"No problem." My eyes roam her spacious office, take in her packed bookshelves. She reads a lot, both fiction and nonfiction, but also poetry. I know she writes plenty. What sorts of things does she write when she isn't working on her column? Winnie said she made a submission to M. Des Jardins but didn't mention any details. I would think she'd be an incredible catch for any agency. Surely, she already has an agent. Why would they want me and not her?

"There," she says. "Would you like a cup of tea?"

"No, thank you," I say.

"Are you sure? This is a delicious Japanese green tea. Healthful," she says. "Calming."

Perhaps she senses how nervous I am.

"I'm sure I don't want any, but thank you, Mrs. Harris," I say.

"Please call me Nellie." Mrs. Harris pours a cup of tea out of a beautiful cast-iron pot that sits immediately to her right. "We're fellow writers, peers."

"Well, I don't think I yet rise to the level of being a peer. I have no experience, comparatively speaking."

"But for some reason the fabled M. Des Jardins is interested in representing you. I've been wondering about how that came to be?"

"The usual way. I queried them and sent them my manuscript . . . blind."

She nods. "I recently ran into an old friend of yours."

"Oh *really*?" Is she talking about Kiyo?

"Yes, I believe you were girlhood friends."

Definitely *not* Kiyo. "Who?" I ask.

"Jennifer Peoples—she lived across the street from you on President Street in Peakview."

"Jennifer Peoples?" How could Nellie Harris have crossed paths with her—unless she had been trying to? "Yes, Jenny and I were friends for a time when my family lived on President Street," I say. "I haven't heard from her since before my eighth birthday. How did you *run* into her?"

"I misspoke. I *found* her—I didn't run into her. I've been doing research on the Vicious Circle for almost as long as you have been alive," she says. "I had a particular fascination for Mihana Sakura, the founder of M. Des Jardins, the grandmother of the current head of the agency—Kiyo Flores." She looks at me pointedly. "Hana, as she was known in the circle, was enigmatic—unknown. Shortly after she signed Dorothy Parker, they found her dead on Peconic Beach on Long Island. The papers reported it as a likely suicide, suggesting the cause was a 'nervous breakdown' after the birth of her daughter, Kiyo's mother. Others, however, speculated that one of her business associates murdered her—there were a number of conspiracy theories."

I don't react. Kiyo told me that his grandmother had died shortly after his mother was born but didn't mention anything about the cause of death.

"Last year I finished writing my book on the circle, and I sent it to M. Des Jardins, thinking that they would have an obvious interest in representing it, given the historical ties."

"Why?" I ask. "Surely, you must already have an agent."

"Of course I have an agent," Mrs. Harris says. "I was curious what response I would get, and I got my answer."

"M. Des Jardins specializes in literary fiction—is yours a work of fiction?" I say.

"Not exactly, but it relies on conjecture, which makes it fiction as far as I'm concerned. It doesn't matter, though, because they turned me away. I had hoped that Mr. Flores would take an interest in setting the record straight. The rejection letter referenced my storied career, so they rejected me knowing who I am—maybe *because* of who I am. Nobody wants to feed the yellow-journalism beast."

"That must have hurt," I say. I bet they figured out who Nellie, Nanci Heart, was by her writing style, which has an unmistakable flair—a bite.

"Only after you told me they are *your* agency. I couldn't make sense of that, so I sent my investigator out to do some digging. I can't help myself from investigating a mystery. It didn't take her long to discover your deep ties to the Sakura family, a fact that was confirmed when we were able to locate your childhood friend Jenny. She lives off the beaten path down in rural North Carolina and was surprisingly eager to share with me—for a price, of course. She still cares about you, you know."

No idea what Jenny shared, or if any of it was true. She was my best friend. She would never say anything to intentionally hurt me or Kiyo.

"Like I said, I haven't heard from her since before my eighth birthday. I can barely remember anything from those times." Of course when Mrs. Harris reads my novel, she will know that I lied, but I don't care.

"What about the romantic relationship between

Jennifer's mother and yours? What about what happened at the fort? What about Anna Gonzales's murder? Does any of that ring a bell?"

"Well, yes, but—"

"Did you know that Kiyo's grandfather and grand-mother may have had ties to the yakuza?"

"I have no idea what you're talking about. What *is* the yakuza?"

"It's organized crime—what the mafia is to Italy, the yakuza is to Japan. For many years, people have speculated that your beloved Mr. Sakura was *oyabun*, or a leader of one of the crime families that had been established in Los Angeles before the war, but nobody ever had any definitive proof of that. So when they found Hana on Peconic Beach, a handful of people speculated—"

"I never saw anything amiss with Kiyo's family. His grandfather was a gardener. He lived in a house down the street from us, and he took care of Kiyo because his mother traveled a lot for work."

"Do you know what line of work his mother was in?"

I'm unsure where all this is leading, but given Winnie's warning, I'll say nothing more. Nellie Harris poses an imminent danger, given her position at the *Post*. She makes and breaks people for a living.

"I don't know what to say, Mrs. Harris. I don't know anything. For me, when I was a child, Mr. Sakura was the gentlest man on the planet—he kept a beautiful garden and brought hope and magic into our lives."

"I'm saying that maybe you should step carefully in your dealings with *that* family—particularly Kiyo, and I am not saying this out of envy, although I can see you might read me that way, given the rejection. Supposing they are not yakuza, given the outrageous wealth that Kiyo has been able to amass in a relatively short time, it's possible that a criminal element is at play," Mrs. Harris says. "I'm trying to help you because you may be treading dangerous waters. I like you, and I don't want you, or those in your care—my children—to be endangered."

I reflect on Kiyo's "business associates" at the Round About, Kiyo's *be careful* farewell, the man in a black suit that keeps showing up wherever I am, Mrs. Tuzova's *bad feeling*. Mrs. Harris could be right, but I refuse to feed her any more information than I already have.

"What do you want from me?"

"I want you to be my inside girl. I'll pay you, and you can spend your days doing whatever you want, but *not* taking care of my children. It will give you time to write."

"I don't want to be your *inside girl*," I say. "In fact, I quit, given your worry over your children's safety in my care." I get up to leave. "If you write one negative word about Kiyo, his family, or mine for that matter, I'll tell the world about the affair you are having with your brother-in-law and how you gaslight your children. I have the photos to prove it," I lie. "I admired you until now."

Mrs. Harris's expression is priceless. "Margaux, I promise you, I am not your enemy, nor am I Kiyo's."

I leave her office without a look back, stopping briefly in the kitchen to tell Mariana, Pedro, Katie, and John that my employment has come to an end.

I should have asked more questions about Jenny before losing my cool. I'd like to talk to her before my book comes out. If Mrs. Harris's investigator was able to find her that easily, surely I can find her too.

* * *

WHEN I GET HOME, I pick up the phone and dial Kiyo. He *did* say to call anytime.

"M. Des Jardins Literary Agency, answering service," a chirpy voice answers. "May I ask who is calling?"

"Yes, this is Margaux Andrews. I'm calling for Mr. Flores."

"Of course. He is expecting your call. I will patch you through."

He is expecting my call?

"Margie!" Kiyo's voice is warm and calm. "I'm glad you called. You got my message?"

I check the answering machine. Sure enough, the light is blinking.

"Oh, I didn't see that you called," I say. "I'm calling about an unpleasant encounter—"

"That you had with Nellie Harris?" Kiyo finishes my sentence. "Winnie called me after you saw her earlier today, which is why I called you. Full disclosure, I already knew you were working for Nellie."

Is there anything Kiyo *doesn't* know about me? How does he know so much? Is he spying on me?

"I should have warned you," he says. "She's been digging for dirt. I'm sure whatever you said to her in response to anything she asked is fine. She's fishing for a story that isn't there. She's persistent—I'll say that for her."

"I didn't tell her much of anything," I say. "But she told me that she found Jenny—she knows that we're connected. She also told me some story about your family and something called the yakuza—and her theory about your grandmother's death."

Kiyo is silent.

"Is there any truth to that?"

"No," Kiyo says. "My grandfather was definitely *not* yakuza, and my grandmother committed suicide; she was *not* murdered, as conspiracy crackpots posit. She had what is now widely recognized as postpartum depression. She felt trapped by motherhood in an era when women were expected to accept motherhood without complaint, but for her it was the death of her *self*, the end of her career as a literary agent."

Kiyo's voice is calm and assured. I believe him. He wouldn't lie to me, would he?

"Look, Margaux, I have something else I want to talk to you about, and this is *real*, and relates to us *now*, not ancient history."

"Okay. Shoot."

"I have a friend in the Peakview Police Department who has been petitioning to reopen the Anna Gonzales case."

"Is that a good thing?"

"Yeah, I think so. It would be good for all of us to know more conclusively what happened, regardless how it reflects on us."

Kiyo goes quiet again. "You there?" I say.

"Yeah, I'm here. Margie?"

"Yeah?" I say.

"Can I come over to see you?"

"Are you still in New York?"

"Look out your window."

Kiyo stands on the sidewalk beside his limousine, phone cord stretched. He's looking up at me, holding a single red rose.

When he gets up to the apartment, I am standing with the door open. I practically throw myself at him. He hugs me tight. I tuck my face into his warm neck. He smells familiar and safe, like the Blessed Abode, the Garden of the Gods, like home. How have I lived all these years without him in my life?

"Don't you worry, Margie. Everything is going to be more than alright."

We pull apart. "Come in, please," I say, "before my neighbor Cassie sees us. She's a bit of a busybody."

Kiyo steps inside. "Nice place!" he says without the slightest hint of irony. He hands me the rose.

"Thank you." Blood rushes into my face. I take the rose to the kitchen and put it into a bud vase.

"No, I mean it! It is everything that you are. Simple and honest. Creative. I knew it would be." He has taken off his raincoat. I take it from him and hang it on the coat tree.

"It's what I can afford," I say.

"That, my friend, is about to change. You'll soon be receiving a handsome contract from one of the world's premier fiction publishers—the Big Five Press. They have so much faith in you, in fact, that they plan to give you a housing stipend on top of your advance, *and* they want to support you similarly for the sequels."

"That sounds too good to be true," I say.

"Isn't life mysterious?" He hugs me again.

"We should have a toast," I say. "I have a presentable bottle of cabernet—it's not Nagasawa, but—"

"Absolutely!"

I fetch the bottle, two glasses, and the corkscrew. I struggle to remove the foil.

Kiyo gently takes it from me. "Let me show you a trick I know." He waves his hand over the top of the bottle and, as if by magic, the foil lifts up and off the neck. "A cheap party trick my mother taught me."

"You're quite the magician!" I take the bottle, pour the wine, and hand Kiyo a glass.

"To us," I say.

"Yes, I like the sound of that," Kiyo says. "So, what did you have planned tonight before I showed up unannounced?"

"Other than looking through the want ads?" I laugh. "Well, before you showed up, I planned on reading the last three chapters of *One Elysium Street*. I'm supposed to meet with Theo and Winnie tomorrow to talk about it."

"So I've heard," he says. "Winnie is special, isn't she?"

"Yes, I like her, and I have to say, she's a perfect match

for Theo. How *did* that happen? Theo said a school friend arranged things, but Winnie and I think there might have been another interloper involved."

Kiyo raises one eyebrow and smiles. "I have no idea what you're intimating. Like I said, life is mysterious," he says. "How about we read the last three chapters out loud? We can alternate sections," he says.

"You don't mind?"

"It would be my pleasure. I have nothing but time tonight, and there is nobody I'd rather spend it with reading." He leans over, looks me in the eye, and gently kisses me on my lips. "And after we finish with your story, who knows what might happen?"

"I have a pretty good idea," I say.

ONE ELYSIUM STREET

CHAPTERS 16 TO 18

16

YEAR OF LOSS

SEPTEMBER 1967 TO MAY 1968

SECOND GRADE STARTS IN A WEEK, and Mama says, "Honey, I have some sad news for you. You and Beanie are not going to be in the same class this year."

"Whaaat? Why not?"

"Mrs. Armstrong recommended that you two be separated. She thinks you'll pay better attention apart. I know how disappointed you must feel—"

"I promise to pay attention! Can't you talk to Principal Walters about it?"

"I'm afraid not. You two will get to be together at recess and lunch, though."

* * *

BEANIE IS in Mrs. Robinson's class, and I'm in Mrs. Packard's. She's okay, I guess. She has red hair piled high on top of her head, real pretty long polished nails, and she wears blue-green eye shadow that matches her eyes. I liked

Miss Pancake better, but she doesn't exist anymore; she's the mean Mrs. Armstrong now, and I'm real mad at her for separating me and Beanie. On the first day of school, when I say hello to her, she acts like she doesn't know who I am. So much for being the teacher's pet.

At the end of the second day of school, there's an assembly in the auditorium. Principal Walters gets up and introduces all the teachers, and then different teachers come up to talk about after-school activities and clubs we can join. Mrs. Packard introduces the Brownies and the Bluebirds.

"If you are in the second or third grades, you can join the Brownies or the Bluebirds. Both clubs meet in the cafeteria—the Brownies on Tuesdays after school, and the Bluebirds on Wednesdays. Raise your hand if you are interested in joining either of these clubs. Mrs. Robinson will bring you some papers to take home to your parents."

I raise my hand and see Beanie raise hers. Mrs. Robinson passes papers down the rows of seats.

On the walk home, Beanie says, "I'm going to be a Bluebird!"

"You already know that?" I say.

"Yeah, my mom was a Bluebird, and then she became a Camp Fire Girl."

"I don't know what my mom was, or if she was anything," I say.

"Well, you should be a Bluebird. It's better than being a Brownie."

"Why do you say that?"

"The uniforms are a lot cuter!"

* * *

When Mama gets home from work, I run to her with the papers that were sent home.

She looks briefly at each of the brochures. "You'll be a Brownie."

"But I wanna be a Bluebird. Beanie's gonna be a Bluebird!"

"Well, I don't like the organization—it's sexist," she says.

"What's that mean?"

"It means they think girls should be pretty, not smart."

"I'm smart *and* pretty."

"Yes, and that's why you're going to be a Brownie."

I run outside and across the street to tell Beanie. I hope she'll change her mind.

Marta realizes too late that she started a small civil war on Elysium Street between Beanie and Piglet when she insisted that Piglet join Brownies instead of Bluebirds. In some ways it mirrors divisions that are rising between her and Barbara and between liberals and conservatives in the country at large. During the months leading up to Christmas, Beanie and Piglet bicker incessantly about which is better. They are insufferable.

In response to the Bluebird-Brownie wars, Barbara said, *Let them be girls, Marta. Everything doesn't have to be political. I was a Camp Fire girl and I turned out okay.*

Marta considered her point. *Well, that may be, but I still would rather that Piglet join Brownies.* Plus, it's debatable that Barbara turned out all right. She is firmly entrenched in the feminine ideals of the 1950s and believes that men are inherently superior.

Marta has been reckoning with some of Barbara's and her fundamental differences. Barbara is much more conservative than she is in almost every way. Marta's school friends align better with who she is.

In the fall, Marta joined a Society of Friends peace group on campus. She has been attending meetings and gone to some demonstrations against the war in Vietnam. She invited Barbara to one. Barbara said, *I could never do that. I support my country and the brave men in uniform, no matter what. Attending a protest is like slapping those young men who are serving in the face.* Marta said, *How would you feel if you had a son? Would you send him to Vietnam as cannon fodder?* Barbara said, *I'd be proud to, and my son would be proud to serve, like Neil did.*

Marta knows what warfare does to the men who survive. Doug and Neil are two examples of what happens to boys ruined by war, but they are the *lucky* ones; they didn't come home in body bags.

* * *

THE THING that Marta fears most arrives in early February, on the heels of the Tet Offensive, in which thousands upon thousands of young American men and Vietnamese civilians were senselessly murdered, tortured, and raped. She gets home from the lab and finds Kit sitting slumped at the dining room table with his head in his hands.

"What's wrong?" Marta says.

Wordlessly, Kit hands her a crumpled piece of paper. Marta's eyes fill with tears as soon as she sees the header: "SELECTIVE SERVICE SYSTEM: ORDER TO REPORT FOR INDUCTION."

Nineteen sixty-eight is starting off badly.

"Oh, Kit, I don't know what to say."

"There's nothing to say. I'm *not* going."

"What are you going to do?"

"Not sure yet," he says.

"I'll help you. I have friends—draft counselors." Marta has been attending training to become a draft counselor herself. She hasn't advertised it for obvious reasons.

"That would be aiding and abetting a draft dodger," he said. "I don't want you to do that."

"I won't let you go into that immoral war," Marta says. "I think your father would agree with me on this one." Doug, although a career military man, thought the Vietnam War was wrong from the start. Marta is pretty sure his opinion hasn't changed. As a trauma surgeon, he has seen it all.

* * *

MARTA SPREADS the word in her activist circles about Kit's notice and gets the name of someone who can help. She's careful, doesn't use the phone. There have been reports of bugs planted and phones tapped. In her training, they advise counselors to communicate only in person, outdoors or in noisy public environments.

"Well," she says to Kit. "I don't want you to go to Canada, but that's what people are doing."

"If I go, I can't come back," he says. Kit's eyes fill with tears. He looks away. "We might not ever see each other again."

"Oh, we'll see each other. Canada is a hop, skip, and a jump away. I'd rather know that you are safe and living in Canada than—"

"I'll meet with your contact," Kit says. "I'm not going to tell you anything about my plans, though. You'll know when it is done. One day, I'll be gone. I'll let you know where I land."

Marta starts crying. They hug each other tightly. "I love you, Kit."

"I love you, Mother."

* * *

THE NEXT MORNING, Marta goes over to Barbara's for coffee. "Well, Kit got called." She starts crying.

"Oh, he'll be fine. He's a bright boy. He'll be fine over there. He'll come back a hero, no doubt." Barbara speaks with unfounded certainty.

"My God, Barbara, listen to yourself! I don't think we can be friends anymore. I'm sorry I told you about Kit. Forget it." Marta doesn't dare tell her more, knowing how Barbara feels about draft dodgers and peace activists. "You're right. He *will* be fine." She gets up. "Well, I need to get to work. Thanks for the coffee."

"Don't leave like this," Barbara says, eyes wide. "I can't stand the thought that you are mad at me. Is this the end?"

"The end of what? You've never wanted to call our relationship anything. It isn't anything. Whatever it *was* is over. I'm not mad at you, but I know we will *never* understand each other."

* * *

THAT AFTERNOON, as Marta drives home from work down Vista Boulevard, she comes upon a terrible traffic jam about a half mile from the house. Sirens were blaring when she left campus, but she didn't think much of it—just that there must have been an accident of some sort. Drivers get out of their cars to see what is going on up ahead, and Marta does the same. She sees the flashing lights of a fire truck and an ambulance. *God, I hope none of my kids have been hurt.* She gets back in her car and maneuvers it to the side of the road to park it. She'll walk the rest of the way home.

As she approaches the intersection of Vista and Avenue A, a surreal scene unfolds. Barbara's station wagon appears to be suspended between the limbs of a large oak tree.

"Oh my God!" she says, turning to a man watching the

scene with intense interest. "That's my best friend's car. How did it get up there?"

"I don't know. Another guy said she was going crazy fast when she hit that tree," he says. "I'm so sorry, your friend definitely didn't make it."

Of course he is right. The ambulance personnel are not in a hurry.

"Was she alone?" Marta asks.

"Yep, far as I could tell."

Marta wanders the rest of the way home in shock, tears streaming down her face. What will she tell the kids? What will happen to poor little Beanie? How did this happen? *Was this my fault? This could be my fault. Only hours ago, I ended our friendship.* She named what it was, when she told Barbara that they couldn't be friends anymore.

As soon as she gets close to home, she makes a beeline for the Jones's and rings the doorbell to see if Neil is home. Nobody answers, and Dottie doesn't bark either. That's unusual.

The kids are not home from school yet. Marta plans to intercede and bring Beanie over to their house. She hangs around on the front steps until she sees them headed down the street, but Beanie isn't with them.

"Where is Beanie?" Marta asks without saying hello.

"I don't know," Piglet says. "She wasn't at lunch recess either. Maybe she had a doctor's appointment or something."

Marta repeatedly tries calling Neil at home but gets no answer. What is going on?

She turns on the local news to see what they have to say about the accident. Of course, the reporter is no other than Holly Riggs—always perky when reporting the most awful news.

"A woman was killed in a tragic accident on Vista Boulevard today when her car hit a large tree at a high speed.

Witnesses say she was traveling westbound and suddenly swerved into the tree for no apparent reason. The car flipped upward into the branches, where it is still suspended. The driver was ejected from the vehicle and likely died on impact. The victim's identity is being withheld until next of kin have been notified. We'll let you know when we learn more on this developing story. Thank God nobody else was injured."

What the hell? Neil and Beanie don't know? Something isn't right. Neil is on the police force. How could he *not* know?

Five days ago, Martin Luther King Jr. got murdered, and today is the funeral procession. Birdie can't pull herself away from the TV. Her mother let the kids stay home from school to watch the news coverage, but the rest of the family left her there in front of the black-and-white glow alone. Everything is so sad and terrible in the world, in *her* world. Barbara died, Kit left without saying good-bye, and then Rob broke up with her because he decided to date Catrina, so now she's gone too. Tears run down Birdie's face as she watches the Kings on their endless procession. What does it feel like to be his children? To know the whole world is mourning his loss? Mourning the lost hope that he embodied?

Birdie gets up from the TV and goes into the kitchen to get a snack. Her mother looks up from the newspaper she's reading.

"Hi, sweetheart, you doing okay?"

"No," Birdie says. "I'm so sad I can hardly stand it. I haven't been this sad since . . . well, ever." She was going to say *since you left Daddy*, but then changed her mind. It would only make her mom feel worse than she already does.

"Yeah, me too," her mother says. "Come sit by me."

"I'm gonna make a sandwich first," Birdie says. "You want one too?"

"No thanks."

Birdie gets the sliced bread, Skippy, and Welch's grape jelly out.

"Mom, I've been thinking about something."

"What?"

"With all the bad stuff that has been happening here in Peakview, I was wondering if maybe I could go visit Dad, now that he's stationed in New Hampshire?" Birdie studies her mother's face for a reaction. None.

"That's a good idea. I'll write to him to see if when school gets out you kids could go visit for a couple of weeks."

Birdie didn't expect her mother to be convinced so easily. Lately her mother lives in another place. Barbara's sudden death; the disappearance of Neil, Beanie, and Dottie; the investigation of the alleged accident, all weigh on her mother, but Birdie doesn't understand why her mother hasn't been upset about Kit's sudden disappearance.

Birdie pours herself a glass of milk and slides in next to her mother in the nook.

"Mom?" Birdie asks.

"Yeah?"

"Where do you think Kit is? Why hasn't he called us?"

"I don't know where he is, but he must have had a good reason to leave."

"How do you know that?" Birdie says.

"I can't say."

Birdie feels the weight of her mother's loneliness. She, too, is lonely. She misses Neil in spite of how he hurt her the last time she saw him.

17

BODY

MAY 30, 1968 TO JUNE 8, 1968

On my birthday, I run out and get the newspaper for Mama. Today the paperboy threw it into the juniper bushes. After retrieving it, I slide the rubber band off and open to the front page. "MISSING SMITH GIRL FOUND!"

It feels like my fifth birthday all over again, but it's my eighth. This time, Maddie hasn't gone missing; she's been found—dead—"in a shallow grave in a field adjacent to the railroad tracks that run along Vista Boulevard." They found her up by the train tracks, less than a block from where we built *our* fort, the fort where that horrible boy held us captive with a knife. Did *he* kill Maddie? I also can't help thinking of Tree telling me, Kai, and Beanie about his first attempt to build a fort when he was six up near The Apartments. He said it collapsed, and luckily nobody was inside. But maybe someone *was*.

As soon as Tree hears the news, he runs downstairs to the basement. He's crying, making strange animal sounds like I've never heard come from a person before. Maybe he, too, thinks it was his fault.

Now that Beanie is gone, Tree and Kai let me hang out with them. Birdie and Willie have also been extra nice. Catrina and Rob vanished from their lives like Beanie and Stella vanished from mine. I miss Beanie. I hope she's okay. I miss Stella. I miss Kit too. I hope he's okay. I want *everything* to be okay. I don't want any more people to disappear. This world's a scary place.

Mr. Obata says we need to make magic because it makes the world better. Maybe I can make some magic that disappears all this pain. Gotta figure out how.

* * *

MAMA INVITES MIMI, Vivi, Mr. Obata, and Kai over for a birthday dinner. Nobody's in the mood for a party, but Aunt Vivi brings over a store-bought cake without *happy birthday* written on it, and Mimi brings a couple of pizzas and a salad from Angelo's. We're sitting out on the back patio, finishing our cold pizza, when Mr. Obata says, "I have a surprise for you, little one."

He pulls out a box that is about twelve-by-twelve inches and six inches deep. It's wrapped in beautiful paper with a geometric design.

Kai says, "I helped make it."

I give the package a shake. "Hmm . . . what is it?" Something loose rattles inside. Sounds like a wooden object. I'm careful as I open it so as not to ruin the beautiful paper. When I get the paper off, I see a polished block of wood that has five sides and an intricate pattern of different colors of wood. In the middle there's a pale-yellow rose—*And yellow roses represent friendship.*

Mr. Obata says, "This is a *himitsu-bako*, a puzzle box where you can keep your secrets."

Mr. Obata must know a thing or two about secrets.

Kai, visibly excited, says, "And you have to figure out how to open it to find out what's inside."

Tree says, "Wow! That is cool. Mr. Obata, can you teach me how to make one of those?"

"I'd be happy to," he says.

I pass the box around for everybody to admire.

Mimi says, "That's a real work of craftsmanship, Hiro."

"And Kai." Mr. Obata beams with pride. "Kai helped at every stage of making this. And it was *his* idea."

Mama says, "Truly spectacular, Hiro and Kai. You both know how to bring light to a party."

Vivi leans over and gives Mr. Obata a kiss on the cheek. "Yes, they do at that."

"Okay, Margie, you have to figure out how to open it now," Kai says.

I turn it over, look at it from every angle, but I can't see a single seam. It appears solid.

"Here," Kai says, reaching for the box, "let me show you the first move, and it will give you ideas about how to open it." Kai places his hand on one of the five sides and pulls down. It slides easily open to reveal another layer of box below. "Now the rest is up to you to figure out. And here is another clue for you: There are three objects hidden inside the box in separate compartments. When you find the third object, you will have solved the puzzle."

The adults go into the house to get the birthday cake. Tree, Willie, and Birdie have gone to get something else inside, leaving me and Kai alone on the back porch.

"Margie," Kai says, "I've been thinking about that day by the tracks, the day that bully came with his knife. I think we need to tell your mom and my grandpa about what happened. I know we promised we never would, but we have to now that they found Maddie's body."

"Yeah. I agree." I put the box on the table. "I give up for

now! Can we wait for another time to tell them so it'll be only the two of us? I don't think Tree can take it."

"Of course, and I think you're right about Tree."

Tree brings out his guitar. Everybody sings "Happy Birthday" to me and we eat cake. In spite of the sad news of the day, we're happy—for the moment.

It's Sunday morning again. Marta makes her coffee, gets out the Farberware griddle, and plugs it into the middle of the table.

As usual, Piglet, who wants to be called Margie now that she is eight, is the first one to the kitchen. Like Birdie, she's always been an early riser.

"Hi, Mom," Piglet says. There's a bounce in her step, something Marta hasn't seen recently. "Can I do something to help?" she says. Her youngest is growing up. Who knew that her eighth birthday would bring about such changes? Too bad Tree didn't experience the same transformation. At almost ten, he's more of a baby than Piglet. Boys.

"Well, yes," Marta says. "How about you set the table. After that, maybe take the bacon out for me to get it started."

Piglet gets right to it.

"How's your puzzle box going?" Marta asks.

"Got it open. Took me nearly the whole night, but I got it open."

"Well? What secrets were hiding within?"

"Now it wouldn't be much of a secret if I told you that," Piglet says.

"Alright."

"Not really, there's a pretty journal in there that is made with Japanese paper, and a real ink pen, plus this." She opens the top of her shirt to reveal a silver rose with pearls on either side of it hanging from a simple silver chain.

"Oh!" Marta says. "That's extravagant!"

"I love it," Piglet says. "Mr. Obata knows how to make magic."

"Yes indeed, and Kai too."

* * *

ALL OF THE kids have finished breakfast and left the table except Piglet, who slides out and starts clearing the rest of the table.

"You don't need to do that," says Marta. "You've already been such a big help this morning."

"That's okay, there's something I want to talk to you about, but I'm waiting for Kai and his grandpa to get here. There is something *we* want to talk to you about."

The doorbell rings.

"That's odd. Kai doesn't usually ring the doorbell," says Marta. "I better get it."

When she opens the door, there are two men in black suits and sunglasses standing there. Federal officers, most likely, or possibly Mormons.

"Hello, ma'am, are you Mrs. Doug Anderson?" says one of the men. He flashes a badge. He's from the FBI.

"Yes, sir, I'm Marta Anderson." Marta kicks herself for her robot-like response. Probably makes her sound guilty. "How can I help you?"

"My name is Federal Agent Booth, and this is my associate Federal Agent Wilson. We're here on routine business. You are not in any trouble."

Yet. Marta's heart races. "That's good since I haven't done anything wrong—that I know of." She laughs to look relaxed.

"We're here to inquire about the whereabouts of your

son, a Mr. Christopher Anderson. He failed to respond to his Selective Service System notice of induction."

"Lord!" Marta says. "I had no idea." She's sweating profusely. Will they notice? She's rehearsed this conversation hundreds of times, but she's no actress. "Well, Kit—we call him Kit—hasn't been here for quite some time. Last I knew he moved in with his girlfriend in Denver. They had a place on Capitol Hill." Marta pauses deliberately. "Of course I disapproved of that, living in sin and all. All this free-love business has gotten completely out of hand if you ask me!" Maybe too heavy-handed?

"You wouldn't happen to know the name of the girl-friend, would you?"

"Yes, it was Stacey something . . . Edwards, yes, that's it. I told him if that's what he wanted to do, it was his choice, as God is his witness, not me."

"Yes, ma'am, and would you happen to know the address?"

"Oh, no, I don't have a clue. I think it's one of those hippie communes where they sit around and smoke mari-juana all day."

Both men nod their heads like they know exactly what she's talking about.

"Well, thank you, ma'am. Sorry to bother you folks on this fine Sunday morning. Have a good day."

Marta closes the door and falls against it, then goes back to the kitchen where Piglet is still busy.

"Mama?" Piglet says. "Was all that stuff you said about Kit true?"

"Hellooo?" It's Kai and Hiro, finally.

Kai and Hiro's arrival saves Marta from having to answer Piglet's question.

"Yep, we're in the kitchen!" Marta calls. She puts some milk and cookies out. What in the world do they want to talk to her about in private?

"Hi, Mrs. Anderson," Kai says.

"Marta," Mr. Obata says. "Everything okay over here? I thought I saw a government car pull away from the curb. What with all of these people disappearing . . ."

Marta sighs. "They're looking for Kit. He didn't show up for his Selective Service induction."

"Oh, I see."

Piglet says, "Mom told them he moved in with his girlfriend, and she doesn't know where he is."

Mr. Obata nods like he understands. "I see. Well? What do you kids need to talk to us about?"

"Why all the mystery?" Marta says. They look serious.

Kai and Piglet take turns telling them about an incident in the field by the railroad tracks and what Tree told them about his fort up by The Apartments.

"I wish you had come to us sooner. These are quite terrible and serious things. The police need to know," Marta says.

"But we're worried about Tree. We're afraid he'll get sent to jail or that we all will get in trouble, or that mean bully will come and hurt our families," says Piglet.

Mr. Obata says, "We won't let any of those things happen." He puts his hand on top of Piglet's head.

"Tree! Could you join us in the kitchen?" Marta calls.

Tree comes into the kitchen from the basement entry. His eyes are puffy and red.

"Kai and Piglet, I mean Margie, told us about what happened in the field with the bully from the apartments. I think we need to let the police know about it, but they also told me about a fort that you built around the time—"

Tree bursts into tears. "I think it's all my fault. If only Maddie and me had never helped with digging that stupid thing."

Marta says, "Tree, we don't know what happened or if where they found her was *your* fort."

277

Mr. Obata's expression is grave. "Oh, children, this is sad. You should never have had to bear these pains alone. Let Marta and me discuss what to do next. In the meantime, it is probably best to keep these stories to yourselves."

Marta adds, "Don't even share them with Birdie or Willie."

Less than a week after Maddie's body is found, Robert Kennedy gets assassinated. A few days later, Birdie once again sits in front of the flickering television screen watching a funeral procession—first the train ride from New York to Washington DC, then the lengthy procession to Arlington Cemetery. The television news has been full of nothing but ugly images of war, violent protests, and news of civil unrest.

Her mother stands in the doorway between the kitchen and the sitting room, where the TV is. "Birdie, honey, it's not good for you to watch all that news."

"I can't help it," Birdie says. "It's like a car accident—I can't look away."

A pained expression crosses her mother's face at the mention of a car accident.

"I'm sorry," Birdie says. "That was just an example."

"I know, but you have to . . . You have to go do something to make yourself happier." With that, her mother goes back into the kitchen to clean up.

Birdie turns the TV off and goes into the kitchen.

"Mom, have you heard back from Daddy?"

"Not yet."

Birdie gets *To Kill a Mockingbird* from her room and goes outside to sit up in the Y-P-S clubhouse to read—she'll get a head start on the high school reading list her English teacher gave them on the last day of school. Not much of a club-house now that Rob and Catrina don't come over anymore. In the Dark Forest, she passes Tree's tree house. She hears the kids up there having an animated conversation.

Kai says, "Tree, if they found her in your collapsed fort, it doesn't make it your fault."

Piglet says, "Mr. Obata and Mom will get things figured out. Mom said they are working on a plan."

Birdie's left out of everything. Willie is hanging out with his high school friends and has a job at the Dolly Madison Ice Cream Parlor. The kids have secrets they don't share with her. She's a freak within her own family. What other secrets are they keeping?

18

HOUSE FOR SALE

EARLY JUNE 1968

MARTA SITS at her writing desk in her bedroom. She sets pen to paper in response to the letter she received back about the kids visiting New Hampshire. When Birdie asked whether she had heard back from Doug, Marta had been forced to lie.

Doug's wife sent a surprisingly nasty note that said *If you wish to communicate with Doug you need to go through me, or minimally address letters to both of us—he is my husband, not yours.* Unbeknownst to Marta, Darla, although to this point a dutiful step-parent, sending cards and presents, has apparently harbored anger about her role. Darla wanted children with Doug but was unable to get pregnant, which might explain why she said, *You should be aware that I married Doug, not his five children, and I resent the fact that you expect me to take care of them.* Doug got the woman of his dreams, someone who takes care of his every need, makes him feel adored, and puts up a jealous fit when he comes home late for dinner. He doesn't have to compete with kids for her attention like he did with her.

The upshot of the letter is that their new house does not have enough space for *all* of the kids to visit at one time, so perhaps this summer Birdie and Willie could come for two weeks in August without the younger kids. What is she going to tell Tree and Piglet? They are going to be crushed. Neither of them knows their father, as they were so young when Marta left him.

"Marta?" Hiro's voice filters through the back door.

"Come on in, Hiro," she says. She walks out to the kitchen. "Can I make you a cup of tea?"

"No, thank you," he says. "I can't stay long."

"To what do I owe the pleasure of your visit?"

"I came by with a couple of pieces of news. One that may provide you some relief and another, which will likely upset you."

"I don't like the sound of that."

"Well, let me start with the first. I've executed our plan to make an anonymous report to the police. I had a friend of mine drop it through the mail slot at the police station. In it, I explained that our primary concern is protecting the identities of the children involved, but also providing leads that might solve the case. That's all we can do at this point."

"Thank you, Hiro. That is good to know, and thank you for taking that task on so readily."

"It's the least I could do under the circumstances," he says.

"And?"

"And the troublesome news is that the Ito family will not be returning to Peakview and have already made arrangements to sell the house to another UP professor."

"That is *terrible* news, Hiro!" Marta leans against the kitchen counter. "What will we do? What about Leadbelly?" She hasn't been able to save much money. Her lab job plus child support has barely been enough to cover expenses. This year just keeps getting better.

"Maybe ask Vivi or your mother for help? I am sure they would be happy to help if they can. As for Leadbelly, I'll take care of him until Professor Ito is able to come pick him up later this summer."

After Mr. Obata leaves, Marta calls Vivi.

"Hi, Viv?"

"I was expecting your call," Vivi says.

"Did you know about this?"

"Hiro told me this morning. I'm sorry."

"What am I going to do? I don't have enough money to get another place right now, and I am trying to finish writing my dissertation."

"How much do you need?"

"At least enough to get through the summer until I start receiving my stipend again, maybe like fifteen hundred?"

Silence on the other end. Finally Vivi says, "I don't think I can help financially right now—things are tight, but if you can figure out how to get through the next couple of months and back to the East Coast, I have a friend who has offered their beach house for free for six months. With your stipend, you could hunker down there and write. The catch is that someone is living there until sometime in September, so you'll have to figure out what to do for the rest of the summer."

Surely Vivi has the money to lend. *Things* are not tight; she is.

"Let me think about it," Marta says.

* * *

THE NEXT DAY, when the postman slips the mail through the slot in the door, Marta finds a letter postmarked in Canada with a return address of a PO box in Montreal, Quebec. No name, but Marta knows who it is from. Finally, some good news—a letter from Kit. The typewritten letter describes the beautiful landscape and includes a drawing of a young woman. Marta tears up, knowing that Kit is safe and happy and not in some hellish jungle in Vietnam or worse, dead.

Maybe when Willie and Birdie go to visit Doug, she and the younger kids can drive back East to pick them up in New Hampshire, and then head up north to Quebec—a road trip before heading to the beach house. Without knowing exactly how everything will unfold she hatches a plan for the coming months.

Marta goes to the kitchen, picks up the phone, and dials Vivi.

"Hey, Viv. I'd like to take your friend up on the beach house offer."

"And what will you do during the in-between?"

"We'll figure it out. It's summer in the Rockies. We're going to head out on the camping trip of a lifetime."

Now she needs to gather together camping supplies. She has enough money to buy a tent, sleeping bags, a camp stove, and inexpensive fishing rods and reels. Next, she'll need to convince the kids that it is going to be a blast— something we are *choosing* to do, not something we *have* to do —she'll try to spin some of that Obata magic.

* * *

ONE ELYSIUM STREET is not the only house on the block that is up for sale. The Jones's house has been put up for auction, being foreclosed. No one has seen or heard from Neil, Beanie, or Dottie since the day of Barbara's accident. A detective interviewed Marta. That Neil was violent did not surprise him. She learns from a couple of short articles in the Gazette about the bizarre crash and the sudden disappearance of the rest of the family. The police have not definitively ruled the crash an accident, nor have they ruled out murder. One article suggested that Barbara might have committed suicide, but there was no note or any other indication of that. As one mystery nears a conclusion, another one opens.

THE END (for now)

MARGAUX

1985

HEAVY STONES

WEDNESDAY MORNING

I LAY awake with my eyes closed. The sun slants across my face. I don't have to be anywhere since I quit my job. Are the Harris twins upset at my sudden departure? Is Mariana?

Maybe yesterday was all a dream. Did Kiyo and I really read the last chapters of *One Elysium Street* aloud? When I finally open my eyes, to great relief, I see Kiyo lying on his side, head in hand, up on his elbow, eyes softly gazing into my face.

"Good morning," he says. He reaches over and runs the tips of his fingers through my hair and then leans in for a kiss. "I could sit here looking at you all day, but I have some business to attend to, like hammering out the details of your contract with the Big Five Press."

"Me too," I say. "I mean I could lie around with you all day. Not sure what I'll do now that I don't have a job. Was thinking I might try to track down Jenny, or maybe get back to writing the next book."

"Do you *really* think it's a good idea to track down Jenny?" Kiyo asks.

"I don't know. My story includes a lot about her family, not *exactly* her family but still, she should have a chance to read it, like the rest of you. Also, I'm curious as to why she felt compelled to talk to Nellie's investigator?"

"I'm pretty sure she needed the money," Kiyo says. "One of my old friends tracked Jenny and her dad to Ashland, North Carolina. The police know where they are. They're living in some sort of Evangelical Christian community. I suspect that she hasn't had a wonderful life. After she and her dad left Peakview, well, you can imagine the lies he must have told her, not to mention the emotional and physical torture he may have put her through. Remember, he's a highly skilled animal trainer, gifted at making creatures submit to him, including his wife and daughter. Jenny likely has buried the truth so deep that it may take many years to find it, if she ever does."

Ned Peoples taught Paloma to train dogs—first Dottie, then Leadbelly—they became close. Paloma thought of him as a surrogate father, until she suddenly didn't—she never told me why. I envied their relationship, but after everything that happened, I wonder if I should have.

"That's pessimistic, don't you think?"

"It's realistic. There *is* hope for her," he says. "In fact, I have been working behind the scenes to get her help ever since I heard about her situation. Until she can get away from her father, she doesn't stand a chance. He's a scary guy, possibly evil. The Peakview Police Department is convinced that he murdered Roz, but they've never amassed enough evidence to charge him. What I know is that I don't want you to get near him, or to give him cause to think of *any* of us."

"I had no idea. It breaks my heart to think of all the pain and suffering Jenny has endured."

"Yes, it makes me sad too."

"I wonder if she'll ever read my book?" I say. "I would hate for it to make matters worse for her."

"*One Elysium Street* is a sad story, but it's also a story about resilience and overcoming adversity, about how we're often afraid of the wrong things. It's about the power of imagination and how magical thinking and magic lift us up. It's about love. You've left Jenny's story unresolved in your novel —there's still room for a happy ending for her. It might be good for her to read it, to know how much she meant to you. How much she *still* means to you."

I get out of bed and traipse to the bathroom to pee, leaving the door open, as I always do. I watch Kiyo get up. His lean muscular body emanates strength. Save for a scar on his chest, his skin is unblemished—a beautiful man. What is the story of that scar? When I asked him, he said it resulted from a "sword fight." I didn't probe—but how likely is it that he was *really* in sword fight?

I long ago convinced myself that I don't need anyone. I've dated, but never someone I would want to keep. I don't believe in living happily ever after. People always disappear, and the idea of Kiyo disappearing from my life scares the hell out of me. What will happen with us?

"What will happen with us?" Kiyo says.

"Did you just read my mind?" I say as I wash my hands. He and the people around him have uncanny abilities.

Kiyo laughs. "Unfortunately not. Speaking my own thoughts aloud. I wish I *could* read your mind!"

I walk over to him. He's half dressed, still shirtless, and I am still naked. He reaches out and we hug. He runs his hands down my back to my buttocks and squeezes. I pull back to look into his face. My fingers draw a line down his scar.

"I never want to let you go," I say.

"Well, my car is waiting downstairs." Kiyo kisses me on my forehead, my nose, my chin, and as a final touch, each of my nipples. "I *really* have to go, but I'll see you and the rest of the gang tonight at the Round About."

"I can't believe you can leave me here like this."

"All is fair in love," he says. He hurriedly slips on the rest of his clothes and gives me one last kiss on the lips before saying goodbye and heading out the door.

He loves me.

* * *

AFTER I HAVE MADE my coffee and toast, I settle down in front of my typewriter. I haven't written a word for days. I don't know where to begin.

The reality of my situation settles over me. I will have a book contract with the Big Five Press—an aspiring author's dream. Am I a fraud? Maybe Paloma is right. Maybe I don't have the right to tell stories, including wholly fictitious ones, let alone stories that harken to some of the darker events that took place in our childhood.

The phone rings. "Hello?" I say.

"Hi, is this Margaux Andrews?" It's a woman's voice.

"Yes, this is she."

"My name is Detective Hillstrom, calling from the Peakview Police Department. We recently reopened the unsolved case of Anna Gonzales, and we believe you and your family may have some germane information. Also, we are reinvestigating the automobile accident that killed Roz Peoples, your neighbor on President Street, and we've been trying to reach your mother, but she hasn't responded to any of our messages."

"I'm not sure why you think we can help."

"Because Kiyo Flores suggested that you could."

What has Kiyo done? Jesus, Kiyo, why couldn't you have forewarned me?

The detective says, "He said that his deceased grandfather drafted an anonymous tip to the police department about some things that you kids did and experienced nearly twenty years ago. We haven't been able to find that note in the evidence locker but would be interested in knowing what it might have said. Ms. Andrews, Mr. Flores plans to come in later this week to tell us what he knows, and he would appreciate having you and your brother Theo come too if you are willing. He said that he will cover all expenses, including any legal expenses, should that be necessary."

The truth will set you free. Knowledge is power. What is Kiyo up to with all of this? Surely, he has a plan. I have to trust him, but I still am not entirely sure that I can. There are too many unknowns.

"Let me talk to my brother and Kiyo first. I *do* want to help, but I'm afraid of the consequences."

"I totally understand," the detective says. "You all were young children when these events took place. You've been carrying the weight of these secrets for too long. Perhaps it's time to lay these heavy stones down."

"And Jenny? Jennifer Peoples?"

"We've reached out to her," she says. "She may or may not be of help."

* * *

WHAT THE FUCK? Does Theo know about this already? Does Paloma know? Does our mother?

I dial our mother's number. She has become reclusive since we all dispersed into the world. She probably hasn't bothered listening to her messages, and if she has, she wouldn't reply to the police no matter what. When my brother Keith dodged the draft, she learned to be cautious in her use of the telephone, and although sentiments have largely turned in support of draft dodgers since the end of the Vietnam War, she still holds a significant fear of law enforcement officers.

After five rings, her answering machine picks up—the greeting is bare-bones. "Hi, leave a message at the tone."

"Hi, Mamacita, call me ba—"

"Hello? Margaux?" She screens her calls.

"Mom! I am glad I reached you."

"Likewise. Things have gotten weird around here."

"Here too," I say. I give her the recap of my week, beginning with the meeting with M. Des Jardins at the Round Table.

"Your sister mentioned that," my mother says. "I always thought Kiyo would come back into our lives, but I would not have predicted this!"

"Paloma told me you had concerns about my book getting published. I'm afraid that with the Gossip Gal on the case, all of our secrets will be spilled long before my book comes out. We should be prepared."

"I never had any concerns," she says. "Paloma is worried, but not about secrets. I understand how she feels. Your book accurately portrays her as a kind and generous child, but also an extremely insecure one, someone who yearned for acceptance—attention. We kept secrets from her deliberately, and that hurt her then and now, makes her feel excluded. Your book confirms all of that."

"Well, about that, like I said, a Detective Hillstrom from the Peakview Police Department called me today to say they are reopening the Anna Gonzales case and are also interested in talking to you about Ned and Roz Peoples—they're convinced that Ned murdered Roz but haven't been able to prove it, could never establish a motive."

"Oh dear," she says. "I guess our day of reckoning has come. Nothing good comes of too many secrets. I'll return Detective Hillstrom's calls. She has left me several messages —you know how paranoid I am about the police. Let me know when you all will be arriving in Peakview."

* * *

GETTING through the day proves difficult. I replay the events of the week and the events from my childhood that led up to this moment. What is going to happen if the Gossip Gal catches wind of these latest developments? Surely someone as enamored with the Vicious Circle wouldn't wish to destroy the modern reincarnation of it or ruin the legacy of Mihana Sakura, but maybe Nellie is like Paloma, always the odd person out—trying to be popular, trying to belong— and she wants in on secrets. Sharing other people's secrets gives her a sense of importance, power. Maybe it's time to include her. What better person to spin our story?

With that thought, I pick up the phone and dial Kiyo and leave a message telling him my theory, and I ask him to meet me at the Mulberry branch at four. Next, I dial Paloma and invite her to have drinks and snacks with Kiyo, Theo, and me. Last, I leave a message with Mrs. Harris's office. I say, "If you want a scoop, please join us at the Round About at the round table tonight at six—and be sure to bring your New York Public Library card. The address is 10 ¾ Jersey Street, a few doors down from the Mulberry branch library."

THE VICIOUS CIRCLE

WEDNESDAY EVENING

SHORTLY BEFORE FOUR O'CLOCK, I head to the Mulberry branch at a brisk pace. The air is crisp, and a cold breeze blows. Multicolored leaves tumble along the sidewalk.

When I get to the library, I look through the window. Rosie is helping someone at the reference desk. I pull the door open, setting off the sound of a single entrance chime. Rosie greets me with her eyes and returns to the customer at the counter. While I wait, I study an exhibit in a glass display. "The Wonderful World of Children's Literature." Looking at the books in the case takes me home. *A Wrinkle in Time*, *Just So Stories*, *Alice's Adventures in Wonderland*, The Chronicles of Narnia, The Goops, Winnie-the-Pooh. What a rich literary heritage our mother gave us.

"Beautiful stories, full of imagination and humor," Rosie says from behind.

"Yes, every single one of these stories influenced my life!" I say, turning to her.

"Well, your own story has taken an interesting turn," Rosie says. "And I am not talking about the deal with the Big Five Press."

"No doubt," I say. "It's been a strange week, and promises to get weirder."

"Speaking of which, Kiyo is here. Follow me."

Rosie pads along in front of me, past the reference desk, deeper into the building. The Mulberry branch is much larger than I'd thought. When we reach an area that is gated off, she enters a code and the gate slides open. Inside are multitiered book stacks—an elaborate sliding shelf system.

She turns to me. "These are the closed stacks. Only approved patrons and employees are allowed back here." She pushes a sequence of buttons on a complicated modern-looking panel, and the shelves begin moving. Some move up and down, while others slide beneath them like a giant block puzzle. When they stop shifting, we proceed down an aisle with high shelves on either side, at the end of which is a tall door. "Through there," she says. She pulls a pencil from behind her ear and waves the eraser toward it like a magic wand. The door slides open.

"You'll know where to go, and Kiyo knows the way out," she says with a wink. "He's been here before."

My heart rate suddenly increases as I approach the portal. When I step over the threshold, the door slides shut behind me, and the sound of the bookshelves reshuffling reverberates. A magnificent combination lock. I am standing in a long empty hallway lined with doors. Can I escape, or is it a trap? *You'll know where to go.* No place to go but forward.

The hallway is disorienting. Each door is unique in style, design, and color. After passing perhaps ten doors, I stop at a red door on my left that has the number five emblazoned on it—my lucky number. I open the door. Inside, a trail of red rose petals winds across the floor and up a spiral staircase.

At the top of the stairs, I find a beautiful loft that has five tall arched windows, each with a different circle motif at the top. The floors, hewn of clear wide-plank maple, bring light to the space. Japanese midcentury-modern furnishings add an air of sophistication. I recognize some of the items from our house on President Street. How did they end up here?

"Welcome." Kiyo's voice floats down from somewhere above. I look up—he's smiling at me over the loft railing. "Make yourself at home. I'll be down in a minute."

I remove my shoes, slide my feet into the provided slippers, and hang my jacket on a hook near the entrance. The sitting area emanates warmth and comfort—not the coldness sometimes present with modern style. I take a seat in one of two George Nakashima lounge chairs from my childhood. Kiyo's grandfather told me that Professor Abe, who owned our house on President Street, was a big Nakashima fan.

"I bet this house feels familiar to you," Kiyo says, surprising me from behind. He didn't waste any time coming down. He sits in the other chair.

"Well, I recognize a few things from the house on President Street," I say.

"Aha . . . like the chair you are sitting on? Mr. Abe gave those to my grandfather."

"Is this *your* place?" I ask.

"Yes, it is," Kiyo says. "Surprise!"

"Have you been living *here* the *whole time* that I have been living blocks away?" How could I have never run into him, or he into me? Manhattan neighborhoods are villages.

"No. I travel a lot for business. I didn't know where you were. If I had known you were here, I wouldn't have wasted a minute in getting reacquainted . . . *trust* me."

"Speaking of trust—I received a call from your friend Detective Hillstrom earlier today."

"Yeah, about that, I'm sorry—I didn't know she had reopened the case until after I left your place this morning, and had *no* idea she would call you so quickly. I planned to

talk to you about it first. As for all of *this*"—he gestures—
"it's part of my inheritance."

"That's some inheritance," I say. "When you mentioned
your mother's success, I never imagined anything like this." I
understand now why Nellie is so suspicious.

"It didn't *all* come from my mother. This whole block,
and more at one time, belonged to my grandmother, so
when it came under my stewardship, after my grandfather
died, I decided to do something that would honor her New
York legacy, hence the connection with the New York Public
Library and the creation of the Round About. I'd already
resurrected M. Des Jardins, so it made sense."

"You mean to tell me that you own the Round About?"

"Yes, the magic you've experienced as a child and in the
Round About is part of my legacy too. My grandfather was
one of the greatest Japanese magicians to have ever lived.
He came from a tradition of magic that has largely died out
in Japan," Kiyo says. "I'm one of the last living keepers."

"The rose garden in the empty lot?"

"Yes, that was conjured."

"What a fantastic trick," I say.

"It wasn't a *trick*," Kiyo says. "Our magic exists in spiritual
realms, in nature, in love, and in art—in imagination. It's not
a simple matter of creating illusions or putting on spectacles.
We create, transform, and build worlds to bring harmony and
balance in all that we do—to make the world a better place."

"I don't understand how the Round About, a business,
factors into making 'the world a better place.'"

"The Round About is an experiment in using something
we call 'magic for good.' I'm not enriching myself, nor my
investors. The monies earned from the business go to people
in need. The experiment has been successful, and now I'm
building venues like it elsewhere in the world."

"Wow. Sorry, I wasn't trying to belittle what you do.

Frankly, it's unbelievable—and wonderful. But how did you learn—"

"Through intensive training—first under my grandfather's tutelage, then my mother sent me to Japan to complete my studies, as she did before me. While you were off learning how to create worlds through writing, I was learning to create worlds through ancient magic. It's no different."

"You know," I say. "I returned to that spot in the Elizabeth Street Garden the next morning and found no signs of us having been there. I thought maybe you'd drugged me." I'm not comforted knowing that Kiyo has the ability to conjure realistic worlds and control my experiences the way he obviously has been doing.

Kiyo says, "I thought about deliberately leaving some signs to throw you off—I knew you would go back."

"But how do y—"

"It's hard to explain, and I *can't* explain, except in the most general terms—it isn't allowed. Members of MAGI, the Mystic Arcane Guild of Illuminati, of which I am one, are sworn to secrecy."

"I wish I could do what you do," I say.

"Well, in a manner, you do," Kiyo says. "There is magic in art—words have tremendous transformational power. My grandmother Mihana started her agency to promote magic through writing."

"I have power? You could have fooled me!"

"You have no idea. Everything we create using our imaginations has the power to illuminate, influence, and change the world. Not sure if you remember the box my grandfather and I gave you for your eighth birthday—"

"Of course I do. I still have it. And I have this." I open the top of my blouse to reveal the rose necklace with pearls on either side. "I wear it almost every day. It's one of my most cherished possessions, along with the origami rose you made for me."

"You can't imagine how much that means to me. My grandfather cautioned me as I labored over those objects back then. He said that childhood love is fleeting. I didn't think mine was," he says. "Do you remember what else was in the box?"

"Of course. A beautiful journal and a pen."

"And look at you now! Changing the world with words. Maybe that gift brought to light your destiny—helped you discover your talent for words."

"Hmm," I say. "I'd never connected the two, but that is when I started writing."

"And what color was the origami rose I made you for your sixth birthday?"

"Red—for love."

"Love is transformative."

"Well, I don't believe in fate, but that's a good story, Kiyo!" I say, holding my hand close as I always do. He's looking more like a puppet master with each passing minute. I don't appreciate being his marionette.

"We should talk business before heading over to the Round About. Your idea of including the Gossip Gal and Paloma in our planning is brilliant."

"I'm glad you think so," I say. "One thing you should know: Nellie might be a bit of trouble—she's suspicious about how you gained your wealth. She will try to pry information out of you about that."

"I have nothing to hide," Kiyo says with confidence. "Along with my inherited wealth, I have investors, like every other growing business out there. I am not at liberty to divulge who all of them are, but they're legitimate, or so I believe."

"Okay, that makes me feel better, I guess."

He must sense my reticence, because he follows up with,

"Everything will work out, you'll see." He stands up. "We should get going."

Kiyo takes my hand as I rise to my feet. He pulls me in close. "You know what?"

"What?" I say.

"I love you, Margaux Andrews." He gives me a soft kiss on my forehead.

Kiyo's heart pounds against my chest. "That terrifies me," I say. I have never said *I love you* to him or to any other person for that matter. "The people I love have a way of disappearing."

"I know," he says. "That won't keep me from telling you anyway. One day, you will accept it and will believe me when I tell you that I'm not going anywhere. You can't get rid of me even if you try."

That likely is true. He will be with me forever, no matter what happens.

Still holding my hand, Kiyo leads me down the spiral stairs back to the hallway, where I entered through the red door. We continue down the hallway to the left, passing doors of many different colors, until we come to another red door—this one is on the right and has the sign for infinity on it.

"This is *my* lucky symbol," Kiyo says. "It is a symbol of wholeness, balance, and love." He pushes the door open. "After you," he says with a bow and a wave of his hand.

I step through the door and find myself in the Rose Room at the Algonquin Hotel. The guests are dressed to the nines. It's a costume party from a different era—1920s maybe. People are smoking cigarettes in cigarette holders. The women wear tea-length flapper-style dresses and feathered, sequined headbands. Smoke lingers in the air.

I turn to Kiyo. "I'm underdressed!" I say.

"You look fine." Kiyo waves his hand. The people and the smell of smoke disappear, but the Rose Room remains.

"How'd you do that?" I say.

"You know I can't divulge secrets, but I can tell you it involves using my imagination." He sweeps his hand upward. The walls of the room and the room itself become a rose garden—a rose garden similar to the one in which we dined a couple nights prior. It's real. This one has roses of many colors. When I look up, the Milky Way spills across the sky, as if we're in a planetarium, but we *are* outside—a cool breeze wafts by, carrying the faint scent of roses.

"This is mind-blowing!" I say.

"Follow me. I want to show you 'the back of the house,' so to speak, where the other magic is made, in the kitchen!"

* * *

THE BACK of the house looks like every non-magical restaurant kitchen I've ever seen, which isn't to say that magic *isn't* happening there. Certainly, Kiyo makes it look normal for my sake. I can't trust anything that I see, hear, smell, feel, or touch, now or forever more. I will always wonder whether I am sensing a conjured world or the natural one. Does it matter?

We return to the front of the house, which has been transformed again, back into the Rose Room at the Algonquin for our meeting tonight, but the modern-day version where I first met with M. Des Jardins. Interesting how the terms *back of the house* and *front of the house* get used. Kiyo has used a theatrical metaphor to describe this venue. The Round About is a stage upon which magical dramas get played out in illusory worlds.

Thus far, we're the only guests. Waitstaff scurry around setting tables. We proceed to the hosting podium. Kiyo says, "Margaux, I'd like to introduce you to Alex, our maître d' this evening. In case you're wondering, most of the people you will see in the restaurant tonight are not conjured!"

Alex laughs. "Thank goodness for that. We need paying customers."

"Nice to meet you, Alex."

"Likewise! We're delighted that Kiyo has an interest beyond the realms."

Rat-a-tat-tat-tatta-tat. Alex turns to the patterned knock on the door. He opens it a crack. "Your cards, please," he says.

He lets the guests in. It's Winnie and Theo.

Kiyo says, "Terrific! Happy to see you." He gives both Winnie and Theo big hugs. "I *knew* it would be the two of you."

"That's because you made it so!" Theo says.

Is there *anything* that Kiyo has not made happen?

Alex leads us to the Round Table. There are seven places set—Alex seats me to Kiyo's left, Theo to his right, and Winnie next to Theo.

"Rosie orchestrated tonight—she'll moderate," Kiyo says.

"So you're not the master of the universe?" I ask. Kiyo's control over everything is beginning to disturb me, but I can't let go of my fantasy of him.

"Rosie is skilled at consensus building," Winnie says.

She's smoothing things over, sensing my discomfort. I forgot that she's empathic.

"Somehow that doesn't surprise me," I say, sounding more bitchy than I intend to.

Kiyo raises an eyebrow and meets my eyes with his, questioning. Then he says, "Rosie's outside waiting now— with membership cards for Nellie and your sister."

Rosie and Winnie, no doubt, are also card-carrying members of the MAGI.

"Membership cards?" I say. "You mean *library* cards, don't you?"

"The library cards distinguish paying patrons from

invited guests. Invitations are reserved for members of the Vicious Circle who we always seat at the Round Table. They never pay," says Kiyo. "Rosie is final arbiter on who gets invited and who remains a member."

"I had no idea that's how it worked. I told Nellie to bring her library card." I laugh. The tension between us dissipates as quickly as it ascended. I have fallen back under Kiyo's spell.

"You don't think we admit anybody with a New York Public Library card, do you? This is an exclusive club for *creatives*," he says. We all laugh.

Theo says, "I've never thought of myself that way. I'm more of a hack."

"Well, both you and Winnie share the rare gift of poetry —not hacks."

I say, "Who comes up with the messages on the backs of the cards?"

"That's part of Rosie's magic," Kiyo says. "Rosie comes from a Celtic tradition—she's all about transformation through words."

"I see," I say. "That explains why when I met her that first night at the Mulberry branch, she reminded me of an elf or a fairy, but those aren't real—"

"Don't be so sure," says Winnie.

Kiyo says, "Speaking of which, it looks like our guests of honor have arrived."

Rosie, with her bright-red hair and cheeks, trails Alex with two lanky and attractive well-heeled women in tow. Nellie dons an expression that is difficult to decipher. Paloma looks delighted.

Kiyo and the rest of us stand to greet the newcomers.

Mrs. Harris says, "What sort of *witchcraft* is being practiced here?"

If she knew the half of it.

"I could swear that I walked into the Rose Room at the

Algonquin Hotel and am being seated at the Round Table. What a magnificent reenactment!"

"We welcome you to the reincarnation of the Vicious Circle. You have both earned a seat at the table," Kiyo says.

I hug Paloma. "I'm glad you decided to come." Next, I greet Nellie, extending my hand to shake. She reaches out and grasps my hand with both of hers. "I'm glad you decided to come too. I think you'll be happy you did."

"Thank you for inviting me," she says. "I know that probably wasn't an easy decision."

"Easier than you might think," I say.

We all settle into our seats. A waiter delivers the menus. I smile as I watch the puzzled faces of our guests. The waiter begins with Kiyo. "What do you wish for tonight, Mr. Flores?"

"I'll take the Drink and the Snack."

I say, "I'll have what he's having." Others at the table follow suit. What will arrive tonight?

When drinks and snacks arrive, everybody is quite pleased with what they receive—*what they wanted*. Paloma's snack is a plate of vegetables, each one cut into a beautiful flower shape, served with a yogurt dip. Her drink is a clear pink sparkling beverage with a touch of gin. A sprig of lavender juts out the top. Nellie receives a glass of champagne and a bowl of roasted almonds. I get a glass of Nagasawa Vineyards cabernet and a charcuterie board with pickles to share.

Paloma says, "Now that is Sakura magic! I have so missed you and your grandfather, Kiyo! You always made our world a brighter place."

"Thank you, Paloma. We always missed your family too." Kiyo turns to Nellie. "Ms. Harris—"

"Nellie, please."

"Nellie, I want to introduce you to Ms. Rose White. She holds the title of Top Dog at M. Des Jardins."

"Nice to meet you in person, Nellie," Rosie says.

"Likewise," Nellie says, "I think." She lets out a nervous laugh.

"Oh, I am sincere," Rosie says. "I have long admired you as a journalist."

What on earth is Rosie talking about?

"Your writing is superb, witty, cutting," Rosie says.

I'll give her that.

Nellie's expression indicates that Rosie's attempt at flattery is working. "Well, thank you," she says.

"I imagine you were insulted when we didn't accept you as one of our authors, given your relative literary prowess."

"Well, yes, as a matter of fact—"

"Surely, you understand that we must make difficult decisions every day about which authors we represent, and that many factors influence our decisions. The first thing we consider is whether the work under consideration is a work of fiction. The manuscript you submitted about the Vicious Circle *clearly* failed that test."

Mrs. Harris looks uncomfortable.

Rosie continues, "It's a piece of journalistic writing that relies on conjecture and half-truths, but it is *not* fiction. In contrast, Margaux submitted a semi-autobiographical novel, full of preposterous events that nobody in their right mind could believe to be true, and events *like* them *really* have happened."

Hedging, Mrs. Harris defends herself. "Ms. White, with all due respect, I don't see a difference between conjecture, half-truths, and fiction."

"That may be because it has been your business as the Gossip Gal to sell lies and half-truths about public figures. You are a *wonderful* writer, and you started out as a legitimate investigative journalist. We would like you to return to your better self and have a proposal for you, for which you will be generously remunerated."

"I'm listening."

"As you know, we represent Margaux. Her novel will be published at the end of next year by Big Five Press, and by the time it is published many of the truths that are embodied in it will come to light through the legal system. We want you to be Margaux's secret public-relations agent —a special agent for M. Des Jardins. If you decide to accept this assignment, you will not be allowed to disparage any members of the Circle, nor will they be allowed to disparage you." Rosie looks at me pointedly, and then back at Nellie. "This includes spreading salacious and unfounded gossip about the Sakura or Andrews families, as you are in a position to do."

"And will Margaux destroy evidence she has about me from when she was working in my household?"

"She has turned over everything to me," Rosie says. "And it is safely stored."

She's telling the truth. I turned over all that I had —nothing.

Looking at Kiyo, Mrs. Harris says, "I have always had great admiration for your grandmother and her accomplishments. I never intended to harm her memory or your future. I am a truth-seeker, not a yellow journalist, at heart. I had hoped that you could help me get closer to the truth."

"I would like to know the truth myself and will do my best to help you discover it. For now, we wish to extend an olive branch," Kiyo says. "You will need to prove yourself worthy as a member of the Circle. We can discuss the financial terms in a separate meeting."

"Of course," Mrs. Harris says.

Rosie sets her gaze on Paloma, then Theo. Her face softens. "Paloma and Theo, we invited you both to this discussion because we want to acknowledge that although Margaux wrote *One Elysium Street*, it is clearly your story too —and Kiyo's."

"That's what I have been trying to tell Margaux. She doesn't have the right to tell our stories," Paloma says.

Rosie says, "Did you ever read *Alice in Wonderland* or Winnie-the-Pooh, Paloma? Did you ever think when you read those books that Alice or Christopher Robin were real people? They were characters based on actual people but were not the people portrayed in those books. When people read fiction, a novel like *One Elysium Street*, they will not see you in the characters. They don't know you. They know the characters."

I say, "Paloma, *I love you*. I would never hurt you." Those words, *I love you*, startle me.

Kiyo smiles. Another success in his world-building, I suppose.

Paloma says, "I love you too. But I'm also afraid, embarrassed that people will see me as pathetic."

"You are one of the most kind-hearted people I know, Paloma," Kiyo says.

"I agree," says Theo.

"Paloma, I'm sorry we didn't tell you about everything that happened on President Street. We wanted to, but Mother and Mr. Sakura wanted us to keep it secret. They were afraid of what might happen. Those were scary times. Mother kept a lot of secrets to protect all of us."

"Those were *lonely* times for me," Paloma says. "Not just because of your secrets. I had a few secrets—"

Rosie says, "You are one of us now, Paloma. As the inspiration of a book character, we make you an honorary member of the circle."

"Paloma is *way more* than inspiration for a character; she is a wonderful writer and editor too," I say. "Very well trained at Yale."

"Funny you should mention that," Rosie says. "I was about to ask Paloma if she would be interested in joining M. Des Jardins as a special editorial agent." She looks at

Paloma. "You would work for me. Your job would be to guide young authors in developing their manuscripts for the market."

"Oh my," says Paloma. "I need to think about it, but—"

"Of course you do," says Rosie. "I will be in touch with you later."

The next pins are about to drop.

Kiyo clears his throat. "Glad that all went so smoothly. Now for something less pleasant. It came to light this morning that the Anna Gonzales case is being reopened. The Peakview Police Department has requested that Margaux, Theo, your mother, and I come in for questioning. As a member of our circle, Paloma, we would like you to join us, to tell your side of the story."

Paloma says, "When?"

"Tomorrow. We'll fly to Peakview on my private jet," says Kiyo. "I've made arrangements for legal counsel to be present as well, in case we end up needing it."

"I don't know," Paloma says. "I'll need to talk to my husband first."

"Totally understandable. Let us know what you decide. Either way, we all need to be prepared—by the weekend, the newspapers will be filled with speculation about what happened to Anna Gonzales, and our families will likely be mentioned in connection with her disappearance. Not sure if you are aware, but your mother and my grandfather provided the police with information many years ago in the form of an anonymous letter, evidence that went missing. Your mother has agreed to tell the police what she knows, as have Theo and Margaux. She also agreed to talk to them about the death of Roz Peoples so that they might bring that chapter to a close as well."

Kiyo turns to Winnie. "Winnie, Rosie needs to stay in New York to attend to some library matters, but we would like you to accompany Ms. Harris, as her assistant, if you wouldn't mind. I'm sure she will want to have some help."

Winnie says, "Thank you, Kiyo. Are you sure you won't miss me too much, Rosie?"

"Oh, I'll miss you, but you'll be back in two shakes of a lamb's tail."

Mrs. Harris looks genuinely happy. As people get up and gather to leave she approaches me. "Margaux, I am truly sorry about how things turned out—I want you to know how much the kids miss you. Also, things are not how they appear with my brother-in-law, but that's a story for another day."

"Yeah, I've come to understand that things are seldom what they seem—believe me," I say. "Good night, Mrs. Harris. I'll see you tomorrow."

FULL CIRCLE
THURSDAY MORNING

KIYO'S REVELATIONS have unsettled me. I've lived under the charms of the Sakuras my whole life and always thought they were magical, but in the way that childhood is, not for *real*. I don't know how fully I can embrace an imagined world—a sad statement coming from a want-to-be novelist.

At ten in the morning, Kiyo's car is outside waiting. The driver, who looks familiar for no reason I can think of, opens the door. I slide in. Kiyo is there.

"Good morning," Kiyo says. "I hope you got some good rest last night."

"Well, no, not really," I say. Pre-trip nerves.

"Me either. My aching heart plagued me."

"Don't be so dramatic," I say.

"No, seriously, I'd hoped you would stay the night. My feelings were hurt that you didn't."

"Don't worry. I needed some time to myself with everything going on. So much has happened so quickly. It's scarcely been a week since you reappeared in my life. And besides, I had to pack," I say. I can't share my reservations about our long-term prospects as a couple.

"That must have taken you all night," Kiyo says,

gesturing toward my only luggage, a small travel bag with two changes of clothes in it. We plan to spend two nights in Denver and return on Saturday.

"You don't know how many changes of clothes I had to go through to arrive at the two outfits I packed!"

"Well, I had a wonderful time last night. Every minute I've spent with you has been a pleasure. I'm grateful that you're such an independent spirit. I would expect no less."

It takes about forty minutes to get to Teterboro, the airport where Kiyo keeps his plane. I've never flown on a private plane until today, let alone a private *jet*. We pull up outside an aircraft hangar. A sign over the opening says "Hanami Enterprises." I've seen that name before. Where?

"Thank you, Joe," Kiyo says to the driver. "See you on Saturday!"

"Safe travels, Mr. Flores." Joe exits the car and hurries to open my door.

"Thank you, sir," I say.

"Joe. Please call me Joe," he says. "Have a safe trip, Ms. Andrews."

"You have to call me Margaux if you want me to call you Joe," I say. Is *he* the man in black? Maybe. Why would he have been following me?

Joe laughs. "See you Saturday, Margaux."

The plane sits out on the tarmac. Kiyo leads the way. It's sleek and modern, white with blue striping. We board, ducking through the entrance.

Are we flying on a conjured plane, or is it real? It better be real.

"Good morning, Mr. Flores, Ms. Andrews," a flight attendant says. "I believe all six of the passengers are here now."

"Perfect," Kiyo says.

The main cabin of the plane looks more like a living room than a passenger compartment. Theo and Winnie sit on a modern curved sectional on the starboard side while Paloma and Nellie sit in individual swivel seats toward the tail. James Bond would be envious of this set up. The two seats left open in the main cabin are on the port side: a small curved love seat facing the larger curved sectional. If all the pieces were placed together, they would form a circle. Of course Kiyo *would* have a love seat on his plane. How many of his lovers have sat here?

The takeoff is blissfully uneventful. When it's safe enough to move around the cabin, the attendant offers green tea and coffee. "Please help yourself to the buffet." She gestures to a round table that descends from the ceiling. At the same time, the seating moves inward. Now we are seated at the round table. The center of the table is a giant lazy Susan, the edge lined with plates, each filled with a different selection of small tastes. Every place setting includes a small white plate, Western utensils, and a set of chopsticks.

"I thought you might enjoy a sampling of foods from my childhood—Japanese and Portuguese," he says. "We'll eat a larger meal later today, but I wasn't sure how many of you would have already eaten breakfast."

Nellie says, "Rolled omelet! That's one of my favorites."

I spin the lazy Susan to the charcuterie section. "Mmm . . . what kind of cheese is this?" I point to a wedge of hard cheese.

"That's a wonderful cheese from the island of São Jorge, where my paternal grandfather came from," Kiyo says. "The breads are also made from traditional recipes from there."

I can't get enough of the fried linguiça with the cheese. As usual, there is something for everybody. Winnie and Theo gravitate to the Japanese foods—rice balls, fried tofu, and assorted fermented vegetables. Paloma opts for a couple of the salad options.

"So, how is everybody feeling about what lies ahead?" Kiyo asks.

"Truthfully?" I say. "I'm nervous as hell. How do you know we aren't walking into a trap?"

"Well, I don't. But I believe that if we don't do this now, the four of us will never be at peace with that part of our past."

"I wholeheartedly agree," Theo says. "I need to know whether they found Anna in our collapsed fort up by the apartments. I still have nightmares about that."

"And," I say, "it would be good to know if there might have been other bad actors involved—Bully-Boy, for example."

"Yeah," Kiyo says. "It's too bad we were too ashamed to talk about what he made us do."

Paloma says, "I feel bad that you guys didn't think you could have told me about it. I might have been able to help. You know, I was r—" Paloma stops, averting her eyes. "I was molested too."

A silence falls over the table. I can tell that Nellie is breathing in every word.

"Really?" I say. "By whom?"

Paloma gazes at her salad.

"It's okay, you don't need to tell us," I say.

"I am going to tell the police about it, in case it will help them resolve anything," she says. "I've never told a soul. Talk about feeling ashamed—the person who did it said I was asking for it, and I believed him. I trusted him."

"God!" I say. "I'm sorry." Paloma suddenly shines in a whole new light—her battles with depression over the years make a lot more sense.

"That is beyond awful," Kiyo says.

We fall into silence again.

"This is not at all what I was expecting," Nellie says. "I

want to assure all of you that I will handle your stories with the utmost care if and when the time comes."

She is not the Mrs. Harris I had come to know. Something has changed in her. The hard edge is gone; she is warmer. I respected her before, but now I like her. She must have a compelling story of *her* own to tell.

* * *

THREE SEPARATE CARS are waiting on the tarmac at the hangar. Kiyo and I will go in one car, Winnie and Theo in another, and Paloma and Nellie in the third. Kiyo and I are going to stay in his loft in downtown Denver. Winnie and Theo are driving up to Boulder to stay at his house. Paloma and Nellie will stay at the Oxford Hotel near Kiyo's.

I get into our car. Kiyo is still talking to the others about the plans for the day.

As I wait, I notice that this hangar is identical to the one we departed from, donning the same brand above the opening—Hanami Enterprises.

When Kiyo gets into the car, I say, "Kiyo, what is Hanami Enterprises? I've seen it someplace else before."

He flushes. "Oh, it's the name of the holding company I own for my various businesses, Round About being one of them. You may have seen it there in the back of the house."

Yes, that is where I saw it.

His clipped response indicates a reticence to tell me more, and yet I ask, "Does it have any particular meaning?"

"Yeah! It relates to the name Sakura, which means cherry blossom. *Hanami* is a celebration of cherry blossoms."

"That's beautiful," I say.

"I like flowers." He smiles. "It's in my name—Flores and Sakura." Then he says, "Excuse me for a moment. I need to make a quick call."

"Of course," I say.

Kiyo picks up the handset for the phone located in the seatback in front of him and dials a number. In this moment, Kiyo is a stranger, a wealthy businessman who flies around the world attending to a mysterious magical empire of which I know nothing.

"Hello?" I can barely make out a woman's voice on the other end of the line.

"Hi, Kiyo here. We've all arrived safely. And you, have you been in to speak to Detective Hillstrom yet?"

I strain to hear the voice on the other end, but can't.

"I see . . . Interesting," Kiyo says. "And the attorney? Was she there?" Kiyo gazes out the window as he listens. "Good. Okay, we'll see you for dinner tonight at seven. A car will pick you up."

When Kiyo hangs up, I ask, "Who was that?"

He smiles. "It's a surprise."

"You have an endless supply of them."

HOMECOMING

THURSDAY AFTERNOON

ON THE WAY INTO DENVER, Kiyo says, "I have to be at the police station for my interview by two. I'll stop at the loft long enough to show you around."

"Oh, okay. I figured they'd want to talk to us separately, but—"

"Yes, and fortunately, we haven't rehearsed anything, so our stories will reflect the past as we each recall it."

"Yeah, and we all have slightly different memories."

"That's the way it should be," Kiyo says. "Theo, you, your mother, and Paloma all have your interviews tomorrow, at nine, ten, two, and four respectively."

He continues, "Anyway, I'll call you at the loft if I run into any problems. I doubt I will, but in case. Otherwise, I shouldn't be gone terribly long—no later than five. I don't have that much to tell."

The loft is not far from Larimer Square, an area of town that used to be considered the red-light district. The last time I visited Denver, this area was full of vagrants, considered a dodgy part of town. In recent years it's undergone a transformation. Now it is full of beautifully renovated Dutch brickwork buildings.

When the car stops in front of his building on Wazee Street, we both get out. The building, unassuming, doesn't have a street number or any other identifying feature. Kiyo presses a code into the entrance keypad, and the door buzzes. We take an elevator to the top floor and emerge into an open loft. It's large, but not excessively so. To the right is a well-equipped modern kitchen and to our left, a spacious living area. Above the living area is what I assume is an open loft bedroom.

Directly in front of the elevator, a solid wall of windows rises from floor to ceiling. The entire Front Range looms before us. I make out Pikes Peak to the south, Mount Evans just to the southwest, and Longs Peak to the north in one sweep of the horizon. The sun hangs pretty far south this time of year, and its rays slant through the window, creating a warm spot in the sitting area.

"What a beautiful sight," I say.

"Isn't it? Had you forgotten?"

"No, but I didn't remember the awe of it."

"This is home," he says.

The space is simply furnished, too empty for my tastes. "I love it," I say. There is nothing personal here. It doesn't have a lived-in feeling.

As if he's heard my thoughts, he says, "I don't spend much time here. I'd like to, though." His expression is wistful. "Are you going to be okay by yourself?" he says. "I realize that I assumed you would want to stay with me. We can make other arrangements if you like."

He's reading my mind again. "Are you kidding? I would have been crushed if you felt you needed to ask."

"Make yourself comfortable. Eat, sleep, drink, whatever your heart desires."

"Thank you," I say. I turn to him, wrap my arms around his waist, and we kiss—a short see-you-later kiss.

Kiyo pulls back. "I don't want to alarm you, but if

someone should happen to ring my buzzer and it isn't one of us, it would be best not to let them up."

"That sounds scary," I say.

"Well, I doubt it will happen—I'm not expecting anybody—but I recently received some threats. I can't give you any details . . ."

"Did it have something to do with those two men in suits —your 'business associates' who pulled you aside at the Round About?"

"You don't miss a lot, do you?" Kiyo's expression is serious.

"Well?"

"It did. I *don't* think we need to worry; I have security people all over the place."

"Ah, okay . . . the man in the black suit who I've seen . . . Joe?"

"Yes. I didn't want you to be afraid, but I can see that might have backfired."

"I would like to know more—"

"I'm sorry, I can't say anything more. You have to trust me."

"That's a tall order at this point, now that I know you've been having me watched. I am not entirely sure—"

"Technically, I've been trying to *guard* you, not *watch* you, but your point is well taken. I'm not a stalker. I'm sorry that I couldn't be more transparent about my, and now *our*, situation. I promise to tell you more soon, but right now I need to go to the police station."

"Okay," I say.

"I'll see you soon. And remember, no matter what happens, I love you."

"You know how I feel," I say. Definitely not committing.

"Maybe?" he says. "You're pretty evasive on that matter, but I'm comfortable with that. It's been a brief reunion, and

I can't expect you to feel as I do." He walks onto the open elevator.

After Kiyo leaves, I stretch out catlike on a chaise longue that sits in the slant of sun. I close my eyes. Wow. Kiyo is full of surprises. Nellie's warning reverberates—*maybe you should step carefully in your dealings with that family—particularly Kiyo.* Is it possible that Mr. Sakura was not the man I remember? Was he some sort of godfather? A criminal mastermind? Is Kiyo? Or, alternatively, is he a wizard embroiled in battle with evil forces? My thoughts wander through the yard and house on President Street. How accurate are my memories? I know the map of the house and the yard I created in my novel, but how well do my recollections from childhood match up to any sort of reality? After all, I did have an invisible friend— her name *really was* Stella, like in the novel. I figured since she was make-believe to begin with, I didn't need to think up a new name for her. I was a kid with an active imagination. Now I'm an adult with an active imagination.

Was the thing that happened in the field as scary as I remember? Did that guy, Bud—Bully-Boy, whose real name I know now because Theo told me—*really* have a switch-blade? Do I remember lying skin-on-skin with Kiyo when I was six? Did our mother allow us to play out by the train tracks? Where was she when we were doing that? Or how about the times Theo crossed over the outside railing above the highway? Knowing what I know now, I certainly would not have allowed my children the same freedoms we had. What about the Butcher Lady—and after that, the Hatchet Lady? Fiction and fact all meld together. I can't keep all of the characters straight anymore.

The sound of the door buzzer raises me from my reverie. My heart pounds. I get up and walk to the intercom next to the elevator. "Hello?" I say. Nothing. "Hello?" I say again.

"Margaux?" It's Nellie Harris.

I breathe a sigh of relief. "Hi, give me a second. If I can figure out how, I will buzz you up—top floor." I push a green button on the panel. I sure hope she hasn't been intercepted by one of the bad guys, whoever they are.

"Worked," she says.

The elevator chunks and churns as it makes its way up. The doors open.

To my relief it is Nellie, and she is by herself. "Hi, I hope I haven't interrupted anything."

"No," I say, "I was resting, enjoying some Colorado gold." I gesture toward the now fading spot of sunshine.

"Marvelous light. You must hate New York."

"No, I quite like it. It feels real—although not so much this past week, or at this moment."

"Tell me about it. That's what I came to talk to you about. I knew Kiyo was having his interview this afternoon and that you'd likely be alone. I owe you an explanation about the thing with my brother-in-law."

"Everybody has secrets," I say. "You don't owe me an explanation."

"I *want* to tell you. I want someone to know. Someone I can trust."

"That's definitely me. I've spent a lifetime keeping my own and other people's secrets."

"You're a fiction writer—secrets are a tool of the trade." She's smiling and warm—not a side of her that I'm familiar with. Can I trust her?

"Okay, I'm listening."

"My husband and I have been divorced for five years."

"Wow, that's a revelation I hadn't expected," I say.

"We divorced when the twins were two. The reason we married was because I had careless sex with a handsome man in the back room at a party and got pregnant. We never loved each other. God, I could *never* love a Wall Street man!" She laughs.

"Why does he live with you if you're divorced and you don't love him?"

"Well, he wanted to be there for the kids, but he wasn't, never has been. The man is a dog, fucking every bitch in sight, which is why we divorced in the first place. I didn't love him, but I didn't want that."

"Awful."

"That isn't the worst of it. Before he moved out, he would come home and tell me all about his conquests in graphic detail. One day it'll catch up with him. I wouldn't be surprised to learn he has caught the clap or some other sexually transmitted disease. Anyway, Chad took an interest in his role as an uncle and spent weekends hanging out with me and the kids. And, well, we fell in love. When Jake found out, he was furious—as if he had the right."

"That's pretty nutty," I say.

"The day you saw us at Caffè Reggio together—I *did* see you there, by the way—Jake had sent me legal papers suing for sole custody of the twins."

"Oh, I'm so sorry. I remember the envelope you handed Chad."

"So you weren't wrong about me. I *was* gaslighting the kids about everything. They didn't know that their father and I were divorced. They know now. If you hadn't threatened me, everything would have blown up in the news soon enough. Nothing more fun than reading gossip about the Gossip Gal. Speaking of which, I resigned from the *Post* yesterday."

"Congratulations?"

"And you know the book I wrote about the Vicious Circle . . . I was testing, looking for an *in* with Kiyo, not seeking M. Des Jardins's representation. I never planned on publishing anything. But that said—"

"You *do* know that I don't have any proof, don't you?"

"I figured you were bluffing, but like I said, it didn't matter. And now you have indirectly given me a second chance at doing meaningful journalism again. I want to thank you for that."

"Thank Kiyo, not me. I never would have offered the gig to you in a million years."

"Can't say I blame you."

"And I owe you a thank-you too—" Before I finish thanking her for her warning about Kiyo the elevator whirs into motion—it must be him now, or at least I hope so. "Sounds like he's home. I hope everything went okay."

"Me too," Nellie says.

The elevator door opens. Kiyo stands there smiling, holding a bouquet of red roses.

"You are a sweet man," Nellie says. "Well, I have done what I came to do. I'm going back to the Oxford to get ready for our dinner tonight."

She brushes past Kiyo into the elevator and disappears.

"I take it by your expression that things went okay?" I say to Kiyo.

"Yes, they did. Detective Hillstrom requested that I not say anything about my interview until we've all been through the process. After that, we're free to discuss our involvement as we like."

"Makes sense," I say.

* * *

KIYO MADE a reservation at a place within walking distance of the loft, on the corner of Market and Sixteenth Street. From the outside, Kabuki Lounge looks like a place that might have strippers. An animated sign of a geisha juts out from the building corner above the entryway. She shuffles her feet, hands in prayer position in front of her chest, and her head wobbles from side to side—a stereotypical image of Japanese women from the 1950s.

"I know," Kiyo says as we approach. "But it isn't anything like you are imagining."

He opens the door, and we walk in. It's almost as if we've stepped into the Round About. A woman dressed in geisha attire greets us in Japanese. She clearly knows Kiyo.

"Nice to see you, Kiyo," she says in English. "Please, your table is ready."

Not sure why, but the absence of an accent surprises me. Clearly she's American.

We remove our footwear and step up a level. The floors are covered in tatami matting. I like the way it feels underfoot. We follow the woman to a separate raised dining platform. The table is low and square, with a hollow beneath it for the comfort of legs and feet—two place settings on each side. Who is the eighth seat for? She guides Kiyo and me to the furthest seats with an outward-facing view.

After we are seated, Kiyo says, "Margaux, I want you to meet a dear friend of my mother's—Momoko Fujita. She owns this restaurant. My mother and she were friends since the war; they met at Amache when they were children."

"It's a pleasure to meet you," Momoko says. "I should say, to meet you again. You probably don't remember me, but I was at your house once on President Street. Kiyo's grandfather was showing me the Garden of the Gods—you were blessed to have such a magical environment to grow up in."

"Yes, I agree about being blessed, but I'm afraid I don't remember you. I'm sorry—"

"No worries. I wouldn't expect you to."

"You're right that it was magical, and this place feels like it might be too."

Kiyo says, "It is, which is one of the reasons I wanted you to see it." He goes on, "As a boy, I was fascinated by the transformation of this restaurant—during the day, it serves the needs of Western business people, mostly men, with Western cultural seating and food sensibilities, and at night, it becomes a beautiful and traditional Japanese venue that includes geisha performances, with traditional Japanese seating. It's the inspiration for the Round About—to be what people want it to be."

"You know how much your saying that delights me," Momoko says, then turns to me. "And, Margaux, I hope you enjoy your experience tonight."

"How could I not?" I say.

"Thank you, Momoko," Kiyo says.

She bows slightly and backs down the step.

"Wow, who knew there was a piece of Japan right here in downtown Denver?"

"A lot of Japanese people?" Kiyo laughs. "This area once was important for the Japanese community, since the turn of the century until recent years. Maybe you've heard of Sakura Square, where the there is a temple?

"Of course! I never made a connection to your family. How wonderful."

Kiyo has caught sight of something. He looks expectantly across the table.

Momoko returns with the rest of our party. My mother walks alongside a woman I don't immediately recognize—Jenny Peoples! She is the surprise guest.

Kiyo and I stand to greet the new arrivals. Theo and Winnie sit to our left, and Jenny and my mother to our right, with Jenny closest to me. Paloma sits across from me and Nellie opposite Kiyo. I couldn't have imagined a better homecoming if I'd tried. I hug Jenny and grab my mother's hand.

"Mother, I want to introduce you to Winnie and Nellie." My mother wears a grin like I haven't seen in a long time.

"Delighted to meet you both, and so happy to see you again, Kiyo. It's been far too long."

"Oh, Jenny, I didn't think I would ever see you again!" I say.

"Yeah, me either," she says. She looks older than I do, like a person who's lived a hard life.

"Well, these are not the circumstances we would wish for to bring us together again, but I'm happy to see you, all the same," I say.

"You have no idea how much I've missed you over all the years. You're the only best friend I ever had, and until Kiyo's investigator showed up, I didn't know where you were." Jenny looks at Winnie. "Thank you for finding me."

"Winnie? You're the one who tracked Jenny down?"

"Yes, I confess."

"Kiyo's investigator?" I look at Kiyo.

"Winnie is indispensable." He smiles. "She takes it upon herself to do what is most needed."

"I see."

I'm dying to know what happened to Jenny, but I don't pry. Our homecoming dinner focuses mostly on lighter topics.

"It's a wonder to see all of you kids together and all grown up," my mother says. She looks at Kiyo. "Kiyo, I've followed your story from afar. I read in the paper about your grandfather's passing," she says. "I was so sorry to learn that. He was wonderful to our family—we could not have survived those years without his help."

"Thank you, Mrs. Andrews—"

"Please call me Cami," she says. "Mrs. Andrews was my mother-in-law! I kept the name to have the same last name as my children."

"It's strange to call you by your first name, but I'll try. Anyway, as I began to say, your family was important to my grandfather and me at that time too. My mother was away

328

most of the time, and I needed a loving family. Between you and my grandfather, I certainly had that." Kiyo clasps my hand under the table. "The implosion that happened in our lives when they found Anna and the sale of Mr. Abe's house added to an already stressful year marked with other significant losses."

Kiyo avoids mentioning Roz's death or the sudden disappearance of Ned and Jenny, but I can see from Jenny's pained expression that it registers. I reach over and squeeze her hand.

She sniffles. "I didn't have any idea that my mother had died the day we left."

My mother puts her arm around Jenny. "We don't fully know what happened, but it looks like your dad took you out of school *before* your mother's accident."

"He told me so many terrible things about my mother and about you. He said she didn't love me—"

"That simply is not true. You were the light of her life. Your father was the darkness. You have to believe me."

"I do. Many things have begun to make sense now that I didn't understand before. I'm not sure I'll ever recover."

My mother says, "None of us completely recovers from the trauma of living, but we do learn from it. If we don't allow ourselves to fall into the mindset of being victims, we can use our experiences to become better people and to do good things in the world."

"We're all here for you, Jenny," Kiyo says. "No matter what comes out of the current investigation."

"Thank you," Jenny says. "Thank you for finding me and for helping me develop the strength to leave."

SPILLING BEANS
FRIDAY

THE NEXT MORNING I get up and prepare for the day. I didn't sleep well, and am moving more slowly than usual. Maybe it's the altitude. Maybe all of the uncertainty. I had a massive headache and was unable to shut down my brain.

The phone rings downstairs. Kiyo answers. After a brief conversation, he calls up to me, "The car is waiting for you."

I go downstairs, and Kiyo hands me a cup of coffee in a paper cup with a lid. "You can take that in the car," he says. "You have to get going or you'll be late."

I give him a kiss and step into the elevator. I'm still upset that he didn't tell me about the threats, that I have no clue about what is going on. Part of me has shut him out of the long-term romantic picture, but the other part can't stop thinking about him. For now, I need to focus on the immediate.

Outside, I see the driver standing in wait. "Good morning, Ms. Andrews," he says.

"Thanks. Good morning to you too," I say, and slide into the back seat. My security guard for the day, I'm guessing. I close my eyes as we pull away from the curb. I'd forgotten how blindingly bright the Colorado sun is. My headache threatens to return.

Traffic is light, and it takes about twenty-five minutes to get to the Peakview police station. The driver rushes to open my door. "I'll be right here when you are finished, Ms. Andrews," he says.

"See you soon, I hope." I pull open the glass door and approach the desk under the check-in sign, which is staffed by a female officer in uniform. "Hi, I'm Margaux Andrews, checking in for an interview with Detective Hillstrom."

"Thank you," the woman says. "Please have a seat until we call your name."

I sit in a molded plastic seat against the wall. Theo emerges from a door on the opposite side of the room. He looks fine. He's not in handcuffs at least. When he finally sees me, I stand up. Without a word, we hug like never before, communicating everything I need to know. He's going to be okay. I'm going to be okay. "See you in a bit, Sis," he says. And with that, he goes out.

"Ms. Margaux Andrews, please proceed to conference room number five." Lucky number five. At least they didn't call it an *interrogation* room.

I follow the sign for the conference rooms until I reach the room where Theo came out. The door is already open. Inside are two women dressed in street clothes. When they see me, they both stand.

"Hello, Ms. Andrews, I am Detective Hillstrom." We shake hands. "We spoke on the phone a couple of days ago. And this is Ms. Fisk, the attorney that Mr. Flores has hired to attend these interviews."

"Nice to meet you, Ms. Andrews," Ms. Fisk says. "Mr. Flores speaks highly of you."

"Nice to meet you too," I say. Kiyo has told me nothing about her, but there are many things he hasn't talked to me about.

"Based on what we've learned so far, I don't believe you'll be needing any representation, so Ms. Fisk's presence is precautionary. If anything comes up, Ms. Fisk can intervene on your behalf," says Detective Hillstrom. "Is that okay with you?"

"Yes, thank you."

"Please have a seat," Detective Hillstrom says. "Would you like a cup of coffee or some water?"

"No, I'm fine, thank you." Sweat trickles down my sides. "Is it okay with you if I record this conversation?"

"Yes, that's okay," I say.

Detective Hillstrom presses a button on the tape deck. She says, "Today is Friday, November first, nineteen eighty-five. This is an interview with Ms. Margaux Andrews concerning case numbers 86060165 and 86052068."

Ms. Fisk says, "A formality—those are the case IDs for the Anna Gonzalez and Roz Peoples cases."

"I figured," I say. "Thanks."

Detective Hillstrom says, "First, let me thank you for coming in. I realize your participation in this interview is completely voluntary. If at any time you wish to take a break or stop altogether, say the word."

"Okay," I say.

"Let's begin by going back to May twenty-ninth, nineteen sixty-five. Do you remember anything about that day?"

"No, not particularly. It was the day before my fifth birthday, but there was nothing special about it."

"How about the next day?"

"Yes, I remember the next day as if it were yesterday," I say. "That was the day of my first *real* birthday party, when the four of us kids got to invite friends. I invited a friend; my sister, Paloma invited a friend; one of my older brothers, Wendell, invited a friend; and Anna was the friend that Theo invited. He had a crush on her. They were in the same class at school. When she didn't show up, he was upset.

Then Paloma, Wendell, and their friends ditched me to go to the playground. That's when they found out that Anna was missing."

"And how did Theo react to the news?"

"He cried and cried, that's how. How do you think an almost seven-year-old would react? He was distraught for a long time. He's still distraught if you ask me."

"And do you have any ideas about why he would have been so distraught?"

"He was in love with her. I know it sounds crazy, but he recently told me that he has always believed that he lost his one and only that day."

"Did he ever tell you anything about the day before?"

"Not that I remember, I'm sorry."

"That's okay. You were young," Detective Hillstrom says. "Did Theo ever tell you anything about an underground fort he built?"

"Yes," I say. "He told Kiyo Flores, Jenny Peoples, and me that he and some other boys from the apartment complex had dug a fort by the tracks."

"When did he tell you that?"

"Uh . . . I was finishing first grade so late spring of 1967 —we were building a new fort, and he wanted to make sure we did a better job than he and the kids had done on their first fort. He said the first one collapsed shortly after they built it."

"Do you know the precise location of the fort that collapsed?"

"No, I'm sorry. I don't have that information, but I'm sure Theo could show you where it was."

"Did he mention any names of other kids who helped build the fort?"

"No. He said kids from The Apartments."

"Okay, that's all of the questions I have about the original fort. Tell me about the fort you were building when Theo told you about the old fort."

I tell them about how Jenny and I came upon Kiyo and Theo, and the part where Jenny's dad helped us make the fort safe.

"What happened to that fort?"

"We tore it down."

"What made you decide to tear it down?"

"Well, there was this guy Theo knew from living at The Apartments. His name was Bud something—he was just Bully-Boy to me. I didn't know him, but of him. He came into our fort and pulled what I now know was a switchblade knife on us. I'd never seen a knife like that. It was scary."

"And then what happened?"

I pause. "Well, it's been a long time, and I was six, so I don't remember it all perfectly."

"That's fine. Do your best."

"He tried to get me to suck on his penis." It was the first time I had ever heard the expression *blow job*. His ugly voice reverberates in my head.

"Did you do what he asked?"

"I started to, but then he decided we should all get undressed instead. He used coarse language the whole time —words I didn't understand."

"Like what?"

"He told Theo 'fuck your sister in the ass,' but we had no idea what he was talking about. Then Kiyo said to Theo, 'Here let me show you, Theo.' Kiyo whispered in my ear as he climbed on top of me 'Don't worry, you can trust me,' or something like that. I don't remember his exact words, but I understood that he was trying to protect me. I knew he would never hurt me. Bud made Theo get on top of Jenny and told him to stick his 'dick into her cunt,' and when he didn't understand the instructions Bud said, 'Stick your wiener into her slit, you faggot mama's boy.' Then he told us to keep doing what we were doing for the next ten minutes and threatened to kill us and our families if we ever told a soul. When he left, we felt lucky to be alive and unharmed. We destroyed the fort immediately."

"That must have been terrifying," Detective Hillstrom says.

"It was."

"And did you tell any adults what happened?"

"Yes, after the police discovered Anna's body—around my eighth birthday. Kiyo and I told my mother and Mr. Sakura, but we didn't tell them the whole story. We told them about Theo's involvement in building the collapsed fort and about Bud threatening us with a knife, but we didn't tell them all of the detailed sexual stuff. I think we felt ashamed or embarrassed. I don't know . . ."

"And then what happened?"

"Nothing. I learned years later from my mother about the tips she and Mr. Sakura provided to the police. But I also knew they weren't the *whole* story."

"And you mentioned Ned Peoples. Did you know him well?"

"No," I say. "I was jealous of Jenny that she had a dad, though. He played ball with her and held her in his lap, gave her kisses. Paloma, my sister, knew him a lot better than I did because Mr. Peoples and she had an interest in dogs in common. Paloma spent a lot of time over at the Peoples' house babysitting and working with Mr. Peoples on training her dog, Leadbelly."

"Did she ever say anything to you about him?"

"Not really. Once she told me that he wasn't always nice to his dog, which seemed weird, but I wasn't always nice to our dog either, so it wasn't a big deal."

"And Mrs. Peoples. Did you know her well?"

"Yes, she and my mother were close friends, and she

drove us kids a lot of places—vacation Bible camp, the pool, and Sunday school."

"Were your mother and Mrs. Peoples *more* than close friends?"

"What do you mean?"

"I mean did they have a romantic relationship?"

I had hoped not to have to answer this question. I say, "Not that I was aware. I didn't know anything about sex or adult relationships. I now understand that they were more than friends, because I have spoken with my mother about it, but it was mostly a flirtation. My mother said that Roz didn't want more than that, because she was terrified of what would happen if Ned found out. He was an abuser, like my own father had been. He threatened to kill her if he ever found out she was cheating."

"You said *mostly* flirtatious?"

"Well, one time, I walked in on them when they were locked in a passionate kiss."

"And what did you do?"

"I snuck away as quietly as I could!"

"Did you ever tell anybody?"

"No. You are the first people I've ever told. I'm *good* at keeping secrets, and honestly, I didn't think it was wrong for them to kiss; it was just a grown-up thing."

* * *

BACK AT THE LOFT, Kiyo and I are decompressing.

"Kiyo, about the day in the fort. We never spoke of it, and I don't know if my memories are real anymore. Do you mind if I ask you a question that has bothered me?"

"Of course not. Ask away. We are on a truth-telling mission here."

"Why did you volunteer to take over for Theo when Bud was trying to get him to, quote, 'fuck me in the ass'?"

"Well," Kiyo says, "I wanted to protect *both* of you. I knew that brothers and sisters were not supposed to have sex."

"But how did *you* know?"

"I'm not sure how, but I knew that incest was wrong. My mother talked to me about a lot of adult topics."

"Theo and I didn't know anything," I say. "Did we have sex? I never thought we did, but it occurred to me that I could be in denial."

Kiyo laughs. "No, we pretended. Theo and I were so terrified we couldn't have mustered an erection if we had wanted to . . . Other than smooshing our groins together, we didn't do anything."

"That's what I remember too, but I've always been worried that I remember what I want to."

"Theo and I've talked, and believe me, we remember! It was humiliating, which was part of the guy's objective."

"I'm relieved to know that, not that it was humiliating for you guys, but that my memory of it is accurate. I've always felt sullied by that whole event."

"I'm sorry, but rest assured, your first time was *not* with me."

"Thank God!" I say. "Actually, that's too bad. And how would you know you weren't my first?"

HARMONY

FRIDAY NIGHT

Kiyo and I spend the rest of the day in the loft. I'm tired and go to lie down. Kiyo sneaks up the metal spiral stairs, which clang in spite of his efforts to be quiet. When he sees that I'm still awake, he says, "Mind if I join you?"

"Of course not."

"I wasn't sure. You've been a little cool toward me the last couple of days."

He strips off his clothes, slides in under the duvet, and snuggles up against me. I have on a T-shirt and underpants. His warm body feels comforting.

"I feel like you're controlling everything too much," I say, "like you are some all-powerful puppet master. I don't appreciate being controlled."

"Yikes," he says. "That's not my intention—to control everything—I just want to make everything perfect for you, for us . . . I guess that *is* controlling."

"I'm not your project—you can't conjure everything. I need time to process my feelings, and to feel like you aren't hiding things about yourself from me."

"I'll tell you everything about myself soon, I promise. My life has some abnormal complexities in it. Please, stay with me long enough to work through them." His brown eyes stare intently into mine. How can I resist?

"Will you tell me the truth about your scar?"

"I did already. I got it in a sword fight."

"Where? When? With whom? You're leaving out some critical details."

"In time, you will know the whole story. You have to trust me."

"I'm trying to," I say.

He runs his hand down my side and says, "I think you might be overdressed for the occasion." He lifts my shirt and I sit up to help him pull it off. I slip off my underpants. "Have I mentioned that I love you?" he says.

"I love you too, in spite of myself." Finally I have said the words out loud, against my better judgment, especially under the present circumstances.

"I've got you," he says, and then we make love and fall asleep in each other's arms. When we awaken, it's almost five o'clock.

"Well, we better get up," Kiyo says. "Tonight, we'll have a house full of guests. The caterers will arrive soon."

"That was brilliant planning—getting a caterer," I say.

"I'd like to take credit, but it was your mother's idea. She thought it might be good to have a time and place to debrief."

* * *

KIYO and I have barely finished showering and dressing when the intercom buzzes. He scurries down the stairs. "It's the caterers," he calls up to me.

When I get downstairs, I'm surprised to see Momoko there with a young woman and a young man. All three are dressed informally in jeans and T-shirts.

"Oh, hello again, Margaux," Momoko says.

"Fancy meeting you here!" I say. "You look different in street clothes."

"Yeah, I hate wearing that costume, but it won't be for much longer. I'm getting ready to close the Kabuki Lounge forever. I can't afford the rent anymore, and there aren't as many customers as we once had," she says. "Much as I have loved building the business, it's time to say good-bye."

"That's a real shame," I say.

"All things change. Speaking of which, I want to introduce you to my children, who will be preparing your sushi dinner; they're both in training to become *itamae*—chefs. This is Kiki." She gestures toward the young woman. "She'll be the first female sushi chef in Colorado, as far as I know. Now *that* is meaningful change!"

"Nice to meet you, Kiki."

"Likewise, I've heard about you a lot over the years and am looking forward to reading your novel when it comes out." She smiles.

"And this is Ken," Momoko says.

"A pleasure to meet you, Ken," I say.

"It's about time!" He cracks a big smile. "Kiyo talks about you and Theo a lot. I always thought he made you up."

"Maybe he did," I say. "He *does* have an active imagination."

Everyone laughs in agreement.

Momoko looks over the set-up at the counter. "Everything looks good here. I need to get back to the restaurant, as it's our busiest night of the week. You're in good hands with Kiki and Ken." She says something quietly to Kiyo and gets on the elevator. Kiyo follows.

I notice a stack of wooden boxes on the counter. "What are those?" I ask Kiki, who's cutting up a beautiful piece of tuna.

"Those are *masu*—boxes for drinking cold sake."

"Wow, is that like a new fad or something? I haven't heard of drinking cold sake."

"No, it's not new. Like grape wines, sake comes in many varieties and qualities, and some of the more refined brews are preferable to drink cold. We often drink it cold for celebrations."

The elevator door opens and Kiyo is back, carrying a smallish barrel decorated with Japanese characters in a black, red, and white design.

"*Komodaru*," Kiyo says, as if I should know what that is.

Kiki says, "A ceremonial sake barrel. Kiyo will break the top tonight to kick off the party. It symbolizes harmony and good luck."

* * *

THE GUESTS START ARRIVING at around seven—Nellie, Theo, and Winnie arrive first. My mother, Paloma, and Jenny arrive together later than I expected.

"Wow, I thought you guys would've been here earlier—you said you were coming straight from your interviews," I say.

Paloma and our mother look at each other. My mother says, "Let's say things turned out different than we expected. Our interviews ran long." She puts one arm around Jenny and the other one around Paloma. They both look as though they have been put through a wringer.

I automatically go to them, and we join in a four-person hug, heads together. We all begin to cry. Our relief is palpable. This day is finally over.

Kiyo says, "I hate to break into the sisterhood's tête-à-tête, but I think it is time to kick off the next phase of this party, and our lives. Please, come and join us in the kitchen area for a special ceremony."

I pull myself away from the circle and am suddenly

stricken by an uncontrollable desire to laugh. Once I start, I can't stop, and soon all four of us are laughing and crying at the same time. When we stop, Theo says, "What's so funny over there?"

"Oh, nothing. I guess we're all feeling better than we have in a long time," I say.

We follow Kiyo over to the kitchen counter, which is now filled with the feast prepared by Kiki and Ken. He stands next to the barrel that he brought in earlier.

"Welcome, all. Although not exactly the way any of us might have imagined our reunion, I believe this day will change all of our lives in a positive way. As a momentous occasion, I wish to mark it with a tradition that my family always followed called *kagami biraki*, in which we begin our celebration with the breaking of a sake barrel. The barrel, as you can see, is decorated with Japanese symbols; each one of these symbols corresponds to each of you. Momoko graciously helped me arrive at these symbols and painted each character with love, as I am not fluent in Japanese, neither in the language nor the calligraphy." He holds up a wooden mallet. "I'll be the first to strike the barrel, then my cadre—Margie, Theo, Jenny, and Paloma—will all get a whack too."

"Kind of reminds me of a piñata," I say.

"Yeah, but try not to spill the sake!" Kiyo says.

Kiyo strikes the top and hands the mallet to me. I strike it, but not more than a dull thud results. Jenny whacks it a bit harder than I, and it cracks—a split. Paloma steps up and bangs it harder. It still hasn't broken open. Then Theo steps up. Grinning, he smacks it sharply—it splinters.

"Well done!" Kiyo says, and he fishes out a wedge of wood and removes the other pieces from the top. "Now for the fun part." He picks up a wooden ladle, fills it, and pours it into a box, repeating until ten boxes have been filled and passed around.

Holding his sake high, Kiyo says, "Here's to the love and magic that brought us all together. *Kanpai!*"

We instinctively lift our cups up and say in near unison, "*Kanpai!*" The sake is cold and smooth going down, with a hint of sweetness.

I lean in to Kiyo to kiss his cheek, but he turns his head and lands a kiss on my lips. We both start laughing. "Thank you," I say. "Thank you for everything you've done."

After we've had our fill of sushi, sashimi, seaweed salad, pickles, dumplings, and other delicious snack foods, we all move to the living area, where we sit on a modern sectional that surrounds a large round marble coffee table. A gas flame burns in the center—an indoor fire pit.

"Please, help yourselves to more sake if you wish." Kiyo sits next to me.

Ken and Kiki finish cleaning up in the kitchen and say a quick good-bye.

After they have left, Kiyo says, "I don't know about all of you, but I'm eager to hear the stories that emerged today and yesterday in the interviews."

"First," I say, "Nellie, this is the part where you can take out your tape recorder."

"Not to worry," she says. "I've been taking notes since we left New York. Being a fly on the wall has never been quite this pleasurable! Does anybody prefer that I don't record?"

Winnie chimes in, "When Nellie writes about us, we will be the final arbiters and have the last say, rest assured."

Everybody agrees that it's okay for Nellie to record.

Kiyo says, "May I suggest that we go in the order of our interviews—me, Theo, Margie, Mrs. Andrews, and Paloma? Jenny, I put you at the end, since they interviewed you twice, at the beginning and the end. Nobody has to talk at all— only if you want to. We've been through a lot!"

My mother says, "That's a great idea, Kiyo."

Kiyo begins. "Well, my interview was relatively brief, as my knowledge of everything that happened on President Street and before—when Anna disappeared—is limited. I told the story of our fort and the day Bud McIntire—I learned his last name today—threatened and molested the four of us. I also told the detective about Theo's previous fort, the one that we all assumed had collapsed on Anna Gonzalez. I didn't know the precise location, only what Theo told me—it was by the UP apartments near the tracks." Kiyo nods at Theo.

Theo says, "I, of course, was able to supply greater detail regarding the whereabouts of the first fort, and Detective Hillstrom and I are going to visit the site tomorrow morning."

I say, "Yeah, they asked me if I knew where it was—I didn't."

Theo continues, "They asked me how I came to build the fort by The Apartments. I told them Anna and I were hanging out and saw Bud McIntire and Bobby Hill, both older boys, digging in the field behind her apartment. We went over there to see what they were doing, and they told us they were digging a fort, so we asked if we could help. They were more than happy to let us have turns at digging, like Kiyo and I were when Margie and Jenny volunteered to help us. When Anna and I left, Bud and Bobby were still working on it. I never saw it when it was finished. I went over there a week later and there was nothing there; it was all filled in. I assumed it had caved in."

The room is silent.

"Wow," I say. "It sounds like Bud and Bobby had something to do with Anna's death."

"Maybe," Theo says. "I guess we'll know more as the investigation continues, but at least it is a tangible lead."

"They also asked me some questions about Jenny's parents, but I didn't have much to tell them."

My mother says, "That's as it should have been."

Eyes turn to me next. "I didn't have a lot of new information to add. They asked about the forts and about Jenny's parents too. I think everything I said pretty much matched with what Theo and Kiyo had to say." I didn't see a need to recount the details again.

Kiyo says, "Mrs. An—, Cami, do you want to tell us about your interview?"

"Yes," she says. "The detective first asked me about the forts. She was shocked that I hadn't known about them and that I had done such a poor job of monitoring the activities of my children."

Theo says, "You wouldn't have wanted to know what we were up to most of the time." We all laugh.

"Well, it does make me wonder if I was a terrible mother," she says.

"You were a great mother," I say.

"Well, you may change your mind. Anyway, after all of the business with the forts, they asked me questions about my relationship with Roz. Most of you know by now that we had a romantic interest in each other, but before she died, things started falling apart. She refused to leave Ned, because she was so terrified of the consequences, and apparently rightfully so. The morning of her accident I had broken off our friendship due to irreconcilable differences of a political nature. You can see how that ended." Cami looks into her sake cup.

Jenny says, "My mother's death was not *your* fault." Her certainty is loud and clear, like maybe she has inside knowledge.

"I'm not sure. If I hadn't pressed her to leave your father, she might still be alive. I don't know if she killed herself because I was pulling away, or your father murdered her because she wanted to leave him. Either way, it would have been my fault."

I get up and cross over to her, bend down and hug her. "Mother, you didn't do anything wrong." Paloma scooches over to make room for me to sit.

My mother is weeping into a handkerchief that Kiyo handed her. We all sit in silence until she finishes.

"Well," Paloma says, "I guess it's my turn to go."

Kiyo says, "Only if you want to. I know this is hard for everyone."

"I *want* all of you to know my story," Paloma says. "It's been unspeakable for so long." She pauses. "When I was in seventh grade, Ned Peoples serially molested and then raped me. It all started with our dog-training sessions. I never told you, Mother, because I was ashamed. Ned had convinced me that I was the one who started it, that I wanted it; he said I flirted with him. I *did*, it's true. I wanted attention. I knew it was wrong then, but now I realize that it wasn't my fault—he was a bad man. I'm horrified to think of anything like that ever happening to either of my children."

A deep silence fills the room. This is worse than I imagined.

A small voice says, "My father raped me too." It's Jenny. "He started molesting me when I was six and raped me multiple times after I turned twelve and until I moved out of the house at age sixteen. By then I knew there was nothing right about it. Like you, Paloma, I thought it was my own doing. I never told my mother, because he said it was 'our little secret.' And at first it didn't hurt. My daddy loved me —he was showing me how much. He'd *never* hurt me—I trusted him.

"Then the night before my father pulled me out of school—on the day my mother died—I heard my parents fighting. They were talking about me. My mother yelled 'What kind of monster does that to his own child?' Some-how, she had discovered our little secret—maybe she saw it happening? I'll never know. She told him she was leaving him and taking me with her. 'I will kill you before that happens,' he said. I didn't know my mother had died the day we left. He told me that she had left both of us. I didn't *know* she was dead until Kiyo told me. I think my father did it. I think he caused my mother's car accident somehow."

Nellie turns off the tape recorder. "This is not exactly what I thought was going to happen. It is more terrible than I could have imagined."

"I agree," I say. "What you and Paloma have suffered is unfathomable."

Theo says, "Funny, how the little mistakes we made as children have their way of catching up to us, isn't it?"

My mother says, "None of those things should have happened to any of you, to us."

"But they did happen, and now we need to move forward," Kiyo says. "And today is a first step. I'm pretty sure we'll all face some hurdles ahead, but fortunately, we have each other."

AS GOOD AS IT GETS
UNTIL THE NEXT TIME

I wish everything had been tied up more neatly, but things are about as resolved as they're going to be. The next morning, when we stop by the house on President Street before departing, I'm struck by how ordinary and middle class our old neighborhood is, how small everything is. Our house and yard are the same as when we lived there—recognizable —but the iron gate has been replaced with a slatted wooden one. The gardens and the yard are smaller than I remember, run-down—Mr. Sakura's magic is gone. Like the Elizabeth Street Garden on an ordinary day, the President Street yard is missing something fundamental—love, the love that we all experienced in the Garden of the Gods, in the Elysian Field, while sitting on Persephone's Couch under the Tree of Knowledge, or when wandering in the Dark Forest.

* * *

Back in New York the next day, Kiyo and I, inseparable, have finished our morning coffee and are reading the paper when the phone rings.

"Hello?" Kiyo says. He's quiet for a few moments. "One

second, I'm gonna put you on speaker. Margie's gonna want to hear this." He turns to me. "It's your brother."

"Hi, Theo!" I say. "What's up?"

"I was telling Kiyo that I learned yesterday, after you guys left for the airport, that they discovered Anna's body about twenty-five yards west of the first fort, so the first fort *didn't* collapse with her in it—it looks like it wasn't an accident."

"That must make you feel better?" I say.

"Yeah, I guess. But we still don't know who did it."

"Well, now at least they know about Bud and Ned Peoples—maybe it was one of them?"

"Yeah, about Bud—I got a call from Detective Hillstrom today—they tracked him down. Turns out he committed suicide—hung himself—shortly after Anna's body was discovered, back in sixty-eight. If it was him, we'll never know. Hillstrom did say there are some new forensic techniques they might be able to use if Bud wasn't cremated—they don't know yet what happened with his remains. For now, though—"

"Wow," says Kiyo. "It sure sounds like it could have been him."

"And she said they managed to track down Bobby Hill. He's a teacher at the high school. Turns out he and Bud were *not* that close of friends, but Bobby knew that Bud had had a hard home life, gave the detective a few details about Bud's family."

"That's not a surprise, I guess," Kiyo says.

"Not at all," I say. "Clearly, he was a messed-up guy, messed up by *someone*."

"Did Detective Hillstrom say anything about the Peoples case?" Kiyo asks.

"She told me that for Paloma's part, the statute of limitations long ago passed according to Colorado law, but because

Ned Peoples took Jenny across state lines and is implicated in a number of felonies, they turned her case over to the FBI. Technically, it wasn't a parental kidnapping, since Roz and he were still married, but the Feds have some flexibility that the state doesn't have—for them there's no statute of limitation on kidnapping, *and* charges could include rape, and possibly even murder. Plus, they may be able to triangulate more recent cases with Ned Peoples now that he's identified as a pedophile. So there's a modicum of hope that justice will be served."

"Well, that's something," I say. "I wonder if we'll ever know about Roz?"

"Yeah, she didn't say anything about that, but at least now we have a good idea of the motive. He certainly had the opportunity and the means, but those might be more difficult to establish after so much time has passed. Mother feels some resolution, though—she no longer feels like it was her fault."

"Do you think Jenny and Paloma are gonna to be okay?" I say. "I'm not sure how Jenny will ever recover from so many years of abuse."

"I have the feeling that both of them will come out of this on top, especially with help," Kiyo says. "And our support. I can't imagine carrying those secrets—"

"No kidding. And we thought our story was terrible," I say.

"It is terrible, but we had each other," Kiyo says. He puts his arm around me. "Paloma and Jenny both had it worse, *and* they were alone."

"One more thing that the detective told me that may be of interest: they believe that Ned possibly stole evidence out of the Anna Gonzales case file—one of those items was the anonymous note that your grandfather and our mother wrote. Ned was the last person to check out the file, and he did it the day before disappearing with Jenny."

"Wow, that's interesting. So do you think Ned could have been involved in Anna's murder?" I ask.

"Good question," Theo says. "Looks like it was either Bud or Ned at this point."

"Someday in the not-so-distant future, we're gonna get an answer," says Kiyo. "I read about a case in England where they are using DNA analysis to identify rapists and murderers. The technology is going to get better and better."

"Well, Kiyo, if ever there was someone to help speed it along, it is you," I say. "Mr. Magic."

"The last bit of news I have to share is that Paloma told me today that she's invited Jenny to come live in her guest house in Darien, and Jenny has agreed to it," Theo says.

"That's great!" I say. "Knowing what an organizer Paloma is, she no doubt has already set up therapy sessions for the two of them. They'll surely be of help to each other. Now, maybe I'll go out and visit them."

Suddenly, Darien's more interesting than it was a couple of weeks ago. Paloma is no longer the person I thought she was. Now I understand more about her need to feel and appear perfect—she felt flawed, like an unworthy person— and also her need to control things.

* * *

THE WEEKS PASS, and the holidays are bearing down. Out my window, snowflakes meander to the ground, and the wind whistles. The radiators crank out so much heat that I strip down to a tank top. I'm looking forward to moving into my new space, but I'll miss this one. In the short time that I've lived here, so much has happened.

I sit down in front of my trusty Smith Corona and am working on my next novel, the sequel to *One Elysium Street*, when the phone rings.

"Hello?" I say.

"Yes, is this Margaux Andrews?"

"Yes, may I ask who's calling?"

"Hi, my name is Alice Baintree. I'm a PR person from Big Five. Do you have a moment to talk? I have a few questions for a Q-and-A piece I am putting together about your next book."

"Sure, I have time," I say. Truthfully, I'd rather be writing than talking to her, but I guess this is now part of my life too.

"How is the work going?" she asks.

"Well!" I say. "I've plotted out the main story, which wasn't too difficult since I scaffolded it loosely on my own childhood, as I did with the first novel."

"What do you mean by *scaffolded?*"

"I say *scaffolded* because the bones of my story and the trajectory are familiar from my own life—that's the starting point, but everything diverges rather quickly as I start developing the specifics."

"Can you say more? How do you develop your themes?" she asks.

"The questions that drive the story come from my lived experiences, which is likely the case for most writers. The last novel focused on the question of whether the world is more dangerous today than it was in nineteen sixty-five. The answer is *definitely not.* That question came about because one day when I was talking to my mother, she said she thought today's world was much more dangerous than the one she grew up in."

"And what about the new novel?"

"The new novel explores the question of how people in the same family can live through the same experiences and have such different views of them."

"And how do you come up with your characters?" Ms. Baintree asks.

"The characters are fabricated of whole cloth—new people who have predefined roles in a family, situated in a particular time and place, like my own family was, but they're made up—this is the hardest part—creating characters that will write their own stories in their own voices, characters that are believable."

"So are you saying that your novel is *not* autobiographical? I was under the impression that it was." She sounds incredulous.

"Yes, that's what I am saying. Do you *really* think all of those things could have happened to one family in such a short time? And then there is all that silly magical stuff."

"It does seem preposterous."

"Yes, well, that's fiction, isn't it?" I say. I've convinced her.

The buzzer sounds.

"Excuse me," I say. "Someone is at my door."

"No problem. I think I have enough information to put together the piece I am working on. I'll pass it by you. Thank you for your time."

After I hang up, I get up and go to look through the peephole—looks like a courier. I leave the chain guard attached and open the door. "Yes?" I say.

"Delivery from Nellie Harris at the *New York Times*." He hands the packet through the opening.

I take the packet. "Thanks."

He offers his card. "Call me if you have any edits, and I'll come pick them up for Ms. Harris."

"Thanks again," I say.

After he leaves, I open the packet. Nellie has landed a new gig at the *Times*, has become an overnight sensation. The first story she sold to them was called "Good-Bye, Gossip Girl!" It was another tell-all, but one she backed up with facts from her own life and experiences as a yellow journalist.

After receiving rave reviews from readers, she proposed a Sunday column in the Book Review entitled Literary Circles, focused on the New York literary scene. This is her first installment. The headline reads "New Kids in Town: The Story Behind M. Des Jardins." At the top is a group photo taken at the Round About. The caption says "We are M. Des Jardins" and lists the members with their titles. The story documents the early days of the agency and its relationship to the Vicious Circle and Dorothy Parker. It features photos of Kiyo's grandparents and describes the many challenges they faced as Japanese Americans. It ends with the reincarnation of the Vicious Circle and M. Des Jardins's seminal role. She says nothing about her trip to Denver or anything deeply personal about the Sakuras. I'm mentioned as one of several talented writers they represent.

* * *

NINETEEN EIGHTY-FIVE COMES TO AN END, and the movers have packed up the last of my belongings to take to my new home. My little fifth-floor walk-up on Elizabeth Street served me well. I'm going to miss it, but I've secured a nice loft close by, within a stone's throw of the Mulberry branch and Kiyo's.

Out of habit, before leaving the building, I peek through the glass window on mailbox number eleven, as I've done every day since moving in. I have mail. I turn the combination lock through familiar turns—*L-O-V-E*—and the door pops open. Today's mail arrives in a thick ten-by-twelve envelope from the Big Five Press. It's a copy of the finalized contract for *One Elysium Street*. My family unanimously gave their blessing to my publishing it. My mother said I had done a good job at capturing the truths of that part of our lives. She liked how I had made our life seem charmed instead of cursed. It *was* charmed, and it still is.

I take my last walk on the familiar route to the Round About. I have a meeting with Rosie and Winnie—my agent and her assistant. Joe, my security detail, is still ever present —that situation is still hanging in the air. Theo has decided to move to New York, "so that we'll all be closer," he said. I know he wants to be closer to Winnie.

Kiyo has gone to visit some of his neglected businesses abroad. I hope he is safe, but if there is one thing I have learned, it is that this world has always been dangerous, and it still is. Fortunately, I have lots of work to do of my own, a place to do it, and before he left, Kiyo gave me a present that I need to learn how to use—a new Apple Macintosh computer. Things change, and sometimes the new stuff is better than the old.

ACKNOWLEDGMENTS

I write in the company of my characters, but getting to a finished book from an early draft is a communal effort. I owe gratitude to many—my family for their unwavering support, whether financial, spiritual, or emotional. Special thanks go to my life partner, ken anderson (and yes, he spells his name in lowercase). I can depend on him to tell me the truth about what I have written, even when it isn't what I want to hear. His insights are usually spot-on.

I also owe thanks to each of my siblings who have supported me as readers and cheerleaders along the way. This book would not have a story if it weren't for them and all of our shared memories and unbelievable experiences. Finally, I am indebted to our mother, Megan McClard, a wonderful writer, artist, and role model. She passed away in 2023 while I was writing this book—it is a tribute to her memory.

My team of beta readers deserves credit for their contributions to the evolution and improvement of this manuscript. For the first time, I recruited authenticity/sensitivity readers in addition to general readers; it was worth the effort, and the changes they suggested improved the story. Specifically, I want to thank Val Gryphin, Carol Stimmel, Kathleen Balgley, Christopher Keener, and Judy Blankenship for their in-depth comments. Additionally, thank you to Nancy Henry and Judy Blankenship for their detailed eyes on the final draft.

Final thanks go to my editor, Erin Cusick. She earned my trust when she edited my first novel, *Butterfly Dreams*, and has once again proven her worth, demonstrating that a writer is only as good as her editor.

ABOUT THE AUTHOR

Anne McClard earned her Ph.D. in Anthropology from Brown University in 2005. Her dissertation research in the Azores inspired *Butterfly Dreams*, her first novel, and her adventure-filled childhood inspired her new series, The Margaux Chronicles. *Margaux and the Vicious Circle* is the first book of the series. Anne currently lives in Portland, Oregon with her husband, daughter, and two dogs. In addition to writing books, she enjoys writing poetry, songs, and playing bluegrass mandolin and fiddle.

Would you like to purchase a signed book? Interested in scheduling a book club appearance or other event with the author? Send her a message! She offers discounted pricing for book groups.

https://butterflydreams.mcclard.com/
https://anne.mcclard.com/

 facebook.com/annemcclard.author
 instagram.com/amcclard
 amazon.com/author/anne-mcclard

SELECT ARISTATA PRESS TITLES

LEAVINGS: Memoir of a 1920s Hollywood Love Child, by Megan McClard, 2022

This Rough Magic: At Home on the Columbia Slough, by Nancy Henry and Bruce Campbell, illustrated by Amanda Williams, August 2023.

Butterfly Dreams: a Novel, by Anne McClard, September 2023.

Women Caught in the Crossfire: One Woman's Quest for Peace in South Sudan, by Abuk Jervis Makuac and Susan Lynn Clark, October 2023.

Raising Owen: an Extra-ordinary Memoir on Motherhood, by Suzanne Lezotte, October 2023.

Coming in 2024

Echoes of the Lost Boys of Sudan, by Susan Clark and James Disco, June 2024.

High Noon on Come Along Slough, by Bruce Campbell, August 2024.

Aristata Press is non-profit organization. We depend on charitable contributions and volunteers to keep the lights on. We are a tax exempt–501(c)(3)–organization (EIN 92-0281706), which means that your contributions are tax deductible. Contributions that we receive will go directly to supporting the publications of deserving literary works by authors that for one reason or another would be unlikely to find a home in the for-profit publishing sector.

Please visit us at: https://aristatapress.com